LOVE AND SORCERY: DISILLUSIONED

ROXANNE MCNEIL

BUTTERSCOTCH BOOKS

LOVE AND SORCERY: DISILLUSIONED

Love and Sorcery, Book 1

by Roxanne McNeil

Published by Butterscotch Books

www.roxannemcneil.com

This is a work of fiction. Though there are some obvious references to the geography and cultures of various countries, the characters and places in this book are products of the author's imagination.

Cover design by Blue Valley Author Services

See back page for printing information.

ISBN: 978-1-7356614-3-8 (e-book)

ISBN: 978-1-7356614-2-1 (paperback)

For my sisters, original and acquired

With many thanks to the Z girls and my critique group for all their wonderful help

CHAPTER 1

Dan

Dan Forell should have been overjoyed at his moment of triumph. Instead, he found himself taking some steady breaths and slowing his horse to a walk. There was no reason to be nervous. He knew exactly what he was getting into. This assignment was the fulfillment of seven years of grueling work and sacrifice, and no one could take that away from him.

He allowed himself a small smile as he studied the chattering guests approaching the stately hilltop manor house. They didn't know that one among their number tonight was a sorcerer, one of the most powerful in the country and the reason Dan had traveled to this remote place. He paused in the shade of a copse of trees to look back down the road toward the village of Perch Harbor and the ocean beyond. It was a peaceful place. Hopefully the sorcerer wasn't attached to it. Dan would be guarding him for the next several years, perhaps even decades, and the sooner they left to start their work, the better. He might have enjoyed the moment if not for the tiny flicker of movement from within the trees.

He was being watched.

Dan casually reached for his throwing blades, wishing his bow and quiver were more accessible.

"Enough of that, Forell, my friend. Enough of that." Coordinator Madsen rode out from behind the trees, one large hand raised placatingly. "I've been waiting for you."

"Yes, sir," Dan grunted. Madsen had been in the army for decades before being promoted to coordinator of the Kalmarian sorcerers, and though he'd never been Dan's friend, he still should have known better than to spy on him from behind the trees. Relief and irritation pounded against Dan's rib cage. Killing his employer, not to mention the person responsible for Dan's current assignment, would not have been a commendable way to start his career as a defender.

"I trust that I've chosen the right man," Madsen muttered as he guided his horse to walk beside Dan's. "You can't be too obvious about your role, you know, and having a hundred weapons on you is a bit of a giveaway."

"Twelve, sir."

Madsen's gaze flickered over Dan. "Just so. And don't 'sir' me here. This is a private party, not a military one. As a matter of fact," he said, nodding at the manor house, "no one here should know you're still involved with the army. You'll need to be particularly careful if you're to get this assignment."

If? "My orders say I'm assigned already, s—"

"Yes, on our end, of course," Madsen said irritably. "But you have to convince the *sorcerer* too."

Wait. No one had ever said anything about that in his training. He wasn't a puppy to be looked over and chosen. Defenders were assigned by the coordinator to protect a sorcerer until reassignment or death of the defender, and this sorcerer was extremely lucky to be getting him.

Madsen seemed to read his thoughts. "Your sorcerer is

possibly one of the five most powerful in all of Kalmar. If joined to the army, our advantage would be tremendous."

Dan's horse tossed his head and tried to break into a trot before Dan reined him back. "I was told the sorcerer already *planned* to join us," he said through gritted teeth. "I wouldn't have taken the assignment otherwise."

"It will be worth the convincing you'll need to do, Forell. You won't have an opportunity as good as this for another fifty years, maybe longer. Don't ruin it." A smirk twisted Madsen's weathered face. "You shouldn't have any trouble. Top of your class at the academy in everything you tried, weren't you? Your law teacher thought you could be the next high judge. Your magical theory instructor claims you should take his job. The weapons master wants you for His Majesty's personal guard. But I tell you, Forell, if you mess this up, I will *bury* you. I don't care how talented you are."

Dan wasn't surprised by the threat. Madsen hadn't earned his current position by being gentle. A dozen questions rose in Dan's throat, but they were almost to the stable, and he couldn't risk being overheard.

In a whisper Madsen added, "We have more riding on this than your career aspirations. Filip Reznik is sending more Kazat envoys to the Northerners. Last time he did that, he'd already convinced half the other Kazat clan leaders to declare war on Kalmar. We only managed to avoid the conflict by buying out a few key clan leaders. Reznik's richer than he was five years ago, and we need this sorcerer more than ever. I'll tell you more about it later. I'm so glad you could come, my boy." The last was louder, clearly for the benefit of the liveried stable hand approaching to take their horses.

They dismounted and handed their reins over. "This way, Forell," Madsen said. "I can't wait to introduce you to our delightful hostesses. My friend, Lucas Loraine, the baron, won't be here. His sister manages this estate."

Dan adjusted his coat and hurried to follow, wishing he was wearing his army uniform.

"And be forewarned," Madsen muttered under his breath once Dan reached him. "I have work to do at this party. Stay out of the way of my men."

"Yes, s—Madsen."

"And to be sure that you do, why don't you see if you can guess the identity of your assignment, eh?" Madsen said as they walked up a few steps to the mansion. "That should keep you busy."

What? But it was too late to protest. They stepped through the entryway, and Madsen swept off his hat, handing it over to a maid. Dan copied the motion with a murmured thanks. He turned to follow Madsen, who had paced forward to bow over the hand of an elderly woman.

"Madsen," she said in clipped tones. "So happy you could make it." She turned her piercing blue eyes to Dan. "And you must be the friend he told us about."

"Ladies, allow me to introduce Daniel Forell, a friend of mine from my army days. Seems he was just as unenthusiastic about staying as I was. You don't see many pretty girls in the army, I'm afraid." Madsen sent a flirtatious wink at their hostess.

Dan tried not to stare at him. Madsen had a generous sprinkling of grey at his temples, but the woman was at least another twenty years older.

"Forell, my boy," the coordinator said, "this is Lady Svea Ellstrom."

Dan bowed over Lady Ellstrom's lined, tremoring hand, not missing the assessing look-over she gave him.

"And her niece, Miss Lillian Loraine," Madsen added, nodding to a young woman standing further in the shadows.

Dan mechanically took her white-gloved hand and bowed over

it. He had a strong aversion to young, unmarried females. They were man hunters, and he never could have finished his training if he'd allowed one to snare him. Judging from the size-up from her aunt, the girl wasn't yet spoken for. When he straightened and met her gaze, she smiled sweetly. She was a pretty enough girl with large hazel eyes and shiny waves of light brown hair, but her smile was her best feature. It transformed her into a dimpled fairy.

"A pleasure to meet you, Mr. Forell," she said in a voice he was certain must have taken years to cultivate into such honeyed tones. It was almost as mesmerizing as her lips.

He snapped his mouth shut, embarrassed that he'd been staring and not defending himself from the man-eating siren. "Miss Loraine," he said abruptly before turning away and leading Madsen into a large parlor teeming with guests. He might as well get to work.

～

Lillian

"What a charming young man we just met, Lillian," Aunt Svea said dryly as Mr. Forell disappeared into the parlor, his brown hair missing the door frame by only a few inches.

"The poor thing, Auntie. We should be kind to him. You get almost the same scowl when you've been around Madsen for more than three minutes."

"True," her aunt agreed. "I'm already sick of him, and he's only been here thirty seconds. I'll try to reserve judgment. Oh, look. Here's Melina. She managed to get away from her mother's brood after all, and she brought her nitwit younger brother instead of her fiancé."

"Shhhh. Geoffrey's not a nitwit, and we *invited* him."

5

Svea sniffed. "The idiot thinks he's got special license to hold your hand because he's Melina's relation."

A few seconds later Lillian's friend, Melina, strode into the room. She kissed Svea on the cheek and grasped Lillian's hands. "You look divine. I'm sorry I'm late. Our baby brother put muddy hands all over my white gown, and I had to change."

"The blue is perfect on you. It brings out the gold shades in your hair," Lillian said with a laugh.

Geoffrey pushed his way forward, practically knocking over his sister as he seized Lillian's hand. "I hope you'll be my dinner partner, Lillian," he said, pressing a kiss to her hand and looking deeply into her eyes.

"Thank you," she said, withdrawing her hand as quickly as was polite. "But Sir Malick was sweet enough to ask me."

Geoffrey didn't try to mask his disappointment, and Melina rolled her eyes.

Aunt Svea broke in. "I think it's time to start, dear, before Malick faints of hunger." They moved toward the parlor, and Melina said in a low voice, "Who is that man and why is he *glaring* at you?"

Lillian looked up, instantly regretting it as she met the disapproving gaze of Mr. Forell. Madsen's men usually ignored her, and none of them had ever stared at her this way in her own house. She nodded politely at him before quickly looking away. "A friend of Madsen's, just out of the army."

"If he offends you, Lillian, I'm sure I can take care of him for you," Geoffrey offered, straightening his coat.

She laughed with good humor, but before she could answer, Melina said, "Don't you dare, Geoff. He looks like he'd tear you to pieces if you looked at him the wrong way."

"Ha. He's the gangly sort. I wouldn't have trouble with him."

Lillian glanced toward the parlor. Mr. Forell still frowned at her, as though she'd insulted him somehow. His presence was increasingly disturbing, but he was *not* gangly. His build was tall and slender, but even with his plain dress coat, it was clear there were muscles to go along with the broad shoulders.

She and her aunt ushered their guests into a large dining room with three long tables. Even if Madsen had insisted on bringing some of his men, she would still try to behave as though it was only a party of friends to celebrate Aunt Svea's birthday. There would be an even larger group tomorrow for the dancing, though Svea hadn't danced in years. They probably would have combined the celebration into one night if Madsen hadn't insisted he needed his man, Octens, to be seen in public for at least a couple nights. Lillian wasn't looking forward to managing the man's appearances. She'd never met him, just seen him at a distance and studied his portraits, but she had to get his illusion right. Her future depended on her being able to prove herself invaluable to the crown.

When she found her own seat, she was unnerved to find Mr. Forell holding her chair for her. It clearly wasn't a post he would have chosen for himself, but Sir Malick stood several paces away, speaking with Coordinator Madsen. She smiled politely and thanked Mr. Forell as she sat down. He took Madsen's chair next to her, making her so nervous that she nearly jumped when Aunt Svea tapped a glass. Sir Malick quickly took his seat on Lillian's other side.

Aunt Svea stood. "Thank you all for coming. I know it's difficult to believe I'm another year older, but I haven't lost my appetite yet, so let's see who can keep up." A group of young men from another table cheered, and she smiled at them before motioning to the servers, who immediately uncovered their trays.

"Well, little Lillian, this is just fine," Sir Malick said. "I suppose you ordered these quail eggs just for me."

"You're the only one who likes them, Uncle Malick," she said with a grin.

"I do like them, but it's nothing compared to how I feel about your aunt. Do you suppose Svea's ever going to marry me?" he asked, black eyebrows furrowed. "Then I could really be your uncle."

Lillian laughed. "You know she thinks she's too old for you."

"Five years is not too great a distance. What say you, young man?"

Lillian cringed inwardly as her friend pointed over her shoulder. She wished the quail eggs were raw, so she could smash them on Malick's head for his meddling.

He smirked as though he knew what she was thinking.

"Pardon me. I didn't hear the question."

Lillian sighed and sat back in her chair, quickly introducing them before Malick could repeat the question. "Sir Malick, this is Mr. Forell, recently of the army. Mr. Forell, may I present Sir Malick Mbaye of Saloum. Sir Malick was an ambassador to Kalmar and decided to remain here when his term was complete."

"Mostly because a political enemy took power and would have had me killed if I returned home," Sir Malick said with a wry smile. "But Perch Harbor held opportunities for business and other pursuits, and I couldn't leave." He glanced toward Svea. "Now tell me what you know of the skirmishes along the eastern border."

Her dinner companions immediately began discoursing on battles far away, leaving Lillian to make observations about Mr. Forell when politeness demanded she look at him. He was young, she was almost sure, though he carried the unusual alertness common among Madsen's most seasoned soldiers. His thick eyebrows were a little uneven over his grey-blue eyes, and his hair looked as though it could be combed a little more neatly. She wouldn't call his face handsome necessarily, but it was certainly fascinating. A small scar on his upper lip drew her attention just as he glanced at her. She blushed for looking at his mouth but met his eyes as though she was interested in the conversation. He frowned and turned back to Sir Malick.

Aunt Svea watched them with interest, and Lillian raised a questioning eyebrow. Her aunt only shook her head and mouthed, "I'm fine." Aunt Svea expended a lot of energy at these gatherings, and while her mind was still as sharp as it had been at thirty-five, she was now almost twice that age. Lillian fidgeted anxiously with her necklace, worrying about her aunt and the rest of her guests.

Madsen sat a few chairs away, looked disgustingly comfortable, as though he was present to watch his grandchild perform a song rather than to assure she fed misinformation to the Kazat spies he'd arranged to have in the room. Madsen directed all the sorcery done for the king, and the look in his eyes when she'd agreed to take more work from him had been entirely calculating. The coordinator certainly made her nervous, his men even more so.

Especially the one sitting next to her. She'd never realized how little space there truly was between the chairs at the table.

She covertly scanned the room for unfamiliar faces, occasionally glancing at her dinner companions or nodding at something they said. Her aunt's gaze often flickered toward them, and Lillian knew Octens needed to arrive. She took a slow breath and let Octens' image form in her mind.

CHAPTER 2

Dan

Miss Loraine obviously wasn't following the conversation, which was fine with Dan. He didn't enjoy the scrutiny of those hazel eyes. He wished the coordinator hadn't insisted on trading seats. She was distracting, and in his new line of work, distraction could be catastrophic. Her gaze often flickered around the room, most likely sizing up the single men. Perhaps the coordinator wanted to avoid her too, or perhaps this seat afforded a better view of the sorcerer.

"And do you feel His Majesty is taking that clan leader, Reznik, seriously?" Sir Malick asked directly.

"I believe so," Dan said, wondering if Sir Malick could possibly be his assignment.

The former ambassador's eyes, only a few shades darker than his deep brown skin, seemed particularly assessing as he surveyed Dan. It would be foolish to hope Coordinator Madsen would make it this easy for Dan to identify the sorcerer, giving him a seat so close to him at dinner. Still, Dan couldn't quite suppress a small bubble of hope. Sir Malick's dress sword was typical of the most elite fighters of Saloum. If they worked together, he could likely teach Dan another style of fighting.

"I understand Reznik's hold on power in Kazatania was solidified a month ago with the assassination of the Kazat heir apparent," Sir Malick said.

Dan nodded. "The king has been watching the situation carefully."

"With all his plays for power, you'd think Reznik would be too busy for war," Sir Malick said with a frown. "But I'm told it's only the army sorcerers who keep him from attacking Kalmar."

Miss Loraine had lifted a glass to her mouth, but at these words, she set it back down, her eyes wide. Of course she would be one of those people frightened at the mere mention of sorcery. And why should that disappoint him?

"Have you ever seen sorcerers in battle?" Sir Malick asked, his eyes distant. "I've always wanted to."

Dan fought to hide his disappointment. Judging from the wistfulness in his tone, Sir Malick couldn't be his reticent assignment.

Miss Loraine looked down at her lap and swallowed.

"A time or two," Dan said, surprised to find he didn't want to frighten her further by explaining. The majority of sorcerers were harmless, but the army sorcerers more than made up for that. Someone like Miss Loraine wouldn't know the difference. He changed the subject. "But surely you have gifted people here?" Perhaps his dinner companions would give him a clue to the sorcerer's identity.

"We have two," Miss Loraine said with a small smile. Everyone loved to gossip about magic. "Our school teacher can predict storms coming, a valuable gift in a harbor town. And we have a fisherman who always knows where the most fish will be."

"Both are useful of course," said Sir Malick, "but an actual sorcerer, someone who can change nature? I'm told we haven't had one here in over fifty years."

Miss Loraine's cheeks paled a little, though her lips still turned up pleasantly.

To avoid looking at her, Dan studied the dinner guests, marking off each one mentally. He quickly disregarded anyone appearing less than forty years old. The youngest age a sorcerer had ever come to power was thirty-eight, but Madsen had been wanting a defender for this sorcerer for years, so he was likely much older.

At one end of the opposite table, Miss Loraine's friend spoke animatedly to a companion. Dan shifted uncomfortably in his seat. He'd thought Miss Loraine had looked at him with special favor when he'd met her in the entryway, and he'd been disgusted by it. But when she'd greeted her stunning friend and the boy with matching chestnut hair, Dan had realized Miss Loraine had merely been *polite* to him. For them, her entire face lit up. And when the young man had kissed Miss Loraine's hand, Dan had been torn between embarrassment and anger. The boy had straightened and pushed his disgusting curls out of his eyes before giving Miss Loraine an overly intimate look. Dan had repressed the unfounded urge to do him bodily harm.

"And the king," Sir Malick said. "I heard his counselors are trying to marry him off to a nice Kalmarian girl before he has a chance to meet a Kazat siren."

"They wouldn't let a girl like that near the king, and there's plenty of time to shackle the poor man to a wife later. He has work to do."

Miss Loraine turned curious eyes on him, and Dan bit the inside of his mouth to keep himself from apologizing. She smiled blandly and sipped her drink before turning away again.

This was not the demeanor of a girl remotely interested in him. He'd been beyond foolish to imagine it.

Her eyes flicked around the room again, this time settling on her aunt. Lady Ellstrom nodded almost imperceptibly to her niece and then looked to the doorway.

Dan followed her gaze and almost dropped his drink. There, flirting quietly with a pretty serving girl, was Blevin Octens, wearing no disguise at all. The spy's thin-lipped smile and red-tinted hair were a dead giveaway. It wasn't surprising that he was flirting; the man was a notorious chaser of women, but what was he doing *here*? He was supposed to be hundreds of miles away, ferreting out information and providing bribe money deep within Kazatania. Nothing in Perch Harbor was worth bringing Octens back.

Octens led the serving girl back into the corridor behind him, and Dan glanced around, wondering who else had recognized the spy. The coordinator's men would know better than to show any recognition, so the two dinner guests with eyes trained Octens' back had to be Madsen's targets. One even excused himself from the table and left by another door.

Dan resisted the impulse to follow. Madsen hadn't wanted him to interfere. He went back to studying the dinner guests, trying to shake an ominous feeling about Octens' presence. By asking about a wall hanging behind them, he had the excuse to turn around and glance over the guests at the third table. Three older men fit the general profile of a sorcerer: mature and confident. The only other obvious candidate was Lady Ellstrom, who certainly had the poise of the army sorcerers, though she was much older than he would have expected.

"My grandfather procured those tapestries almost a hundred years ago," Miss Loraine answered. "When he was a young man he lived in Medan. He met a sorceress there who specialized in weaving."

"Did he marry when he lived in Medan?"

"No. Years later, and his wife died shortly after the current baron was born."

"I see. And she had only the two children?"

Miss Loraine paused, and though her expression remained polite, Dan knew his questions were rude. But he needed information and didn't have time to humor her, even if he wanted to, which of course, he didn't.

"Aunt Svea is the daughter of Grandfather's second wife, who also died in childbirth. Grandfather never married again."

Sorcerers had few children, so that kept Lady Ellstrom a possibility.

Miss Loraine looked out the window, and he followed her gaze to see Octens outside, still chasing after the same serving maid. He was an idiot to be out in the open where anyone could put an arrow in him.

Dan pretended to look back at the tapestry, ruling out another guest at the table behind them as he did. Satisfied now with his short list, he addressed Sir Malick again and tried, without much success, to forget about the pretty girl next to him.

When dinner was finished, Miss Loraine was claimed by a following of no less than ten young people, most of them male, and was quickly pulled toward a dais where they took turns playing music. She spoke happily with her friends, including the young man who had kissed her hand earlier, and Dan forced himself to look away.

The coordinator appeared at his shoulder. "Nice little party, eh? Though of course, you might find the dancing tomorrow evening more to your taste."

"Tomorrow evening, s—Madsen?"

"You don't already know who your assignment is, do you?" he asked quietly, dusting invisible lint from his embroidered jacket.

"I've narrowed it down to the gentleman with a pipe in the corner behind me, the grey-beard to your right, and Lady Svea Ellstrom."

Madsen studied Dan, who kept his expression neutral, not

allowing a trace of smugness to show.

"Well done, lad." There was an unmistakable gleam of humor in Madsen's eye. "I'll be sure to arrange a meeting with Lady Ellstrom after the other guests are gone."

He moved away to talk to one of his men, and Dan's stomach plummeted in disappointment. Lady Ellstrom had to be sixty-five. Of course, sorcerers often lived longer than others. She might have another decade or two of work in her, but to join the army sorcerers at this point didn't seem likely, especially considering her tremor.

He turned at a light laugh behind him and stared helplessly in the direction of Lillian Loraine. The annoying young man pressed a lute into her hands, but she shook her head.

"Oh, Geoffrey. Don't be ridiculous. You only want me to play so you can show me up afterward." She laughed affectionately, but pushed the lute back into his hands with finality. "Save me the embarrassment and everyone else the noise." As she turned away from him, her eyes met Dan's. Her perfect eyebrows knit in confusion for a fraction of a second before her gaze slid past him and focused on the next young man vying for her attention.

Dan shook himself and strode purposefully away. He hoped Lady Ellstrom could be convinced to join the army, because he couldn't stay in the same house as that girl.

Lillian

Lillian fixed a smile to her face, but Geoffrey must have noticed how Mr. Forell's glower had unsettled her.

"Is that man bothering you, Lillian?" he asked, putting down the lute.

Lillian cringed at his overly loud voice. "Not at all."

Melina rescued her by asking Geoffrey for a particular song.

15

She gave Lillian an apologetic glance before her fiancé, Bennet, came to claim her attention. The look that passed between the two made Lillian sigh. Bennet and Melina were just right for each other and very much in love. The last man Lillian had chosen to love had been such a disappointment, but that was no reason to envy her friend's happiness.

It seemed hours before guests began to take their leave, and she and Aunt Svea stood by the door for almost another hour after that, exchanging pleasantries with their departing guests. Luckily, Madsen's men left quickly with only murmured thanks. She never knew what to say to them. Madsen and his new recruit lingered in the background, and she wished they would leave as well. Mr. Forell was so disconcerting. When Madsen steered Mr. Forell into the library, Lillian's heart fell an inch in her chest. "Not another meeting?" she whispered without much hope. "We're tired. Isn't he tired?"

"Madsen's never tired, darling. Perhaps he only wants to congratulate you on your work."

Lillian highly doubted it, but if she was to prove herself invaluable to the crown, she'd need to take the next assignment he'd offer. Surely it couldn't be much longer before the baron would want his home back, and she needed to find her own, one nice enough to include Aunt Svea. The king paid her well, but she still didn't have nearly enough saved.

In a louder voice, her aunt said, "Yes, goodnight, my dears. So happy you could come."

Several of the guests stared at Lillian's image of Octens as they left. She kept him sulking at the side of the house, occasionally checking his pocket watch. A few older women smirked at his evident failure to snare the maid.

Once the last guests were gone, Aunt Svea took Lillian's arm, either for support or to keep her from running away. Coordinator Madsen set down a book when they entered the library, and he and Mr. Forell waited for them to take their seats before joining them at the small table. "I hope you enjoyed your birthday party," the coordinator began.

"Let's just get to it, Madsen," Aunt Svea said. "You know I detest hosting your little evenings of amusement. You said the change in plan was urgent. What's that matter?"

"It is urgent. The Kazats nobles are rallying, unifying for the first time in over a hundred years, all in support of Filip Reznik."

"The clan leader?" Aunt Svea asked.

"Yes. The only one who could have checked him was their heir apparent, but the poor man was assassinated before he could be crowned, so the Kazats are still without a king, leaving the power in the hands of the clan leaders."

Lillian looked between the two, trying to understand the extra meaning in their eyes.

"And we expect Reznik to dispatch the next in line for the throne?" Aunt Svea asked.

Madsen nodded. "He's aligned himself with Andrej Strihat, the commander of the Kazat army, and with the money and support the two are amassing, Reznik is close to beginning his campaign."

"What campaign?" Lillian asked.

Mr. Forell looked at her as though she'd done something impolite.

"Kazatani soldiers outnumber ours three to one. It's our sorcerers who've kept them in check the last several decades. Octens has learned that Reznik intends to wipe out our Kalmarian sorcerers," Madsen said grimly. "Then his army would invade."

"It would take a full-scale war for the Kazats to annex Kalmar," Lillian protested. "Tens of thousands dead on each side. The Kazats fight among themselves, but surely their people wouldn't stand for *this*."

Mr. Forell arched an eyebrow, but she ignored him.

Madsen waved his hand. "They are not like us. The lower classes are horribly uneducated and tightly controlled by their nobility. Reznik exaggerates the riches of Kalmar and the ease of conquest. The Kazats nobles who oppose him will die, and the others will follow him."

"What's being done to stop him?" Lillian asked.

Madsen gave Aunt Svea a questioning look.

"Is this the boy you told me of?" she said, ignoring Lillian's question. "He doesn't look old enough."

Lillian stared at her aunt. She rarely took interest in Madsen's men, probably because they played such dangerous roles. Attachment just meant potential heartache later.

"He's twenty-five, Svea. And as I told you, his credentials are perfect. Two years with the army sorcerers, five years at the academy before that. None in his regiment could beat him at hand-to-hand fighting, and he's one of the top ten swordsmen on the continent."

Aunt Svea raised a skeptical eyebrow as she surveyed Mr. Forell.

"I hand-picked him, you know," Madsen said convincingly. "Every single one of the army sorcerers vouched for him. Incredible fighter and very knowledgeable. You couldn't get better."

Svea looked to Lillian, who began to understand where this was leading.

"No, Auntie," Lillian whispered. "You promised."

"I promised we would wait, and we did. It's time now. You're doing too much not to be noticed eventually. Things have grown too dangerous." She gave Madsen an accusing glare.

"But, it isn't good for us to-"

"Miss Loraine," Mr. Forell interrupted. He looked at her as though she was an unwelcome child at a conversation for adults. "Your aunt can only benefit from having a defender. I promise I will do my utmost to keep her safe and—"

It was his turn to be interrupted. "You told him it was *me*, Madsen?" Aunt Svea said with a laugh. "That wasn't kind."

"No less kind than *you* not telling *me*," Lillian muttered, clutching her skirt in tight fists under the table. Lillian had done all she could to shield her aunt and friends from the coordinator. The idea of one of his men living there, trailing her everywhere she went and interfering with their lives, was completely out of the question.

Mr. Forell looked between Lillian and her aunt, disbelief and horror warring in his expression. "Surely you're not suggesting that—"

"My dear Lillian." Mr. Forell was interrupted again, this time by Madsen. "You did beautifully with Octens this evening. Thanks to you, we've almost got the men sent after him."

"What? *Her?*" Mr. Forell said with insulting incredulity. "That's impossible. Is this a joke, sir?" He clenched his jaw so tightly that Lillian thought it might break.

"Forell, Miss Lillian Loraine is the youngest sorceress in centuries and your new assignment."

"I can't defend *her*," Mr. Forell exclaimed before Lillian could protest. "She's not even old enough to..." He faltered under the combined stares of Aunt Svea and Coordinator Madsen. Lillian might have laughed if she hadn't been so furious.

"My age is irrelevant, Mr. Forell," she said into the silence. "Because I completely agree with you. You *can't* defend me. You are nothing like what the coordinator and I discussed. I'm sorry that you had to waste your time coming here." She stood, and both men leapt to their feet. "I hope you get to enjoy a day on the beach before you go," she said in her most pleasant, meaningless voice. "The coast is lovely, and I'm told the fishing is unparalleled. Good night."

She ignored the protests of the coordinator and her aunt and walked through the door and down the hall.

Of all the proud, horrible, self-centered, hateful people. How dare he come here, and without anyone asking *her*? She stopped to lean her head against the wall, almost shaking with anger. If she didn't eat soon, she'd be shaking from all the work she'd done.

Lillian ducked into the dining room to find Liv cleaning up plates. The maid smiled at her and, with a little flourish, pulled a napkin off a large roll.

"You're wonderful," Lillian breathed, immediately scooping up the roll and popping a piece of it into her mouth. Liv grinned, and Lillian slipped back into the hall where she could listen to the conversation still going on in the library.

"I won't convince her to let you stay, Mr. Forell," Aunt Svea said. "That's *your* task. I'll be in enough trouble for allowing you to come."

"Where should I look for her?" He sounded less condescending now.

Lillian stepped close to a potted tree and focused her energy on her own form. Invisibility took a bit of energy, and she'd only begun to manage it the last few months. Altering her appearance into another tree was much easier.

Mr. Forell appeared in the library doorway.

"She's probably as hungry as I am," Aunt Svea said from behind him. "Check the kitchen first."

"Yes, ma'am. Thank you." He strode past Lillian, oblivious to her presense.

Once he was out of sight, her aunt whispered, "I know you're there, dear. Put away the leaves, and come talk to us." Of course Aunt Svea would notice an additional tree in the hall. Madsen stood behind her in the doorway, looking around expectantly.

Lillian sighed and let go of the image before lifting her chin and striding back into the library.

"That was amazing," the coordinator exclaimed in a low voice. "Oh, the places you could go, Miss Loraine. Octens' success would be nothing compared to yours. Why, the work you could do for His Majesty if you would only agree to—"

"Enough, Madsen," Aunt Svea said sharply. "You could never guarantee her safety. A spy's life is not for my niece."

"Of course, you're quite right," he agreed quickly, though Lillian knew he wasn't giving up. "But my dear, you *must* have a defender. The crown has a vested interest in you and wants to protect you, not just for the work you're doing, but for your own safety as well. Your gift is one of the most powerful we've ever seen. It's only a matter of time before the Kazats discover you."

"So you've said," Lillian replied blandly. "But I stipulated that *if* I ever accepted a defender, I wanted a female." The idea of living with someone as distasteful as Mr. Forell caused her stomach to churn. At the same time, her future independence hung on Madsen employing her.

"You know there are only three female defenders in the entire country," he said, "all of whom are already assigned."

"Train more, then," suggested Lillian.

"We have five women in training, but it will be years before they're ready. Forell is the best we have right now, and for you, my dear, I want the *best*." The last was said with such fatherly affection that Lillian almost relented. But no. Madsen would say anything to get his way.

Lillian popped another piece of roll into her mouth, leaving her aunt an opportunity to speak. "I don't see what choice we have, Lillian. We'll have to keep him until another can be found."

"Aunt Svea," Lillian exclaimed around her food.

"A sound proposal," Madsen cut in. "I'll be on my way, then. It's late." He stood and walked briskly to the door. "A room next to Miss Loraine's will be just right for Forell. I know he'll do his best for you." He caught Lillian's warning look and amended, "Until I can find someone more suitable, of course."

And then he was gone.

CHAPTER 3

Dan

D an doubled back from the kitchen in time to see Madsen exit the library. He looked like he was *leaving*. Escaping perhaps.

"Forell," he said quietly as he walked past. "Try not to offend the girl again. I'm counting on you to help her develop her gift and her loyalties."

"I'm staying? What about the ceremony?"

"We barely convinced her to let you stay temporarily. Let's not push our luck with the formalities."

He was gone a moment later, just before Lady Ellstrom and her niece appeared. Lillian Loraine nodded in his direction and moved silently away.

Lady Ellstrom beckoned to him. "We'll send to the inn for your things, Mr. Forell. I'll show you to your room."

Dan followed, speechless. He wasn't sure he wanted the assignment, but he *did* want to be recognized for his worth. He was academy trained *and* first in his class, and they all acted like the girl's opinion of him was the only thing that mattered.

Madsen wouldn't trust him with a better assignment if he didn't prove competent with this one. How could this have happened to him? How could he have been assigned to a spoiled child who didn't understand how he could help her?

Lady Ellstrom led him to a comfortable bedroom, gesturing to doors nearby. "That's Lillian's room, and that's mine. I hope you'll be patient with my niece. She's extremely unhappy with this entire situation."

Dan pressed his lips together to prevent himself from responding that *she* was getting the most qualified defender in the country and that *he* was the one stuck with a sorceress with underdeveloped talent and a distracting smile, a young woman that would probably cause him trouble at every turn.

He thanked Lady Ellstrom as politely as he could and bid her goodnight before entering the large bedroom. His saddle bags had already been placed near the table. Someone had expected him to stay. He quickly removed his boots and readied for bed. Tomorrow he'd start over with Miss Loraine, make her trust him somehow. Then he'd discover the extent of her abilities and help her improve them until everyone saw how vital he was to her success. With those happier thoughts, Dan slept almost as soon his head touched the pillow.

The next morning, he found the breakfast parlor empty except for a maid with white-blonde hair laying out trays of food.

"Excuse me, miss...?"

"Liv, sir." She dipped a curtsy. "If you're looking for Lady Ellstrom or Miss Loraine, they'll be taking their breakfast in Lady Ellstrom's room and making plans for the dancing tonight. Mr. Jensen, the caretaker, plans to take you riding around the estate, sir."

He buried his irritation. It wasn't the maid's fault. "Oh?"

"Miss Loraine said you'd like to see the grounds, sir."

"Yes. Thank you, Liv." It made sense to know the layout of the estate, for defensive purposes if nothing else.

Dan ate his meal in silence, barely finishing before the caretaker presented himself. "Jensen, sir. At your service. Miss Loraine said you may be staying some time and would like to scout the fishing and hunting on the property, sir."

"Yes, that would be appreciated."

Jensen grinned, showing one chipped tooth and many smile lines. He appeared ten years older than Dan and had a burly build and a shock of red hair. "I'll see you outfitted with fishing tackle and this afternoon you could try the river, unless you're too tired from your journey."

They spent the next two hours touring the extensive grounds of the Loraine estate, Dan surreptitiously looking for hiding places and weak points in the manor's security. Jensen focused on the best places in the river to catch trout. Dan had never actually fished before, and finally confessed it to Jensen, who watched him very seriously a few uncomfortable moments before saying, "There now, Mr. Forell. That is a major disadvantage in your life, but we can remedy it before any of the other menfolk around find out. It had better be this afternoon." He nodded decisively. "Then you'll still have time to dress for the ladies tonight." At Dan's blank look, he added, "For the dancing."

Dan suppressed a bubble of disappointment. He'd forgotten about the dance. Such a waste of time. "Perhaps we'd better head back. I'd planned to be of service to Miss Loraine today."

"Oh, she's long gone by now."

"What?" He managed not to shout as an unfamiliar discomfort pinched him under his ribs. She could be in danger.

"Well, yes, sir. She went calling with Lady Ellstrom. And then she'll stop at her friend, Miss Melina Penchant's, to pick up extra flowers. Miss Loraine can never get enough pink roses."

"When do you expect her back?"

"Not before early evening, and then she'll be at her dressing room until the guests arrive. Nearly the entire district shows up for Miss Loraine's dances. I, m'self, am not one for dancing," he said. "But thankfully my wife is expecting our fourth soon, and my oldest daughter is too young, so I don't have to go."

Dan clenched his teeth and considered riding out after Miss Loraine. It would probably anger her further. "Congratulations on the upcoming birth," he told Jensen. He thought longingly of the practice weapons and books in his trunk, which still hadn't arrived. "Fishing, then?"

"My pleasure, sir." Jensen smiled as though he'd just received a particularly nice birthday present.

~

Lillian

"That wasn't very nice of you, dear," Aunt Svea said as she helped Lillian dress her hair.

"What? Denuding Melina's rose bushes? She'll have a hundred more blossoms within the week, Auntie."

"You know very well I meant the way you avoided Mr. Forell today."

"Why should I spend time with him? We mutually dislike each other. He'll be gone soon. Besides, Jensen said they had a wonderful time fishing."

"Any time fishing is wonderful for Jensen," Svea said, holding up different hair ornaments for Lillian to choose from.

"Why should I spend more time with him than absolutely necessary?" Lillian turned away from the mirror and pulled a dark green gown from her wardrobe, ignoring the dress Liv had already laid out for her.

"You should wear the white, dear," her aunt said. "And I think you're simply uncomfortable with him knowing about your gift."

Lillian didn't scoff at the word "gift" as she wanted to. "It's hard to work with him frowning at me, and white is for young girls looking for husbands." She held up the green dress. "The last time I wore this, Mr. Dahlstrom said my eyes sparkled like emeralds."

"Mr. Dahlstrom is sixty years old and colorblind."

Lillian laughed. "Oh, let me enjoy a compliment. I'm sure he meant it, which is more than I can say for any other compliment I've received from a man."

Aunt Svea eyed her a bit warily in the mirror. "It wouldn't hurt you to give someone else a chance."

Lillian sighed. "It hurt last time. Why wouldn't it hurt again?"

"I don't want you to be like me, dearest," she protested quietly.

"Loved by everyone, intelligent, independent?"

"Alone." Aunt Svea had been married only a few months before her husband died of pneumonia. She'd been a widow for almost fifty years.

Lillian sniffed. "You wouldn't be alone if you paid a tenth as much attention to Sir Malick as he pays to you."

That brought a laugh. "The dear. He only flirts to cheer me up. He's been my friend too long to be interested in an old lady like me."

Lillian watched her aunt slyly, an old suspicion resurfacing. "If you promise to see Dr. Prent about your tremor, I'll dance as long as I see you flirting with Sir Malick."

"Done," Aunt Svea said immediately.

Lillian quickly rethought her idea. Perhaps she'd spoken too hastily. "I was only joking about the dancing, Auntie."

"Too late," Svea said dismissively as she turned away. "If I'm going to play the temptress tonight, I'm going to wear something more provocative."

"Aunt Svea," Lillian said, her eyes wide.

"Like my rubies," Svea added with smirk and a toss of her grey head.

Lillian snorted a laugh but wished she'd never suggested the scheme. She liked dancing, but only with Sir Malick and some of his friends, men who had once been fighters, who were profoundly graceful dancers, and who didn't say anything inappropriate. Of course, tonight she was obligated to dance at least a couple times with Octens. The coordinator wanted him seen again.

An hour later, after leading the first dance with Sir Malick, Lillian attempted to melt into a group of matriarchs seated in one corner of the ballroom. Aunt Svea gave her a meaningful look from several paces away before sidling up to Malick and smiling flirtatiously. Lillian had to laugh at the look on his face: surprise and pleasure mixed with concern. What must he think of her aunt's level of sobriety?

There was nothing for it. She had to dance, but at least Aunt Svea would have to see Dr. Prent.

Melina's little brother, Geoffrey, gave her a meaningful look before sweeping his curls out of his eyes and moving toward her. Across the room, Mr. Forell tried to free himself from the clutches of the three Mitter girls. Lillian hid a smile behind her fan. She'd hinted about his eligibility to them when they'd arrived, and judging by their enthusiasm, they'd taken her words very seriously. But Mr. Forell was getting closer, and one of the sisters had already given up, accepting a dance from another young man.

She only had seconds before Mr. Forell and Geoffrey would reach her. Dancing with an imaginary man was preferable to her current options. Lillian took a deep breath, formed an image of Octens firmly in her mind, then feigned surprise as he stepped into the room from a nearby door. His smooth, auburn hair was combed neatly, his dark blue coat was expertly cut, and his mocking smile showed perfect, white teeth. He bowed and held out his hand to her. She quickly excused herself to the sweet woman next to her, and, holding her head high, walked with Octens onto the dance floor. She infused just enough distrust into her expression to make it clear she was not pleased with the arrangement. She didn't need her own reputation to suffer. Octens only smiled more deeply and began the dance. It was a simple one, and Lillian enjoyed the steps, even if she felt utterly ridiculous dancing without an actual partner. Thankfully, no one but Aunt Svea and Madsen knew how ridiculous it really was.

Lillian kept tabs on Geoffrey, who stared at her openly, and on Mr. Forell, who kept an eye on her much more subtly, turning occasionally to keep her in his general line of vision. As the music slowed, Octens led her to a stop just in front of Melina, and with another mocking bow, he was gone in pursuit of the maid he'd followed yesterday, both of them disappearing around a corner.

Keeping his image perfect from every angle had been exhausting, and the last thing she needed was to faint or be sick all over the dance floor. Using her gift to hide what she was doing, she pulled a vial of her medicine from her pocket and placed a dose under her tongue.

"Even if he is the baron's friend, you don't have to dance with him if you don't want to," Melina said consolingly.

Lillian changed the subject. She had no intention of telling even her best friend why she chose to dance with the scoundrel. From the corner of her eye, Lillian saw one of Madsen's suspects follow after the non-existent Octens.

Aunt Svea wasn't finished with her antics, so Lillian had little choice but to accept a dance from Geoffrey and another from a man she didn't know, who asked her twice about Blevin Octens. Lillian scoffed at his inference that she had an understanding with the man, and was glad when the dance ended and her wiry, unpleasant partner departed. She danced the next several sets with different young men of her acquaintance. They were not enjoyable dances, but they were relatively painless.

An hour into the evening, however, she was claimed by Mr. Forell, who swooped in so suddenly that she accepted his request for a dance out of sheer surprise. His hand took hers firmly as he escorted her onto the floor, and, as annoyed as she was, she couldn't help noticing how well their hands fit together. Still, she wished she could have thought of an excuse. Perhaps she could have faked a fever, but there was no point to such hopes. She'd promised Madsen she'd help with Octens, so she had to stay.

"I was disappointed to not work with you today, Miss Loraine. We have much to discuss." Mr. Forell's tone was polite, but she guessed at the frustration behind his voice. If she wasn't so distracted by his proximity, she might have answered immediately. They began the dance, and she was relieved to find he knew what he was doing. He was even as graceful as Sir Malick.

"My day had been planned before you ever came, Mr. Forell," she finally managed, giving him a pleasant smile. She chatted on before he could interrupt her, telling him all about the importance of a well-rehearsed quartet. It wasn't polite not to let him get a word in, but it meant he couldn't criticize her.

By the time the song was over, exhaustion pulled at her limbs. Unfortunately, Aunt Svea hadn't taken a break from her flirting campaign.

"I hope you will dance the next with me as well, Miss Loraine," Mr. Forell said, his brow furrowed. "I'd like to talk with you about your schedule for the week. I thought—"

Lillian lightly touched his arm to interrupt him and nodded toward the far wall. Mr. Forell looked down at her hand with an odd, not entirely pleased expression, then turned to see Octens beckon to Lillian from across the room.

"I'm so sorry, Mr. Forell. I'm afraid I've promised this dance. I thank you for your kind offer." As she left him, she let her polite mask slip. He didn't want to dance any more than she did. He was only trying to do his job, a job he didn't want. Well, that's exactly what she had to do this evening: a job she didn't want.

She moved sideways through the crowd to the empty space where Octens waited. Mr. Forell followed her but was intercepted by the Mitter girls again. What could he *want*? As she neared her illusion, a man suddenly stepped out from a doorway several paces away. He was the same man who'd danced with her and asked about Octens. Lillian's eyes were drawn to the gleam of the large blade clasped in his hand, just before he threw it at the spy's back.

CHAPTER 4

Dan

Dan shook himself free of the girls clinging to his arms just as a wiry man with a knife appeared near Miss Loraine. Dan swore under his breath and sprinted forward, pulling one of his own blades from inside his jacket. Octens moved between him and the assassin, blocking his chance. He was too late, too far away. An unfamiliar pain seared his chest as the assassin's blade flew toward Lillian Loraine. The trajectory immediately proved Octens was the target, but the blade miraculously missed. Miss Loraine uttered a tiny gasp as the knife flew by her, and for a sickening moment, he thought she'd been struck. The fearful "oh" of her mouth instantly disappeared as the knife clattered against the wall, thankfully far from any other guests. Miss Loraine took several steps back, wrapping her arms around herself as two of Madsen's men tackled and disarmed the would-be-assassin. By the time Dan reached Miss Loraine's side, the work was finished.

His heart pounded loudly as Octens' attacker was led forcibly away by Madsen's men. Dan was surprised the spy didn't follow to question the assassin himself, but Octens hadn't been acting himself that evening. His dancing had been too graceful, his mannerisms altered. Dan took a step forward to ask Octens if he was all right, but the man melted into the crowd and disappeared.

Dan stood helplessly next to Miss Loraine while she quieted the guests, and he had to admit she lied impressively. She held her fan against one arm in an indignant stance and gave an explanation that he was sure she'd invented on the spot.

"That Blevin Octens will never set foot in our home again, I assure you. Trying to accost young women and sending their fathers wild with anger," she exclaimed in a carrying whisper to several women nearby. "We never would have allowed him to come if he wasn't the baron's friend." The women scattered to spread the tale.

Once the crowd had finally dispersed back to their dancing, everyone happy with something to gossip over, Madsen appeared at Miss Loraine's side and bowed over her hand. "Congratulations, my dear," he said in a low voice. "That was most impressive."

Before Dan could ask what he meant, Miss Loraine withdrew her fingers and said on an unsteady breath, "Far too much excitement for me, Mr. Madsen." The sparkle in her eyes was absent, and though she smiled, it conveyed no warmth. "I'm going to freshen up and find a cookie."

She left, winding her way gracefully through the crowd, her fan still clasped against her arm as she gave reassurances to guests along her way.

Dan intended to follow, but the coordinator leaned closer to speak even more quietly. "You see what I mean, don't you? We *need* her," he said.

Dan glanced around to be sure their conversation was still private. "Sir? In what way?"

Madsen looked at him as though he lacked judgement. "Have

you ever seen such a perfectly created image? How else could we convince the Kazats that Octens was in Kalmar? There was a question of identity compromise. We had to lay a false trail. And she did it beautifully, neatly catching us the man who was sent to kill Octens. Now his friends will go back and feed a false trail to Reznik."

"Octens is still in Kazatania?"

"Yes, of course. He's been invaluable there. We couldn't pull him out."

Dan blinked as a wave of understanding washed over him. He'd been so wrong. He hated being wrong. Octens had only been an image, one cast so expertly that it didn't even falter when the knife was thrown. That was why Octens hadn't spoken to anyone else, why he hadn't touched anyone else. He'd only been a distortion of light.

"That's why he danced so well," Dan murmured. Miss Loraine wasn't familiar with the way Octens danced. She'd probably never met him. Dan smiled to himself. She'd been dancing alone.

"What's that?"

"Nothing s—Madsen." He thought for a moment. "She cast that image of Octens without any help at all?"

Madsen nodded. "I told you her talent was amazing. We've never had someone with a gift for illusions, and she would perfectly complement the gifts of the army sorcerers. Or she'd be perfect to work directly with the king. Either way, no one would suspect her, not with her youth and social standing. She's pretty, but not so pretty that she should draw attention. Though, come to think of it, she draws much more attention than I would like."

Dan glared at Madsen, though he was much angrier with himself than he was with the coordinator. He'd misjudged Miss Loraine, badly.

Dan excused himself to follow her, a sudden discomfort

plaguing him as he remembered the momentary look of surprised panic on her face before the knife had clattered against the wall.

He walked silently down the hallway, pausing to listen at doors as he went. Silence met him at each until he reached the library. A woman was crying behind that door in muted, gasping, little sobs. He couldn't stand it when a woman cried, and knowing that it was Miss Loraine made it so much worse, probably because she was his assignment.

Dan opened the door very quietly to see Miss Loraine seated at a polished desk, her entire body trembling as tears leaked from between her tightly closed eyes. Blood soaked the sleeve of her dress, and she held a small cloth to her upper arm.

Dan swore once and stepped inside the library, shutting the door behind him. Her eyes had flown open at the sound of his voice, and she leapt to her feet, quickly scurrying around the desk before standing regally before him.

Dan stared.

The blood was gone. Her tears, reddened face, injured arm; had he imagined it all? She raised one imperious eyebrow.

"I came to check on you," he said as he approached. "Why didn't you tell someone you'd been hurt?"

She didn't answer, but as he skirted the desk, she moved too, keeping the desk between them.

Dan halted mid-stride. "Are you really going to make me chase you around the library?" He knew he sounded angry. He *was* angry, angry with himself for not understanding, and angry with her for hiding everything from him.

"What do you want?" she finally said. Her face was smooth and her expression cool, but her voice came out in a hoarse whisper.

"I want to help you care for your arm," he said, taking a slow step forward. "And I want to make sure nothing like this ever happens again." He took another step. "Now, please get rid of the image you're casting on yourself." At his next step, she rocked backward, as though tempted to turn and run. "I know you're hurt, and moving about isn't going to help." He drew out his pocket cloth and closed the distance between them. She didn't run, but she didn't dispel the image either. He leaned forward and gently gripped her hand.

He mostly did it to make sure she stayed still, so he could tend to her arm without more blood loss. He wasn't prepared for the odd sensation around his heart when his calloused hand met her ungloved fingers.

Stop being an idiot. She's your assignment. He frowned. "Release the image, please, Miss Loraine. I can't see what I'm doing."

She sighed. In an instant, the image was gone and her injury visible. Her reddened eyes turned away as he inspected the gash just above her elbow. It was deep, but as he firmly blotted it with the cloth, he couldn't find anything else concerning. "It'll be fine, but it needs tending. Let's get your aunt and—"

"No."

He jerked his head up.

"We can't tell anyone," she said, sniffing. "I just need to bandage it, and then I can go back to the dancing."

"A surgeon should see to this."

"If Aunt Svea finds out, she won't want me involved in these things any longer. She may want me to have a defender, but she doesn't want me to *need* a defender. It was difficult enough to convince her I should work with Madsen in the first place."

"You *want* to work with Madsen?" he asked, not masking his confused disbelief.

"No." She closed her eyes as he pressed the cloth to the wound again. More tears spilled from between her lashes. "But I *can* help, so I should. I want to be useful, and the income means I can be independent one day."

She had motivation. Perhaps they could accomplish something together after all. "Hold pressure here," he instructed, moving her free hand to cover the cloth.

The thrill at touching her hand was beyond irritating, but much less irritating than the strange urge to gather her into his arms.

"You have to stop shaking, so I can tend to this. I'll get my kit. Do you need anything?"

She bit her lip, then said, "Some chilled juice would help me settle down."

He nodded once. "I'll be right back."

"But—"

"It's going to be fine, Miss Loraine," he said, surprised to find he meant it. "Come, sit here until I get what I need to take care of this." He guided her to a seat closer to the fireplace so the heat and light could replenish her energy. Did she even know that's what most sorcerers needed after working? And why was it hard to let go of her hand? He jerked his own away, as though he'd been burnt.

She gave him a very doubtful look but sat, still shaking and sniffling. Perhaps he'd be able to teach her better control over her emotions during their time together.

Satisfied she would stay where she was, Dan turned and strode away, trying to ignore the pleasant feeling in his chest that he assumed was a hope she wouldn't be so terrible to work with after all.

Lillian

Lillian watched with trepidation as Mr. Forell moved briskly to the door. Did she dare trust him? She tried to blame her current shakiness entirely on her recent work and need for medicine, but she knew part of it may have come from the close proximity to an extremely attractive man. He'd seemed almost kind for a moment, and he did have the nicest eyes... She shook her head. How idiotic. He was there because of Madsen, to keep her alive so she could keep doing what Madsen needed her to do for the security of Kalmar.

Although he *had* been gentle when touching her arm.

Mr. Forell returned a few minutes later with his shirt sleeves rolled up, carrying a leather case and a glass of juice.

"I was an army medic," he said, setting down his case on a small table. "And I had further training with healers at the academy." He waved at her bandaged arm. "The scar would be better with a skilled surgeon, but I can manage this well enough."

"What other kind of training did you have at the academy?" Lillian asked, nervous to have him near her again and very conscious over her lack of magical education. There were no academies for sorcerers, and though she'd read all the books on magic in the baron's library a few times through, she'd always wanted another sorcerer to talk to and learn from. Mr. Forell was the closest she'd ever known.

He lifted her hand from holding pressure on the wound. His own hands were damp, as though he'd just washed them. "The bleeding stopped." He sat down close beside her.

Oh. He was *really* close.

He carefully inspected her gash before seeming to remember her question. "Weapons, hand-to-hand combat, magical theory, all sorts of things." He opened a jar of ointment and scooped a small amount onto his fingers. "This will take most of the pain of the stiches away," he said.

Stitches?

Mr. Forell immediately distracted her anxiety by moving nearer still and smoothing the ointment along the margins of her wound. She'd never been so aware of a person's physical nearness. His scent was clean and masculine and hinted of leather and cinnamon. A number of small scars marked his tanned forearms.

"You have to stop trembling, or I can't put any stitches in," he said firmly. "Are you that shaken, Miss Loraine?"

As though having an assassin's blade slice open your flesh was nothing to be concerned about.

Lillian quickly wiped her tears again. The numbing ointment was beginning to work, thank goodness.

"This will help," she said, lifting the glass.

"A serving girl already had chilled cider, though perhaps you need something stronger." He pulled a few packets from his medical kit.

Juice was exactly what she needed, even if it was disgusting. The sugar would replace what her illusion-making had depleted in her blood, especially if she added a few drops of her medicine. With only a tiny bit of her gift to hide what she was doing, she whisked a small vial from a pocket in her skirt and emptied a few drops into her cup. It tasted terrible and sickly sweet, but she sipped it anyway, allowing it to sit under her tongue a few moments before each swallow. Her shakiness faded, as it usually did.

"Feel better?" Mr. Forell asked, the intensity in his grey-blue eyes making it difficult for her to concentrate.

Lillian nodded and said the first words that crossed her mind. "I've never had stitches before. Does it hurt much?"

He gave her a sharp look. "It shouldn't. But whatever you do, don't move."

Did he think she'd have a tantrum like a little child? She'd just been sliced open by that disgusting knife, and hadn't betrayed it to anyone in the entire room. At least, no one but Mr. Forell had suspected it.

"How did you know that I'd been injured?" she asked.

"I'm going to clean the wound first," he said, shaking a small vial. "I didn't know, only guessed. Tell me if this hurts." He drizzled a small amount of pale pink liquid onto her arm, sponging the excess with a cloth.

"No, it's fine."

"Good." He scrubbed the wound more briskly, and she held her breath. *That* hurt.

He set down the cloth and selected a curved needle, threading it carefully.

Oh. Oh, dear. That was an actual needle, and he was going to stab her with it. Her heart sped up alarmingly, and a sheen of sweat broke out on her brow.

She definitely needed a mask for this. She slid the image over her face as he pressed the needle into her skin. The numbing ointment helped, but it wasn't perfect. A sharp sting caught her breath from her and brought tears to her eyes. *Don't look. Don't look.*

He glanced at her and, apparently satisfied with her image of a stoic expression, kept his needle moving steadily. He was half-done when one of her tears splashed his hand. He froze, and she avoided looking at him, but he put a hand to her cheek before she could pull away.

"What is this?" He rubbed the moisture of her tears between his fingers. Then, in clipped tones he said, "I would appreciate it if you would avoid placing images on yourself around me. As your defender, I need to know what you're feeling and thinking if I'm to help you."

Lillian hiccupped and released the image.

"Does it hurt still?"

Well, obviously. "Yes, a little."

"You could have just told me," he said, his blue eyes solemn. "We'll use more numbing ointment." He spread another scoop of the medication along her wound and then looked back up to study her face.

"You needn't be so disapproving, Mr. Forell," Lillian said quietly as she mopped her eyes.

"What makes you think I disapprove of anything?" he said, his eyebrows still furrowed.

"Don't you?"

He watched her a long moment before she turned away.

"What do you want to tell your aunt about your arm?" he finally asked.

Lillian sighed. "I don't think I'll tell her at all."

They sat in silence a few minutes more while Lillian berated herself for the tears pricking her eyes simply because an irritable stranger disliked her.

"My arm is numb, I think," she finally said.

Mr. Forell resumed stitching while she sipped her drink.

He tied off the last knot but gripped her arm when she moved to stand. "One moment," he said. He pulled another little pot toward him and opened it one-handed. "This one keeps it from festering." He smoothed a generous amount of odorless salve along her wound, and the heat of his hands was simultaneously pleasant and disturbing. She jumped to her feet and took a few steps toward the door. "Thank you for tending to my arm. I should get back to my guests. They won't see the torn sleeve, or the blood."

"Wait."

She turned back to face him.

"I hope you don't have any more parties planned for a while."

"Not for a week, at least, though I usually receive callers or go out visiting most days."

"You do have a lot of friends," Mr. Forell said with such a disapproving set to his mouth that Lillian had to laugh.

"You find that strange?" she asked.

"It's inconvenient that everyone likes you so well." He paused a moment before adding, "But they underestimate you."

"Not everyone likes me." Obviously *he* didn't. "No one should know what I can do. Besides, a *different* estimation doesn't mean an *under*estimation. I wouldn't be less of a person without my gift, just less useful to Madsen and His Majesty."

Mr. Forell's eyebrows rose an inch. "You have an incredible gift, and you aren't even fully mature yet."

What a horrid thing to say. Lillian quickly slid an image of a pleasant, blank expression over her face. It couldn't help for him to see her disgust.

His eyelids narrowed, and he leaned forward to study her face. He couldn't have noticed. No one ever noticed when she changed her image.

"Just how old do you think I am, Mr. Forell?" she asked.

His eyes darted about the room. At least he was smart enough to recognize a trap.

CHAPTER 5

Dan

Dan snapped his mouth shut and looked around for an escape. He was such an idiot around her. First, he hurt her with the sutures, then he was silent when she accused him of disapproval, and now he had no idea what to say about her age.

"I wasn't given that information, Miss Loraine," he finally managed. She could be as young as sixteen or as old as twenty-five, but anything he said would be wrong, just as any truthful answer about his disapproval would be wrong. There was no polite way to explain that his disappointment at working with her had everything to do with her youth, beauty, and popularity.

"Perhaps we shouldn't make assumptions, then." Her tone was sweet, but Dan was almost positive she had placed an image over her face. Her eyes lacked their usual brightness, and her hair wasn't nearly as glossy. On the one hand, he'd asked her not to do it, but he also needed to placate her before she got hysterical. "Of course. Of course. Now don't you think tomorrow we'd better start early? I need to learn about your gift, and what I can do to help you and keep you safe. We've wasted almost the entire day."

"Have we, Mr. Forell?" she said with a polite smile, though he suspected her real expression could have cut open his liver. "I spent my day feeding false information to Kazat spies. How did you spend yours?"

"In frustrating idleness."

Miss Loraine blinked her eyes innocently. "Didn't you enjoy fishing?"

Dan shook his head. "Much more than I should have. I think Jensen somehow snuck the first fish onto the line so *I'd* be hooked. I haven't had fun like that for years."

"Really? Don't you get any time off in the army?" True curiosity tinted her voice.

"I never take much. There's always something too important going on, and now I have something much more important to take care of." He clenched his teeth a moment, hating what he had to say next. "I owe you an apology," he said firmly.

He caught himself staring too long into her hazel eyes, and coughed to cover the awkwardness. "I'm very sorry that I allowed you to get hurt. I've only been your defender one day, and you ended up needing a surgeon."

She smiled a little. "That's all right, Mr. Forell. I suppose I didn't let you get close enough to do any defending. I didn't expect to need it."

He shook his head. "I knew better, and still you were hurt, by accident at that. Imagine what could happen when the Kazats find out about you."

"Yes, I see your point."

"Madsen thinks they'll come for you eventually, and he's right. A power like yours..."

She looked up, her eyes solemn.

"What they sent for Octens will be nothing compared to

what they'll send after you." She didn't have a chance without him.

Miss Loraine pressed her lips together and turned to study the line of tiny stitches on her arm.

"I know I am only your defender until you can have the kind you prefer," he said, "but I don't want to fail you again as I did today. So I propose that *I* keep better track of you, and *you* stop avoiding me."

She watched him a moment before nodding once. "I suppose that's best."

"Will you spend tomorrow morning with me and explain more about what you can already do? Then we can decide what to work on from there."

She sighed. "I guess we should. I'm not particularly interested in having a knife lodged in my heart, no matter who it's aimed at."

Dan nodded. "Thank you. May I take you back to your aunt now? Or will you retire early?" He didn't want her around another potential assassin, but he didn't want her to disappear into her room where he couldn't see her either.

She gave a wry smile and shook her head. "No. I'd better get back, but I supposed I'd better clean the blood off the table first. I don't want Liv to see it."

Dan helped her scrub the table with cloths from his medical kit and then followed her back to the party. She spoke briefly with her aunt and then melted into a crowd of matrons.

Madsen appeared at Dan's shoulder. "Come to an understanding, have you?" he asked.

"I'm not sure I'd call it that just yet," Dan said, glancing at her over Madsen's shoulder. A few young men had come to talk to their older female relations, no doubt with the hope of snaring Miss Loraine for a dance.

"Well, take care of it. I want that girl committed and developing her skills for us."

Dan raised an eyebrow at the coordinator's steely tone. "She'll do her best for you, I think, with or without me, and I'll do everything I can to keep her safe, but you'd better stop throwing her in danger."

"She's fine. You saw her."

"I saw her bleeding all over the library. The blade went through the image of Octens and sliced her arm. She's lucky it didn't hit a lung."

Madsen opened his mouth and closed it. "Did you take care of it?"

"It'll heal."

"Svea's going to kill me."

"Miss Loraine doesn't plan to tell her aunt."

"Fast work there, Forell. Good lad."

Dan had a sudden and strange impulse to punch Madsen in the face. "I didn't have to convince her. She didn't want anyone to know." Maybe she was tougher than she looked.

The retired, jovial persona reemerged, and Madsen clapped him on the shoulder. "Well, good. I'm glad to hear it. I'm leaving now." He lowered his voice again. "But I'll send her instructions for the next project soon."

Dan watched the coordinator melt through the crowd. Madsen mostly gave his orders from a distance, but if Miss Loraine joined the army sorcerers, she'd have to work with him more often. And as much as he tried, Dan could *not* imagine Miss Loraine with the army sorcerers. They did serious work, frequently wading into danger to wield enormous power. They struck fear into any who opposed them. He swallowed a curse and glanced to Miss Loraine who was laughing happily with her friends. She couldn't frighten a rabbit if she tried, and yet, Dan couldn't keep his scowl in place. He felt his lips turn up involuntarily. Miss Loraine was sweet and charming...that is, for a spoiled little prodigy who spent far too much time on her appearance and friends. But what a prodigy. He'd never seen anything like it. The army sorcerers could rain fire and ice down on armies, control plants and animals, and travel miles in the blink of an eye, but what Miss Loraine had accomplished that night was unparalleled. The coordinator had been right—her potential was enormous. If she wasn't so weak and delicate, her addition to the army sorcerers would be priceless.

Dan spent the rest of the evening subtly watching her as she moved among her guests. Jensen, the caretaker, had said she invited *everyone* to her parties, and if so, then *everyone* seemed to adore her.

It was a pitiful shame. He'd watched dozens of sorcerers paired with their defenders, watched the way they worked, practically reading one another's minds. Dan had worked so hard, but what did he get? Someone who would waste her talent on small tricks for Madsen while she partied with her friends, someone who'd be a target of the Kazats before she could ever become a threat to them. He didn't have a chance of keeping her safe unless he made her strong first.

～

Lillian

Lillian woke the next morning to someone pounding on her door.

"Miss Loraine, are you awake?"

Goodness. He wasn't going to barge in, was he?

"I'm coming in," Mr. Forell called. The knob turned.

He was!

Lillian leapt from her bed and pulled an image together just as he walked briskly through her door.

"Good morning," he said to the image of herself sitting at her table beside her perfectly made bed. This version of herself was properly clothed with her hair dressed. She paused in writing a letter to frown at Mr. Forell. Lillian *wanted* to throw a mug from her nightstand at him. He'd never know what hit him. His eyes flickered in her direction, bringing her back to reality. She gave up on the mug and began easing around the bed and toward her image.

"I'm glad you're up," he said, a little too cheerfully and far too loudly for the time of day. "Your cook was kind enough to pack us breakfast." He held up a tote of food. "I thought we could find a secluded place in the gardens to begin working."

The image raised an eyebrow at him and didn't speak. She placed her pen in the inkwell and fanned the letter with her hand to dry the ink. Lillian slowly eased into her illusion so her voice would come from the correct direction.

"Perhaps you are unaware that coming into the room of an unmarried woman is considered inappropriate," she said. "As is spending large amounts of unsupervised time together."

A hint of frustration flickered across his face before he casually leaned against the doorframe. "But I'm your defender, at least for now, and rules such as those don't apply."

"But few people know of my abilities, so it would still seem very inappropriate."

"What if you cast an image of a chaperone any time people could see us?"

Lillian held back a groan of exasperation at the way he'd cornered her.

"Give me a moment to get ready," she said. "I'll be out soon."

"I'll wait for you," he said quickly, as though worried she'd get away from him again. "How can I help?"

Lillian bit her tongue. She couldn't tell him she wasn't decently clothed when to his eyes she was wearing a somber grey gown. "Very well," she said calmly before folding the letter that didn't exist and placing it on the dresser. She almost opened the top drawer to pull out a vial of her medicine but then reconsidered. She hadn't had any dizziness in weeks, and it had been a year since her last seizure. They'd be eating breakfast soon anyway. Aside from all that, the top drawer always squeaked. She wouldn't be able to hide what she was doing, and she wasn't ready to explain any sort of weakness to Mr. Forell. He disapproved of her enough already.

He held the door open, and she passed quickly by him, glad he didn't offer her his arm. The appearance of her dress wouldn't match the feel of her bare skin.

They walked through the halls and entryway without seeing anyone and without speaking. Once outside, Lillian focused a moment, letting an image form in her mind before it took shape in the shadow of the doorway and stepped out to join them.

"Who is that?" Mr. Forell asked, glancing at the dark-haired, older woman behind them.

"My imaginary friend, Eleanor." She smiled at the image, who smiled back and looked skyward.

"It is a beautiful day, isn't it?" she asked the image. Eleanor nodded before putting on a hat.

The image walked with them through the gardens. They waved to Jensen, who worked in the distance, and eventually they made their way into a private, grassy space lined by rows of trees on all sides. Eleanor disappeared, and Mr. Forell shook his head. "She was very good."

"Thank you." Lillian looked pointedly at the basket in his hand. Creating images in the morning on an empty stomach was never a good thing.

He reached into the basket but pulled out a pencil and paper.

"You can cast images of other people near you, almost to perfection," he said, writing quickly on his paper, "and you can alter your own image enough that most people don't realize you're doing it."

She raised an eyebrow at him. *Really?*

"We can work on that," he assured her, obviously not understanding the hint. "Could you show me what else you've already mastered?"

"I can change the way an object looks, make it look like something else entirely."

"Could you show me, please?"

Lillian sighed. She *would* be polite to him, even if he did ask for ridiculous parlor tricks. He'd been patient with her last night. She could be patient with him today. She bent and picked up a small rock from the flower bed below them. In her palm it turned into a colorful garden spider. She smiled at the look on Mr. Forell's face.

"Hold it," she suggested. "I can't change the way it feels, or the weight of it. I can only bend the light to alter the image."

He held out his hand, and Lillian dropped the spider into it, making the legs wiggle convincingly. The spider walked along his palm and then, because Mr. Forell looked much too calm, Lillian sent the spider crawling up his wrist and into his shirt. He flinched and then barked a laugh as the rock in his hand became visible once more.

Lillian almost lost hold of the image of her grey dress, and instantly berated herself. Just because he *could* laugh didn't mean she had to go all mushy inside.

"I knew it wasn't real, but it still startled me." He shook his head, still smiling at his palm a moment before looking back to her. He immediately frowned and moved back a few feet, as though afraid of catching something infectious.

He made another note on his paper. "So, small things, but very detailed."

"I can do larger things," Lillian said, trying not to take offense. Octens was six feet tall, for heaven's sake.

He looked at her expectantly, his pencil poised.

"Especially if you let me eat breakfast."

"Oh, of course," he said. "But can we eat after we've finished? We're finally making progress."

Lillian repressed some unladylike words and looked out into the yard. Two benches nearby suddenly turned into sheep, which changed color every few seconds as they frolicked around the yard. She even kept their shadows slanting the correct direction.

"Quite impressive," he said. "What about larger things?"

The sheep disappeared. "I've worked up to altering trees and parts of the landscape."

"Would you show me, please?" he asked officiously.

"I'd rather not," Lillian admitted. "It takes quite a bit of energy, and I haven't eaten yet, so..." She trailed away as he crossed through the lines he'd just written. "You don't believe I can?" she asked incredulously.

"Of course," he said, glancing at her. "I just want to keep notes on the things I observe."

Something inside her snapped. "If you paid *attention*, your notes would fill the page," she said hotly.

He looked at her in surprise. "What?"

"And I suppose you think it's *my* fault you don't pay attention."

"Miss Loraine," he said with forced patience, as though speaking to an overwrought child. "I did not mean to offend you. I simply want to keep careful notes of the things I *see* so the process is more scientific."

Lillian knew she just needed to eat and she'd be able to calm down, but she didn't care. No one ever treated her so rudely. "What right have you to imply I'm incapable of describing my own work?

"I only meant that if you could show me, then I could—"

"Leave me alone? All right. *Fine*. I'll show you a trick if you'll leave me here in peace, since I'm no longer allowed any in my own room." She pointed to the wall of trees lining the eastern part of the garden. She knew she was being stupid. She had no obligation to prove her words, but something about the way he held himself away from her, as though she was diseased, and the way he gave her no credit for the years of work she'd done to get to her present abilities, infuriated her.

She held her breath, watching with Mr. Forell as the wall of trees grew more thickly together, then shot up to more than three times their natural height, shading the entire garden. Then the other hedges grew, blocking out the arched entrance to the garden, at least to Mr. Forell's view. In her current state of hunger, she never could have held the image from other angles, even if she hadn't been concerned someone else would see.

Mr. Forell's mouth dropped.

Lillian's skin went clammy, and her nausea grew. "That's enough, I think," she said coolly. "That is the way back to the house." The archway appeared. "Please take it and leave me alone." She spoke more quickly at the end, beginning to panic as she grew lightheaded.

Mr. Forell clicked his mouth shut, nodded curtly, and strode away. Lillian slowly released the image, light growing in the garden as her own vision darkened. She groped for the basket of food, hoping he'd brought something useful.

CHAPTER 6

Dan

Dan's irritation grew as he stalked from the garden. At least she brought the light back.

"And Mr. Forell..." Her voice was faint but not repentant. Tired perhaps. "I would appreciate it if you'd find my aunt directly and have her send out some juice." Her tone was more polite now, and it grew so quiet he almost didn't hear when she added, "I'm accustomed to drinking juice."

"Of course, Miss Loraine," he said without turning around. He would not shout at her that she was being petulant and impossible. It wouldn't do any good, and he *would* be a gentleman even for his spoiled little assignment. He scanned the grounds as he left, ignoring an uncomfortable voice in the back of his mind that told him to go back to her. She didn't want him there, and he was certain she was safe. He'd give her some time to calm down and then try again.

His anger took him quickly into the house, and every time his mind presented him with images of her beauty or the memory of her scent, he quickly thought of something else. He was old enough to ignore a pretty face, especially the pretty face of the girl who was going to destroy everything he had worked so hard for.

A minute later he found himself in his room. He flung his paper and pencil aside and forced himself back into the hall where he knocked on Lady Ellstrom's door. There was no answer, and he was about to turn away when he heard stirring from within. Lady Ellstrom appeared a few seconds later, still wearing her night cap and dressing gown.

"What are you doing at this unholy hour?" she demanded groggily. "We were up half the night. Military men. *Really.*"

"I'm sorry to disturb you, Lady Ellstrom. Your niece asked for someone to bring juice to her in the garden, and I didn't know where to find—"

Her eyes came suddenly alive. "The garden? What's she doing in the garden so early?"

"We were working and she... said she'd had enough," he said, trying to keep the defensiveness out of his voice. It wasn't *that* early.

"Did she eat breakfast?" Lady Ellstrom demanded as she swept past him. "Was she upset?"

"We intended to, but we were busy. She *did* become upset. She ordered me away, actually," he said tightly, half expecting Lady Ellstrom to console him.

Instead she turned on him, her eyes filled with anger and worry. "You pushed her, didn't you? And on an empty stomach?"

"I... well..." He was oddly glad she wasn't holding a weapon.

He followed her into her niece's bedroom, dread growing in his chest.

"Someone's been in here," Dan said, eyeing the unmade bed. The letter Miss Loraine had been writing had disappeared from the dresser.

"No one's been here," Lady Ellstrom hissed. She muttered

words that sounded a lot like "idiot" and "bumbler" as she searched one of the drawers. "Here it is," she said more loudly, grasping a small vial of clear liquid. "Quickly. Where is she?"

He led her back through the hallway, and near the kitchen they met Liv. Lady Ellstrom snatched a small pitcher of juice and a cup from the maid's tray and thrust them into Dan's hands. "We'll be back with Lillian in a moment," she said. "She may have had one of her spells."

Liv's face fell, along with Dan's stomach.

"Spells?" he asked as they hurried through the corridor.

"Yes," she huffed, her legs not allowing her much speed. Dan wanted to throw her over his shoulder and run with her back to her niece.

"This is medicine for her?"

"Of course." She was panting already.

"May I run ahead and give it to her?"

"If you think you can do it without causing more trouble, yes. Place two drops under her tongue every minute."

Dan snatched the outstretched vial, his heart hammering in fear, and took off at a sprint.

"Where is she?" Lady Ellstrom called.

"The east garden," he said over his shoulder. He ran on, heedless of the small amounts of juice that sloshed out of the pitcher in one hand but very careful of the vial in his other. The next minute seemed to stretch to an hour, and when Dan arrived back at the garden, there was no sign of her.

She wasn't on the bench where he'd left her, but as he approached it, he saw a slippered foot peeking around the side. He was there in an instant, and when he saw Lillian Loraine, he stopped short, his heart in his navel.

She was dead.

He couldn't draw air, couldn't think.

Miss Loraine lay motionless on her back in the grass behind the bench, her arms bent at odd angles and her face ashen.

Dan had never known such torment. Horror and guilt froze his muscles, his logic, his senses.

But then, did he imagine it? No. Her chest rose in a slow breath.

Dan lunged forward, dropping to his knees beside her and slamming the pitcher onto the wooden bench. The clatter cleared his mind a little, and he shook her shoulder.

"Miss Loraine."

No answer.

"Miss Loraine?"

Still no response.

"Lillian," he practically shouted into her ear as he lifted her to a half-sitting position. She may have twitched a little, but it was difficult to say. With his teeth he pulled the stopper from the vial. He tilted her head back and got two drops of the thick, clear liquid under her tongue.

He counted, watching and listening to her breathing as he tried to understand what she'd done to herself. Her grey dress had been replaced by a soft muslin gown that looked suspiciously like a night dress. Her arms were mostly bare, exposing the row of stitches above one elbow. Her hair was no longer pulled tightly into a smooth knot, but was plaited loosely over one shoulder. Only her hat looked the same as it had when they left the house, though it was lying on the ground next to her rather than properly settled on her head.

He patted her hand. Her skin was cold and clammy.

There was no noticeable difference after a count of sixty, so he gave her another two drops. By the third dose, she began to stir, just as her aunt shuffled into the garden.

"She's breathing?" Lady Ellstrom demanded.

"Yes. She's hardly moved, but she doesn't feel as clammy," he said, putting the back of his hand to her cheek. Her warmth was reassuring, but she was still pale. "I don't understand how she could have changed her clothes. What happened? Did she faint?"

Lady Ellstrom found her niece's pulse and then gave him a hard look. "She had a seizure," she finally said. "She's in a deep sleep now. It will probably last most of the day."

"A seizure?"

"Yes," she said hotly, her eyes narrow slits. "And do you *really* think she changed her clothes?"

Understanding washed over Dan, and he closed his eyes. He was an idiot, a thousand times an idiot. How could he not have realized?

Lady Ellstrom felt Lillian's face and hands and watched her breathing for a few moments before turning back to Dan. "You barged into her room without warning, didn't you? So she conjured up clothing for herself."

Defenders didn't have to wait to enter their sorcerers' rooms, but the Loraines wouldn't know that. He studied Lillian Loraine for further signs of life. "I knocked, but I should have waited."

Her aunt mumbled something about "men" under her breath. "If she does too much with her talent, or especially if she works on an empty stomach, her energy is eaten up. First, she becomes nauseated, tired, and irrational. Then, if she continues to push herself, she loses consciousness and sometimes will have a seizure. Didn't you know that sorcerers developing their gifts often have undesirable physical effects?"

"I did know that," Dan said through gritted teeth. "Their energy is usually replenished by sunshine or heat. I didn't realize the cost to her could be different. It was extremely stupid of me, and I won't let it happen again." Some defender. He'd embarrassed her, starved her, and then abandoned her.

Lady Ellstrom studied his face a moment, then, seeming satisfied with what she saw there, nodded once. She took the vial from his hand and gave her niece another dose.

"And Lady Ellstrom?"

"Yes?"

"Will you please help me learn her eating schedule and needs?" he asked, running a hand through his hair in agitation. "I'm not sure she'll tell me."

Her expression softened. "Of course I will." She stood and beckoned to him. "Bring her back to her room. You can keep giving her medicine until she's awake enough to take her juice. It's just as well you learn what to do when this happens."

Dan blushed to touch a girl when she wore only a night dress, but at Lady Ellstrom's raised eyebrow, he quickly gathered her in his arms and stood, allowing her aunt to set a slow pace back to the house.

◊

Lillian

L illian rested in a comfortable chair on the deck of a ship. The setting sun warmed her left side, and to her right sat a familiar couple, holding hands and smiling at her. The woman was young and dimpled, with Lillian's exact hair color. The man beside her wasn't much older, a red-tinted beard giving him distinction so at odds with the mischief in his hazel eyes. They didn't say anything. They never did. They just watched her, love emanating from their smiling faces. She recognized them, and knew she was dreaming because she'd only ever seen her parents in visions of sleep.

The ship stopped rocking, and she woke with a start, realizing someone had just deposited her into bed.

And she had a headache.

She squinted, opening her eyes as little as possible to see the outlines of Aunt Svea and a vaguely familiar man looking down at her.

"Let me sleep," she mumbled, groping feebly for her blankets, her arms barely moving.

The man pulled the covers up for her, but Aunt Svea said, "Juice first. Then you can sleep."

"Leave me alone," Lillian said, truly wishing for unconsciousness.

"She says just what she thinks when she's in this state," Aunt Svea said as the man raised Lillian's head and pressed a cup to her lips. "You might find it refreshing."

"This is disgusting," Lillian muttered after a few swallows. "You know I hate apple juice."

"You have to drink it, dear. You've had one of your spells."

Lillian glared at the cup but drained it. She was so tired, her limbs leaden. She drifted off, but not before Aunt Svea said, "And when she is in this outspoken and honest phase, you can be sure she won't remember any part of it the next day, so feel free to have frank conversations."

Lillian was too tired to contradict her.

She woke again an hour later when someone shook her shoulder. "Miss Loraine. Miss Loraine. Wake up. It's time for more juice. And something to eat."

"Go away," Lillian moaned. Why was he so loud? And why did her head pound so horribly?

"Miss Loraine, it's very important that—"

"*Honestly.*" With effort, Lillian pulled open her eyes long enough to squint at the stranger and say thickly, "Leave now, please. You are *annoying* me." She closed her eyes, hoping to cure her bone-deep exhaustion.

"She's *your* problem," Aunt Svea said from somewhere nearby. "But she has to eat, even if you have to force it down her throat. Though, if you were smart, you might mention that Liv brought some of her little white cookies." Aunt Svea's footsteps moved away.

Liv's cookies? The idea made its way through her mental fog. Lillian opened her eyes to look hopefully toward her nightstand table. Her satisfaction at seeing the little plate of cookies was dimmed by the laughter coming from the person who woke her. She looked at him more carefully.

Mr. Forell chuckled without restraint, and when he straightened in his chair, his familiar grey-blue eyes moved straight to her own. In place of his usual frown was the most attractive smile she'd ever seen, with a small dimple high up on the left side.

How interesting.

"I see I'm going to have to learn a new recipe, Miss Loraine."

"Don't call me that," Lillian said crossly. She wanted to slap him and play with his hair at the same time. It was highly disturbing to have him so close to her when she wasn't even dressed, and this time, he knew she wasn't. "It is very inappropriate for you to be here."

"But I'm your defender," he reminded her, growing more serious. "And since it's my fault you're in this situation, I intend to be the one to take care of you."

Lillian glared at him, annoyed with him for keeping her awake and annoyed with herself for being attracted to him. "I'm the one who pushed myself too far. It's not your fault or your concern, and I told you to go away." Her voice sounded a little stronger, at least.

"No."

"What?" She tried to sit up a little in bed but quickly gave it up. Instead she leaned back against her pillow, closing her eyes. "It's my room, and I—"

Lillian stopped short when something sweet and crumbly was pushed into her open mouth. Liv's cookies. Mmmm. She moved to take the cookie from him, but her hand only made it halfway before she gave up.

"Just relax. I'll help you eat it."

"By eating it yourself?" she asked distrustfully around her bite.

He laughed again. It was a remarkably wonderful sound. She smiled in spite of herself.

"Yes, and if you drink all your juice, I'll give you another."

Her smile halted. "I don't want to drink apple juice. It always tastes like something died in it."

"It's grape juice, so let's sit you up." His arm slid under her shoulders and propped her up.

Lillian's disquiet at his nearness was tempered by the gentle strength of his arms. She drank, having to stop twice to rest before the glass was finished.

"Ah, but you still look angry," he observed. "Is grape juice bad too?"

"You'd be angry if you felt weak and pathetic."

"Yes, I would."

Why should she want to smooth the crease between his brows? "Don't eat my cookies," she warned instead as he eased her back onto her pillow.

His laugh was the last thing she remembered before falling asleep again.

What seemed only seconds later, her consciousness roused when a calloused hand took her own. Too tired to open her eyes, she waited, expecting Dr. Prent to speak.

Instead Mr. Forell's voice came, low and serious. "I'm sorry to do this when you sleep. I don't think you'll want to when you wake, and it's important to me."

She was on the verge of telling him exactly where he could take himself if he thought he could try something inappropriate while she slept, when he began speaking in a quiet, but formal, tone.

"Lady Lillian Loraine, sorceress of Kalmar, I hereby bind myself to you as your defender. I swear to put your needs above mine, to work in your best interest, to shield you from harm, and to protect your life with my own, to my last dying breath."

Oh. How interesting. It was a good thing she'd kept her eyes closed.

He slowly released her hand, and she felt, rather than heard, him stand up next to her bed. He must have been kneeling.

"Normally there would be witnesses, and we'd sign a contract," he whispered a bit sheepishly. "But there isn't anything normal about this situation."

She drifted back to sleep, wondering if he really could have meant the words he'd just spoken.

She woke every hour, each time being roughly shaken awake but then gently helped up by Mr. Forell. Twice she nearly asked him about what he'd said, but both times she thought better of it. If it had been a dream, she'd only make a fool of herself.

"Lillian, you sleep like the dead," he told her once they'd completed the process a few times.

"Then why are you smiling at me?" she asked sleepily, her curiosity momentarily overcoming her fatigue.

"What do you mean?"

"You usually only glare at me. Or frown at best." She gave him a long, curious look. "Why do I disappoint you?" Maybe he'd tell her if he didn't think she'd remember.

"Why would you think that?"

She finished another glass of juice and sighed, allowing her eyes to slide shut again. "It's true. I think it's because you hate women. Or maybe because Madsen told you to get me to join the army sorcerers, and you know I won't."

"You won't?" he asked, obviously startled.

"No," she breathed as sleep claimed her again.

Almost instantly she felt his hand on her shoulder, shaking her awake. "Why not, Lillian?"

She tried to pull away from him, but he must have been used to it, because he held her shoulder firmly. "Tell me why, Lillian. *Why* won't you work in the army?" How did he make his voice pleading and commanding at the same time?

She opened her eyes a little to study him. He sat forward, his shirt stretched tight over broad musculature. Anxiety pulled at his eyebrows, as though her answer held his future. "Why would I *want* to?" she asked in return.

"That's where you can do the most good."

He was very handsome when he was nervous. She couldn't help smiling at him, but her eyes refused to stay open any longer. "That's the most ridiculous thing I've ever heard."

CHAPTER 7

Dan

Lillian sank into unconsciousness, her words ringing in Dan's ears. She thought she could be more useful somewhere *outside* the military. It was madness, but the type of madness that could be reasoned with. Maybe.

He surveyed her sleeping form. She was still a little pale, though nothing like she'd been in the garden. He remembered her appearance with a surge of guilt. He'd been so confident he was the best person for her. He shook his head in defeat. She'd been vulnerable, beautiful, and pitiful all in one, like she needed a protector. She *did* need one, and all she had for now was him, a pathetic soldier far too distracted by his pretty assignment.

Dan let his head fall forward into his hands. He'd been in her room for hours already. It should have worn off. He shouldn't still be so affected by her, but it was getting worse, not better.

He stood as Lady Ellstrom entered, pulling black gloves from her fingers. "Did she eat anything yet?"

"A cookie is all."

She nodded as though that was what she'd expected. "Are

you ready to hear about her?" she asked, waving him to sit with her on a sofa some distance from the bed.

"Yes, ma'am. Thank you."

"You know that Lillian was adopted by my half-brother, the baron?" she said abruptly.

"No, I thought she was truly your niece."

She shook her head impatiently. "She was found as a baby by one of his stewards at a distant land holding. The steward couldn't find anyone who knew anything about her, so he handed her over to my idiot brother."

Dan kept a straight face, wondering if she'd refer to the baron that way if he was present.

"Her forest home had been destroyed and her parents killed. Bandits, the steward thought, but my brother later suspected Kazats were involved.

"The baron adopted her and cared for her as best he could, but when she was six years old, she became very ill. It had been months since I'd seen her, and I couldn't believe the change in her. She was so thin, just skin and bones, even though she ate and drank everything in sight."

She paused, and Dan spoke his thoughts. "The symptoms are the same as sugar sickness, but it couldn't have been. She survived."

Lady Ellstrom eyed him shrewdly. "You *have* studied, haven't you?" She turned speculative eyes toward Lillian's sleeping form before continuing. "Each doctor my brother hired said her body couldn't access the sugar in her blood, and that she'd die within the week, but she lived each week, and then a month, and another. About the same time, strange things began to appear around the house and grounds, rainbows when there hadn't been rain, ponies and puppies no one could catch." She laughed shortly. "My brother thought a sorcerer had been brought in to play tricks on us, but then another doctor came, and not just a doctor, but a sorcerer too. He did all kinds of tests. He said it wasn't sugar sickness, though it was similar. When he tried to prick her finger again, he couldn't catch her."

"She ran?"

"No. She displaced her image by a few inches. She didn't want him to take blood again. He kept reaching for her hand, but it wasn't there. Once he realized what she was doing, he nearly died of surprise. And he said some very inappropriate words, if I recall." Lady Ellstrom frowned. "There's never been a sorceress so young. And then she lost consciousness and began to seize for the first time. I almost fainted in fear, but the doctor just started dripping medicine into her mouth, and soon she came around. He said her gift was eating up her energy, taking the sugar right out of her blood, so it never had a chance to feed *her*."

"I've never heard of that effect," Dan admitted, looking over at Lillian again. "Usually magic leaches something when it's first used a certain way, depleting senses temporarily, or causing fever or pain, but this could actually *kill* her."

"The physician didn't think it would, but he couldn't promise, so we're very careful. She eats on a strict schedule and drinks juice frequently during and after big projects. She hardly notices the little things anymore."

"And the medicine?"

"It increases the sugar in her blood." She sat back in her chair and gave him a long look. "Once my brother realized what she was, he began to find reasons to work away from the estate."

"Why?"

"My brother's a fool," she said bluntly. "I love him, but there it is. He couldn't bear to see his little girl become a dangerous and powerful woman, so he simply melted out of her life."

"But all his responsibilities are here."

He left his daughter because he was afraid of her? Perhaps he was the idiot his sister took him to be.

"He has holdings spread across the country. He claims they

need his attention and that I'm better at managing the estate anyway. Well, I suppose he's right about that last part," she said with a toss of her head. "But the point is, my niece doesn't need anyone else abandoning her. She was twelve when she realized why her adopted father so rarely came home. It—" She paused. "It was hurtful."

"I wouldn't hurt her."

She watched him a long moment. "We shall see." She glanced over at Lillian. "Madsen knew about her gift because the physician reported to the Crown. I wouldn't even let Madsen see her, but eventually she realized she could be helping people and insisted she begin working. So much of her gift came to her naturally that she was able to start early. She's read a few books on diverting energy, and the physician who diagnosed her symptoms taught her exercises to focus her gift, but most of what she's learned has been through careful experimentation."

Lady Ellstrom frowned in Dan's direction. "When Lillian started taking assignments, they were small projects. She looked great distances, found lost things and people, but Madsen's been giving her increasingly difficult assignments, and about a year ago, she started taking more frequent projects, insisting on it. I worry, especially because Madsen doesn't think of her safety like he should." She pressed her lips together and handed Dan a thick paper. "I'm leaving now to go calling. Here's a description of her usual diet plan," she said, pointing at a neat column. "And here I've written out her schedule for after a seizure. The servants and our close friends all believe she has a mild form of sugar sickness, and each knows what to do if you lose this or have questions. I've told Liv to check in with you regularly, so she can help her with more feminine things. Just ring the bell if you need her sooner."

Dan nodded. "I'll stay with her."

Lady Ellstrom gently smoothed a stray hair from Lillian's face and left.

Dan soon settled in a chair next to the bed, a history text for companionship. Liv passed the open door several times, and after an hour she came into the room.

"Still pale, isn't she?" She shook Lillian's shoulder forcefully, and Dan grunted a laugh.

Liv smiled apologetically. "It won't help to wake her gently."

"I learned that a few times this morning already."

Liv shook Lillian again, calling her name loudly. Lillian moaned, and Liv smiled a little too brightly. "You know you scare us when you do this."

"Oh, Liv. How's your foot this morning?" Lillian asked tiredly. "Still bruised?"

Her face was turned, so Dan couldn't see her expression, but relief flooded him at the sound of her voice.

"Hush. Don't worry about *me*," Liv said. "I shouldn't have stood on that dresser, and *you* should have eaten your breakfast."

Liv helped Lillian sit up before Dan could move to assist them. "I know. I let myself get distracted. Stupid of me." Her voice was only a whisper, but her cheeks had color, and the sleepiness was gone. Perhaps it wouldn't take long for her to be back to normal.

"Would you like me to help you up?"

"No, thank you. Maybe later. But would you give me my cookies and try to find my pearl earrings? One catch was loose, and I took them off in the parlor. Aunt Svea will skin me if she finds out."

"You're right. She will. I'll check back in a bit."

Lillian nodded energetically, and Liv placed the little plate of cookies in Lillian's lap before leaving.

Dan blinked as Lillian's image blurred and then resumed focus. Her color and energy were gone. She picked up a cookie in one limp hand, her entire arm trembling as she tried to bring it to her pale lips. As he watched, the cookie slipped from her fingers and fell back onto the plate.

"Drat," Lillian whispered, just as Dan loudly voiced a less gentle expletive.

~

Lillian

L illian's eyes flew open, and she would have screamed if she'd been able. All she managed was a sharp intake of breath. She'd been facing away to talk to Liv and hadn't realized anyone else was in the room. But there was Mr. Forell, sitting much too close to the bed and glaring angrily, as though he had all the right in the world to be critical.

Tears of frustration pricked at her eyes, and she slowly slid an image over herself. The version he could see sat up straighter in bed and brought her arm up to point imperiously to the door.

Mr. Forell quickly reached out to grasp her hand, and Lillian was too slow in moving the image. His hand went right through it. "I *am* going to help you, Miss Loraine," he said tightly, "so you might as well get rid of the illusion."

Her image only raised one haughty eyebrow.

"It's my fault, and it's my responsibility to take care of you until you get a replacement. I was an idiot before, and I'm sorry for pushing you, and I'm sorry I left you. I won't ever make that mistake again, even if you want me to."

He didn't look sorry. Only angry.

"We're stuck with each other," he said, "so let's make the most of it, starting with you eating."

Lillian finally let go of the image. "I don't like to be around angry people," she said crossly.

He frowned a second more before his mouth split into a wide smile. "I see."

Lillian lips turned up involuntarily. "See the influence you have on me? I'm not like this for other people. You should smile more," she added without thinking. "It makes you so handsome that I wouldn't even have to hint about your fortune to the Mitter girls. They'd be after you much more persistently than last night."

"That was you, then? I thought so." A hint of a smile contradicted his narrowed gaze.

Lillian smiled without a trace of guilt. "They're like sap on eligible men, impossible to shake off." As much as she wanted to tease him, she couldn't keep her eyes open any more. "Goodnight."

Immediately his hand gripped her shoulder, startling her awake again.

"Lillian. You have to eat your cookies."

She feebly tried to shake him off until he said, "Otherwise *I'll* eat them."

"Oh, all *right*." She reached for one and made it halfway to her mouth before her arm faltered. Warm fingers suddenly encircled her wrist and took her hand to its destination. Lillian took a bite, trying not to notice the pleasant sensation of his hand on hers.

After two cookies and another cup of juice, he helped her settle back into bed.

They hardly spoke the next two times he woke her. He left while Liv helped her change her clothes, and Lillian didn't misinterpret the raised eyebrows and wink the maid gave her. She didn't know how to respond, so she simply pretended not to notice. She washed her teeth before she got back into bed, hating that Liv had to keep her steady on her feet.

The next time she woke, Mr. Forell was nearby, reading words on a scrap of paper, his brow furrowed.

"What is it?" she asked groggily.

He turned and blinked at her a moment, his lips parted as he studied her face. She grew uneasy under his scrutiny, wondering if she had grape juice stains on her mouth or if her hair was mussed.

He shook himself a little and waved the paper. "A request from Madsen," he said. "He wants Octens to be seen tomorrow in Dalarna. He's deep in Reznik's household, and we can't have him suspected. And in two weeks, Madsen wants you at the capital, showing the king's sister and her husband riding in a carriage through the city. Octens caught a hint of a planned assassination, and we can't have the princess in the open."

"All right," Lillian said around a yawn.

He peered at her. "I already wrote a response, telling him you wouldn't be available tomorrow, and I'm not sure you'll be ready for the next task either, considering the difficulty of the job."

She smiled at the concern in his voice, and he shook his head, as though to clear it, before frowning again. "I mean, it would be better not to go if you can't do it perfectly."

Oh. He was only worried about how it would reflect on him. This was not a man who would have sworn an oath to act in her best interest. She must have dreamt it.

"I'll be back to normal by tomorrow," she said flatly. "Then I can show you how I'll manage the other job."

"If you're sure you're ready."

Lillian nodded and pulled her covers tightly around her shoulders. It seemed only moments later he was shaking her awake to drink again. That went on the entire afternoon. Liv sat with her in the evening, but Mr. Forell split the night with Aunt Svea. Lillian didn't talk much. She still wanted to groan with shame for allowing herself to have a seizure and causing so much work for everyone.

When she woke in the morning, Mr. Forell sat beside her bed, reading a thick book. "Good morning, Miss Loraine," he said, his expression guarded. "How do you feel today?"

"Much better, thank you," she said, adopting his polite tone. "I hope you didn't stay up all night."

"Not at all. Your aunt told me you wouldn't remember much since the incident." He shifted uncomfortably before adding, "I want you to know how truly sorry I am. I won't let it happen again."

Someone didn't like apologizing. At least he knew how.

Lillian shrugged. "It wasn't your fault. I knew better." She considered telling him she remembered their conversations perfectly well. The words sat on the tip of her tongue, but she decided against it. If she ever overtaxed herself again, Aunt Svea's fib could only help her.

He repeated the coordinator's requests, and she responded as she had the previous afternoon, feigning interest.

"I'll take just a few minutes to be ready," she said, but he didn't move until she gave him a pointed look. He turned away too quickly for her to tell if it really was a blush creeping up from his collar.

"I'll get Liv," he promised over his shoulder as he fled the room.

CHAPTER 8

Dan

He was in such trouble. One little smile from her yesterday had addled his brains. At least now he had a better idea how to help her, how to make her see where she belonged.

Miss Loraine was ready in very little time, and, armed with her medicine and several of Liv's cookies, they climbed into the open carriage. "How are your parents, Jake?" she asked their young driver.

They exchanged pleasantries while Dan glared at the conveyance. When he'd explained to Lady Ellstrom that an open carriage was little protection from assassins, she'd told him, very shortly, that the other carriage wasn't as well sprung, and that she'd been up half the night and had no intention of being jostled all the way to Dalarna. She settled back against the seat and was asleep before they passed the village.

The sun was high in the sky, but a shadow fell across Lady Ellstrom's face. Dan looked up, expecting to see their path covered by trees or clouds, but there were none.

Miss Loraine smiled at his evident confusion. "She burns easily," she explained.

"How are you doing that?" he asked, trying not to sound impressed and failing.

"I'm just tilting the light around her."

Dan quickly looked over his shoulder at the young driver. Lillian waved a careless hand. "Jake's hearing isn't very good. He mostly lip reads. He's been teaching me."

"That's a good skill to have." Dan's mind went blank for a pleasant moment as he watched her peaceful smile and the strands of honey brown hair that had escaped the knot on her head.

He shook himself and studied their surroundings for possible threats. "Is tilting that much light difficult?" he asked.

She shrugged, her smile fading a little. "A little shade like this is easy because I'm only shifting the light. But creating darkness takes a lot more energy. Light wants to fill space, to bounce around it. It doesn't like to be blocked."

"So large areas of shade or darkness are the most difficult," Dan said, thinking of the way she'd darkened the garden.

She nodded. "That and invisibility. I can only manage it for a few minutes. Also refracting light so an illusion looks the way I want it to from many viewpoints."

Dan's eyes widened at her casual admission she could cloak herself in invisibility. He swallowed and said, "That's why you usually kept Octens against a wall."

They drove into a small grove of trees, and Dan was instantly uncomfortable. He searched the forest for threats as Miss Loraine slipped a book out of a bag at her feet. "I've been dying to finish this, but Aunt Svea doesn't approve." She narrowed her eyes at him. "And you won't tell her, will you?"

He gritted his teeth. Any reading she did should be on magical theory, but he still felt guilty over letting her have a seizure, so he only shook his head once.

Miss Loraine turned to her marker, her eyes soon flying back and forth across the page. He couldn't see the title of the book, but he didn't have to. It was rubbish, some romantic foolishness. Perhaps he could enlist Lady Ellstrom's help to purge the library of novels.

It took only fifteen minutes to emerge from the woods, but twice he thought he saw something moving out in the trees alongside them. He desperately wished he would have brought a bow.

Occasionally they passed villagers on the open road, and Miss Loraine put her book down to call out greetings. An image of her aunt smiled and waved before dissolving when they were out of sight to show Lady Ellstrom still asleep.

The second time Dan arched an eyebrow.

"She's tired," Miss Loraine said with a shrug. "Liv told me she was up late last night taking care of me, and that you were too." Her happy expression faltered, and she blushed a little. "And I'm very sorry for any rude or unkind things I may have said."

"If you did, I'm sure I deserved it," he admitted, the truth of it painful. But in an instant, his discomfort disappeared, simply because she grinned at him. How would he possibly survive until the coordinator found his replacement? A quieter voice in his mind asked how he would survive without her smile once he did. He crushed that voice quickly. He hardly knew her.

They talked very little before reaching Dalarna, mostly because Miss Loraine's gaze was glued to her book. The way her eyes widened as she bit her lower lip was extremely distracting. The minute her aunt began to stir, the book vanished.

When Lady Ellstrom woke fully, she announced Dan could hold their things while they shopped.

That was a *horrible* idea. "I may need my hands free if a situation arises."

Lady Ellstrom actually chortled a little at that. "You think men in masks will attack us at the fabric warehouse?"

Dan tightened his lips before answering. "Political squabbles and fear of magic put all sorcerers at risk. Just during my years in the army, I saw seven attempted assassinations." They had to understand how much Miss Loraine needed him.

That is, how much she needed a defender.

Lady Ellstrom didn't seem impressed, but she let the matter drop.

Dan scanned the shops they visited, wishing he dared wear his sword openly. As it was, there were several weapons on him, as well as two extra vials of Miss Loraine's medicine and some extra cookies. She carried her own medicine, but he had to be sure she had enough.

Between shops Lillian made sure Octens was seen, always against the wall of a building, in view of several people, and never for more than a few minutes. Dan slipped Lillian one of Liv's cookies every time he noticed Octens, but by the time they had visited two fabric shops, a jeweler, and a florist, her skin had an unhealthy pallor.

When they finished their errands, Miss Loraine insisted on one more stop. "You promised, Aunt Svea. We're going to visit Dr. Prent."

$\sim$

Lillian

"Is that the doctor who knows about you?" Mr. Forell asked quickly.

"Not the man who diagnosed it but the one who treats me now, yes," she said, ignoring her aunt's shrewd look.

Mr. Forell scanned the streets as they made their way to Dr. Prent's office. Reminded of the purpose for their outing, she

formed Octens' image in her mind, then watched as he saun-
tered around a corner ahead and leaned against a building. She
was still tired from her recent seizure, and it must have shown,
because when she turned back to Mr. Forell, he held out
another cookie. It was at least the fourth he'd given her in the
course of the day, and he looked a little pleased with himself, so
she said, "You needn't train me with treats like you would a
hound. I've already learned these tricks on my own."

He looked stricken, and she couldn't hold back her laugh.
"I'm only teasing."

A corner of Mr. Forell's mouth twitched. Aunt Svea smiled
broadly, looking between the two of them, obviously imagining
things.

Dr. Prent met them at his door. "Lady Ellstrom, Miss
Loraine," he said with a bow. "I hardly know which of you is
here to see me today, as you both look in the best of health."

Lillian quickly introduced Mr. Forell as a family friend. "He
knows what I am, so you needn't tiptoe around it," she added,
ignoring a rather sharp look from her defender. Did he not
expect her to mention it? "And we're here because Aunt Svea's
tremors are worse."

The physician nodded, led them to seats, and began examining Svea. "Any more spells?" he asked Lillian as he checked her
aunt's pulse.

Lillian loathed the blush that gave her away, even before Mr.
Forell said, "Yes, just yesterday. Do you think it would help if
she took her medicine *before* working?

"It might," Dr. Prent said calmly, as though it was any of Mr.
Forell's business. "It's concentrated sugar water combined with
a drug to make her blood sugar level rise. If taken in very large
quantities, it would have the same undesirable effects as any
large scale ingestion of sugar, so the only real concern is the
state of her teeth."

Was she a horse to be discussed in this manner? *"Dr. Prent,"* she said impatiently, "what do you think of Aunt Svea's tremor?"

He only smiled at her irritation. For someone she'd known since childhood and who was supposed to be working in her best interest, he could be extremely unhelpful.

Dr. Prent put Svea through a series of hand exercises, then looked in her eyes and ears before pronouncing there was nothing new, only the expected progression of an age-related tremor.

"Delightful news," snapped Aunt Svea.

He grinned at her. "Increase your nightly medicine by a quarter of the cup, and I'll check on you in a couple weeks," he promised.

"And can we get more of Lillian's medicine?" Mr. Forell asked. "A lot of it?"

Lillian frowned, but Dr. Prent looked back and forth between her and Mr. Forell with an annoying smile.

It was a relief to get out of his office and back into the carriage. Aunt Svea discussed upcoming parties for half an hour before Mr. Forell managed to ask the question Lillian had been waiting for.

"You told me you'd be able to show... oh."

Before he could finish it, Lillian quickly slid an image of the princess over herself. The king's sister wasn't much older than she was, and they were close to the same size, so the transformation took little effort. The princess smiled and nodded her head regally, waving at imaginary subjects on either side of the deserted road.

Mr. Forell glanced over his shoulder at Jake, who was too intent on the road ahead to notice what happened in the carriage behind him. Just for fun, Lillian turned Aunt Svea into the prince, who gave Lillian a dirty look. Oops. The prince's expression turned adoring, and Svea sniffed in disgust. "You know the shadow of the image on me makes me dizzy, dear, and I don't like to look like men."

"Sorry, Auntie."

She dissolved both images, and Mr. Forell shook his head. "But Lillian," he began before his face reddened. "Excuse me. Miss Loraine. If an assassin wanted to take out either of them, you, or whatever person you projected the image upon, would still be killed."

Aunt Svea should *not* smile like that. Smugness did not become her.

"I suppose I could project the image several inches forward, as long as the carriage seats were deep…"

"That isn't good enough," he interrupted. "You'd still be in danger, and as your defender, even as your temporary defender, I can't allow it. We'll have to think of something else."

Lillian knew she should have been annoyed, but she couldn't work herself up to it. The defiance in his tone was so surprisingly sweet.

The carriage neared the grove of trees before the turn-off to Perch Harbor. They'd be home soon. Tension seeped out of her shoulders, even as Mr. Forell's hands tightened on the seat beside him and his eyes scoured the trees ahead.

The poor man was going to develop an ulcer if he didn't relax. Soon trees shadowed the carriage, and Mr. Forell shifted almost constantly in his seat to be able to see around them.

"I'd prefer you called me Lillian. That *is* my name," she said, wondering if he'd remember the first time she'd instructed him to do so.

"Thank you. It would be simpler. Please call me Dan," he said, still not looking at her.

She should tell him about her aunt's fib. That would distract him from whatever was worrying him. The words were on the tip of her tongue when something sliced through the air just in front of her nose, something that looked horribly like an arrow.

CHAPTER 9

Dan

Dan lunged forward and, ignoring the women's cries of surprise, jerked them both down into the bottom of the carriage where they landed in a heap.

Jake turned in his seat. "What in the—" he began.

"Faster," Dan roared at him. Jake slapped the reins and yelled to the horses as another arrow hit the carriage near the driver's seat.

Dan bent low, looking over the door of the carriage and pushing Lillian back down when she tried to get up next to him.

"I can change our appearance," she hissed.

"No," Dan exclaimed. "Too risky."

"Why?"

He ignored the question, instead watching the forest. He was sure he'd seen… there. A man on horseback, armed with a bow. Taking aim again.

"Down, man," he shouted at Jake, who mimicked Dan's movement just in time.

Dan quickly drew two blades from hidden sheathes in his

clothes. Over the rim of the open carriage he saw their attacker spurring his horse onto the road just behind them. Dan's first blade missed, but distracted the rider enough that the next arrow wasn't loosed. Dan's second blade took him full in the throat. The attacker toppled off his horse, and Dan stood up from his crouch to see he stayed down. Lillian rose up beside him again, but Lady Ellstrom pulled her down before Dan could push her back to the floor.

"I have to be sure there aren't more of them," he said roughly. His heart thundered in his ears, a new symptom for such situations, but he didn't have time to consider it.

"I can help," she said.

"No," he growled quietly. "If there *are* more of them, they can't suspect you more than they already do. Stay down."

Lady Ellstrom spoke quickly in her niece's ear, and whatever she said must have been convincing, because Lillian stayed put.

It took another ten minutes before they broke through the trees and were back into open fields. Dan sighed in relief to see the landscape deserted, and his heart finally began to slow its strange thumping.

When they neared the house, Lillian convinced him to let her project an image of them all sitting normally, though he insisted both she and her aunt remain in the relative safety of the foot of the carriage. Dan leaned over the side and pulled out an arrow still embedded in the carriage. It was Kazat made.

When one of Jake's assistants approached from the stable, Dan hid the arrow behind his back. The young man held a hand out to Lady Ellstrom to help her down, and she groaned. "You may have to carry me, Peter, after all I've been through today."

He smiled broadly and assisted her down and toward the house.

Dan leapt down quickly in order to offer his hand to Lillian. She paused fleetingly before taking it and stepping down to follow her aunt.

The contact with her hand lasted a brief moment, but a sharp awareness of her touch had him flexing his fingers long afterward. Lillian had exceptionally beautiful hands, and even with so much on his mind, he couldn't help but be affected.

Dan's eyes swept the courtyard, but no one present seemed to think anything was amiss. He quickly motioned Jake aside and instructed him not to speak of the attack to anyone. The young man paused before nodding once, and Dan hurried to join Miss Loraine.

He needed to go check the body, but he had to be sure his assignment was safe first. Once in the seclusion of Lady Ellstrom's parlor, Lillian sank onto a chair and stared at the rug at her feet.

"Why was she targeted?" her aunt asked him as soon as the door was shut.

"We can't be certain the arrow was meant for *her*," he said, striding around the room. The image of what might have happened if Lillian had only been sitting a few inches forward played over in his mind, making it difficult to breathe. What was wrong with him? He'd been in far worse situations than that, and had never felt such terrible panic. He *always* remained as calm inwardly as he was on the outside.

"Someone might think Aunt Svea is a sorceress?" Lillian asked in whisper. "She's in danger."

"It's impossible to say. For the Kazats, a suspicion is enough. Perhaps they saw you change into the princess and back."

"You think the archer was a Kazat?" Lady Ellstrom asked shrewdly.

"I need to go check the body to be sure. And bury it. And then we have to give whoever sent him something else to think about. Maybe another target."

"Put someone else in danger?" Lillian asked with a shudder. "I couldn't do that." Her skin was almost green. Dan automatically fished out the parcel of cookies in his pocket, handing her one as he thought it over. She accepted it with a murmured thanks, though she didn't eat it.

"Or make a new suspect," he said as he thought it through. "Someone to draw attention away from you two."

"Make one?" Lillian said thoughtfully. "I could do that."

"I don't mind being the suspect," Lady Ellstrom said with a shrug. "I fit the profile better, and—"

"Absolutely not," Lillian said emphatically, color returning to her face.

"Then we should make you look less suspect, dear."

Dan snorted. "Impossible."

Both women turned to stare at him coolly, and Dan winced inwardly at the coming tirade.

Lillian

Lillian opened her mouth to retort, but Mr. Forell hurried to add, "What I mean to say is that you are a young woman, hardly more than a girl, really…"

He faltered again, and Lillian raised an eyebrow at him.

Aunt Svea sniffed. "What I think he means to say, dear, is that the problem is not with *you*."

"Exactly," he said, noticeably relaxing.

"It's with *him*," her aunt added.

His head snapped back. "What?"

Aunt Svea gave Mr. Forell a tolerant smile. "While my niece is nothing what people expect in a sorceress, you, Mr. Forell, are exactly what everyone expects in a defender. The Kazats may have followed you here."

The situation wasn't funny, but Lillian still had to suppress a laugh at his dumbfounded expression.

"You are military trained," Aunt Svea said. "You've been in

the company of sorcerers for years, and if anyone looked into your background, they might find out about your academy that you're so proud of."

"Oh."

Lillian bit back comforting words. It wouldn't hurt if Aunt Svea made him feel a little uncomfortable. She did it to *her* all the time.

"You must come up with a reason for staying here," Aunt Svea added briskly. "Fishing could give you an excuse to last a day or two, but if you're going to *live* here, it's got to be more convincing."

Lillian suddenly suspected where this was going.

"You mean I should pass myself off as a relation?" he asked.

"Hardly," Aunt Svea said. "Everyone knows us here. It's a small town. It would never work."

"Then what do you suggest?" he asked.

"Aunt Svea," Lillian broke in.

"Hush, dear," she said calmly. "Mr. Forell, I suggest you come up with a legitimate reason to spend a lot of time with my niece."

Finally comprehension lit his face. "I should pretend to be attracted to her."

"No, you should *not*," Lillian said, trying to ignore the uncomfortable truth he'd just let slip. He wasn't attracted to her at all. She'd already known it, so hearing it aloud shouldn't make her feel worse, but it did.

"Why not?" he said, beginning to pace again. "It's a good idea. It makes perfect sense, unless you have a lover somewhere."

Lillian tried to cool her blush and failed. She quickly used her gift to hide her coloring.

"Too pale, dear," Aunt Svea whispered.

Lillian wanted to run away to hide her embarrassment. "You have no business discussing the idea."

"You're old enough to have a suitor, aren't you?" Mr. Forell asked, apparently oblivious to her irritation. "And men follow you around like senseless idiots, don't they? So what would it matter if I did too?" The idea was obviously growing on him. "Everyone will expect you to be interested in some man eventually."

Lillian felt as though her insides might boil. Men did *not* follow her around. "I appreciate the sacrifice you're apparently considering," she said quellingly. "But I don't think that will be necessary."

"Surely people will simply think you snared me, or that I'm after your fortune. The heiress to a barony," he said.

Aunt finally gave him a warning look, but she was too late. Lillian was done.

"Because it would take a vast fortune or me tricking him for a man to be interested in me?" she asked, anger clawing at her insides and seeping into her voice.

His expression fell. "Well...no. Of course not. What I mean is—"

"Excuse me, please, Mr. Forell," Lillian said. "I find that an attempt on my life and seeing a man killed have made me very tired." She swept past him, ignoring his protests. She made her way to her room, relieved neither he nor her aunt tried to follow her.

A stranger had just tried to put an arrow through her head. That should be enough reason for her tears. And she should be furious with her aunt and Mr. Forell for their ridiculous ideas, but all too quickly her distress and anger were replaced by the old hurt, all of it coming back. She leaned her head against the cool wood of her door. She was almost sure Aunt Svea wouldn't disclose the pathetic details of her two previous suitors. The first broke their engagement when he learned a distant cousin was the heir of the baron's fortune, not her. She'd been so stupid not to realize what he was from the beginning. And *he* should have realized the baron would never have named her his heir.

She was a foundling and a sorceress, though her fiancé hadn't known the latter.

The next time she'd been more careful. She made sure the second suitor who proposed knew of her financial situation.

"Do you think I care about that, darling?" he'd whispered, his eyes full of admiration. Then she told him she had a magical gift. She didn't tell him what it was, and definitely not that she was a sorceress, but the admiration had faded quickly from his eyes, panic taking its place. She hadn't given him a chance to rescind the offer, but gently told him they probably wouldn't be happy together, given her situation. He agreed far too readily and was out the door two minutes later, never to return. A few months later, she heard of his engagement to a young woman from a neighboring district.

She'd been so cautious with her feelings the second time, but it had still hurt. Badly. Not everyone wanted to marry and have a family, but she did. She always had. And she was desperate to leave the baron's home without having to be far from her friends or Aunt Svea. The baron had provided a generous dowry, whether at Aunt Svea's insistence or to get rid of her sooner, she wasn't sure. But even if she wanted to accept it, which she didn't, it still wouldn't be enough to overcome the inherent dangers of living with a sorcereress, not to mention that she might never have children. Most sorcerers, and even the majority of people with simple magical gifts, didn't discover the fact until they were in their forties or fifties. By then most were already married, and their spouses simply had to deal with it. If they'd wanted many children, those dreams had been disrupted before they realized the magic was to blame. But knowing in advance, who would ever want her?

Lillian trudged to her bed and slumped against her pillow. She was usually resigned to her fate. She knew she had every-thing a person could need to be happy: family and friends who loved her, important work to do for her country, a beautiful place to call home. And she was working toward financial independence, so in the near future she wouldn't have to rely on the baron. Everything was lining up as it should.

But now her aunt was encouraging a man to pretend to like her. It did more than simply prick her pride. It was humiliating. If she was going to remain single all her life, which might be a very short amount of time after all, she would do it her own way. On *her* terms. Without play-acting or pity.

Sleep claimed her before long, and she was immediately embraced in her parents' arms. She wished she knew which of them had been a sorcerer and how they'd caused the peacefulness of their love to surface when she was upset. As usual, it worked, and she slept deeply with peaceful dreams. At least the dead loved her.

CHAPTER 10

Dan

Dan cursed his delay as Lillian stormed from the room. Why he had to make such a fool of himself around her was beyond understanding. He verified she was safely in her room, then hurried to the stables. He didn't want to hear the lecture Lady Ellstrom was surely holding back by a thread. Guilt tore at him as it was, knowing that a Kazat assassin may have anticipated his assignment and followed him to Perch Harbor.

He found Jake and explained, with as little detail as possible, that he was going back to find the body.

"I can come with you," Jake immediately volunteered.

"I appreciate your bravery, but it is more important for the house to be guarded. I need you watch for intruders and sound an alarm if you see anything suspicious."

Jake agreed, his expression stony. Dan really did want someone guarding the house, and his search would be more effective without anyone else to worry about.

Hoping to be back before dusk, Dan rode at a gallop until he neared the area they'd been attacked. His senses high-strung and his bow half-drawn, he combed the area without success. It didn't help that his thoughts kept returning to Lillian. Pretending to court her would give him the legitimacy they needed. It was strange the idea wasn't distasteful, but then, he was a rational sort of man, and the idea was logical, even if Lillian Loraine found it repulsive. His hasty words hadn't helped the situation.

His third time back over the ground where their attacker had fallen, Dan found evidence of the dirt being smoothed over. If a do-gooder had found the body and taken it away, they wouldn't have smoothed the dirt. The assassin hadn't been working alone.

He returned to the manor as quickly as he could, stopping at the stable again to leave his horse with Jake.

He took Dan's horse with a questioning look.

"The body's gone. It's not the last we'll hear of all this."

Jake nodded. "I'll keep an eye out for anything strange, Mr. Forell, but I think you ought to tell Jensen, so he can do the same."

"You're right. I will."

Jake nodded once, and Dan hurried to update Lady Ellstrom. She took the news unflinchingly, then insisted they check on her niece.

He was sure Lillian wouldn't want him in her room, but she slept deeply, a faint smile turning up the corners of her mouth. Without stopping to consider what her aunt would think, he pulled the blankets up to Lillian's shoulders. She seemed to get chilled easily, and she'd never know he'd been there.

"She fell right asleep, poor girl. Her work does tend to wear her out."

"Lady Ellstrom," he said when they were back in the hall, "something your niece said at Dr. Prent's made me wonder if Miss Loraine is not happy to be a sorceress?"

What I am, she'd said, as though it was a defect of some kind.

Lady Ellstrom tilted her head to the side and looked up at him. "I don't think she sees it as a benefit, but I don't think she despises it either. She can hardly remember life before her gift."

Dan nodded. "I need to write my report to Madsen. Miss Loraine and I can resume our work in the morning."

"Not too early," Svea said.

Over the next several days, Dan practiced holding his tongue and with positive results. At least, Lillian didn't seem irritated in his presence. It may have helped that he remembered to never barge into her room and to never bring up her aunt's idea of a pretend courtship. He was also careful to never say anything disparaging about all the time she wasted reading her ridiculous romance novels.

She, for her part, practiced for the impersonation of the prince and princess for several hours a day with a level of enthusiasm that Dan found encouraging. And when she wished to walk the grounds, Dan picked a spot nearby to practice his skill with a sword. Sometimes she liked to walk along the river, and she insisted that he fish with Jensen while she did.

"You can keep your bow with you," she said firmly. "I'll stay where you can see me, but I need time outside by myself."

Dan reluctantly complied, but the fish didn't bite for him anyway. Jensen looked over his shoulder and offered various advice.

"You are too used to action, sir," he told Dan seriously as Miss Loraine walked along the river a short distance away. "Fishing is a sport of patience and skill, but patience isn't something I can teach you. You have to let the fish see what you have to offer, and then you have to give them some time to make up their minds." He gave Miss Loraine a sidelong glance and added quietly, "It's sorta the same way with women, I'm thinking."

Oh. "I confess, I'm not making much progress in that sector either," Dan said.

"Well, Miss Loraine, she's something, isn't she?"

Dan nodded, and Jensen took that as encouragement. "Most people only see her as a sweet, pretty girl. They don't know how blasted stubborn she is until they cross her."

"Oh?"

"Been that way since she was little. You know about her illness?" He looked guilty, as though he'd said too much, and his cheeks darkened a shade closer to his red hair.

"She and her aunt told me about it, yes," Dan said.

Jensen relaxed noticeably. "Well, her governess, when she was first sick, was always trying to keep her indoors, keep her from playing too hard or doing anything too difficult. I'll tell you, our little Miss Loraine would have none of that. Wouldn't give an inch when she thought she was in the right. Finally her governess went away, said she'd had enough back talk and disobedience."

Dan smiled. He could well imagine.

"It was for the best. The woman wasn't quite fit, you see. Always swatting at bugs that weren't there, startling at shadows, that sort of thing. She didn't have it in her to take care of such a strong-willed child."

Dan almost choked on a laugh before growing serious. Would he begin seeing things that weren't there? Would she drive him mad too?

"She's sweet as ever, our girl, does so much to please everyone. Just be careful about pushing her. I've only ever seen her back down from a decision once, and that was when she was twelve years old."

"What happened?"

Jensen paused, frowning. "Little Miss Lillian got it in her head she should leave, seek her fortune elsewhere."

Twelve. That was when Lady Ellstrom said Lillian realized why the baron wouldn't come home. "She wanted to run away."

"That's not how Miss Lillian saw it," said Jensen.

"And?"

"And I overheard her aunt, all fierce and angry. She said this was Miss Lillian's home, and she was her family, and no one, not even Miss Lillian herself, was going to take her away."

"And?"

"And she stayed. So you see, you've got to be there for her. Be patient, consistent."

Just then, Dan felt a tug on his pole. He jumped and fought the line for a few moments before pulling out a nice-sized trout.

"See there, Mr. Forell," Jensen said, laughing cheerfully. "You were holding so still with your line while we talked. That was all you needed."

Dan laughed sheepishly. He wished it was as easy to help Lillian, but if she was to make any progress, he couldn't sit idly by.

A few days later, as he watched her practice keeping the image of the prince and princess steady from different angles and distances in the carriage room, he suddenly realized her problem. When she moved her image into the carriage to sit down, the image jostled, ever so slightly.

"You must have never studied theory," he blurted out.

The image of the couple waving from the carriage dissolved, and Miss Loraine looked over her shoulder at him, one perfectly sculpted eyebrow raised, as though daring him to continue.

He wished he'd kept his mouth shut until he found a better way to bring it up. "It's difficult for you to keep your dimensions tight when you're moving. I have a few books on magical theory that..."

There. She did it again. Her expression changed just as the light in her eyes faded. She was wearing a mask. He intended to call her on it, but her eyes flitted over his shoulder to the door of the carriage room, and Dan turned to see what caught her attention. Jensen approached from the courtyard, a rake in hand.

"I'll distract him while you leave," Lillian said in a low voice. "We shouldn't be in here alone." She walked past him and into the sunshine, waving to Jensen, who immediately turned about to accompany her back to the house.

Dan ground his teeth. He hadn't even been able to explain. He waited two minutes more before leaving the carriage room and making his way to a different entrance of the house. As he passed one of the gardens, he heard a familiar whistling. He doubled back to see the caretaker cutting weeds near a small pond, his scythe swinging in rhythm with his tune.

Jensen looked up and nodded in greeting.

Dan's confusion abruptly cleared. "You haven't seen Miss Loraine, have you?"

"Not this morning, sir," Jensen said.

Dan bit back a curse.

"Remember, sir, women and fish."

Dan took his leave with hardly more than a nod. The little minx. The minute he'd opened his mouth to be helpful, she'd tricked him and run away.

Dan combed the house, his irritation growing, without finding a trace of her. He almost collided with Lady Ellstrom when he rounded a corner too quickly.

"What are you doing, Mr. Forell?" she demanded once she'd righted herself. "Why aren't you ready for our outing?"

"Outing?"

"Don't you remember? The picnic at the Penchants' home?"

Blast the picnic. Another excuse for her not to work. Another place her life was in danger. "Have you seen your niece?"

"Lost her, have you?"

It was exceptionally irritating that someone he towered over could look down her nose at him.

"She's probably getting ready," she said. "You should too."

"Thank you."

Of course she was getting ready. Choosing a hat was so much more important than protecting the king's sister.

He stormed into his room, slammed the door behind him, and ripped his shirt off over his shoulders. He threw it angrily onto the bed, his hands moving to his belt before his mind registered the tiny, "Oh!" from across his room.

He spun, unconsciously drawing a blade, only to see Miss Loraine sitting frozen in his chair, her eyes wide as they flickered back and forth between his chest and his knife.

~

Lillian

Lillian could hardly draw breath. How on earth had she managed to get herself in such a situation? Behind a closed door with a half-dressed man, one with ridiculously well-sculpted muscles and a murderous look in his eye, and who held a knife like he might use it to split her open. He'd caught her in his *bedroom,* no less. What kind of idiot was she? And on top of all that, her voice didn't seem to work.

She scrambled to her feet, marking her place in his book with her fingers. The book. That's right. She'd been reading.

"I hope you don't mind me borrowing your book," she managed, her voice shaking embarrassingly. "Magical theory. You said I needed it."

She kept her eyes from his muscled torso with significant effort. "I'll just borrow it for a while, if you don't mind."

She edged around the wall, keeping as much distance between them as she could.

"Wait."

Her feet froze in place, and he stalked toward her, sweeping something off the bed as he came.

He didn't slow. For a moment she thought he'd plow her over, but he stopped abruptly, just inches away. Heat poured off his body and surrounded her. Then again, it might only have been her embarrassment making her fevered. She forced her gaze from his collar bone to his eyes. He studied her intently, his lids lowered. His gaze took in her hair and her...*lips?*

Was he going to kiss her? The room was too warm. Her head was light. She needed air. She sucked a large breath into her lungs, and he quickly took a step back.

"Here," he said, pushing another book into her hands. "This one too."

"Thank you," she said automatically. She took a step toward the door, and another. His eyes bored into hers with intensity that scared her and intrigued her equally. She felt the oddest inclination to walk back to him and kiss him on his scowling lips. Then her common sense returned to her, and she turned and fled the room with little thought for her dignity.

She managed not to slam her own door behind her. The bolt, which she'd started using after his second morning at her home, slid into place silently. Her heart, on the other hand, threatened to be heard on the other side of Perch Harbor.

When she'd decided on his room for a hiding place, she'd never imagined he'd barge into it so soon. She should have disguised herself as a potted plant again, or just gone to her own room after she'd heard him stop looking for her there. But the book she found on his desk had been interesting and exactly what she needed, energy patterns and magical theory combined. The only books on magic in the baron's library were histories of sorcerers, helpful in their own right, but not actually useful for practice.

Maybe if she immersed herself again in Mr. Forell's book, she'd be able to erase the image of him imprinted in her mind.

She'd had two suitors, respectable and courteous men, but she'd never had the desire to fling herself at one of them. And then *he* came along, didn't like her at all, and she had to go all weak-kneed when she saw a bit of his skin.

Lillian buried her face in her hands. He certainly was a distraction. It was difficult enough keeping the image of the princess and prince correct from all angles without him scrutinizing everything she did.

"Lillian," Aunt Svea called from the hallway. "It's almost time to go."

Lillian leaned her head against the wall. They'd accepted an invitation to a picnic at Melina's home almost a month ago. They couldn't cry off now, as much as she wanted to crawl into bed and stay there for a week. She changed her clothes, repinned her hair, and hurried out to the carriage where Mr. Forell stood waiting to hand her up. She couldn't look him in the eye but thanked him politely, slipping her fingers out of his as soon as possible.

"It was just as well that Daniel insisted on a covered carriage," said Aunt Svea as soon as they were settled. "Too much dust on the road to keep your white dress nice."

Lillian nodded distractedly and settled back onto the cushioned seat.

Mr. Forell glared out the windows in turn, obviously expecting trouble, but they arrived at their destination without difficulty. Several women were already there with their daughters, and their laughter soothed Lillian's nerves. Melina hurried toward her, two little sisters in tow, and embraced Lillian affectionately.

"What? A man at our picnic?" Melina's mother, Mrs. Penchant, asked as she approached, her hands fluttering as quickly as frills on her dress. She smiled at Mr. Forell but glanced meaningfully at his dress sword and raised shocked eyebrows at Aunt Svea.

"This is Mr. Forell, Lillian's special guest."

Lillian clamped her teeth shut to keep from denying it. She wished Aunt Svea had said *anything* else, especially in front of Melina's mother, the biggest gossip in the district.

Mr. Forell bowed over Mrs. Penchant's hand. "I hope that you don't mind my intrusion," he said. "I can't seem to leave Miss Loraine's side if I don't absolutely have to." He sent a hesitant smile toward Lillian.

What?

They hadn't given up their mad scheme for a pretended courtship.

Melina's little sisters giggled, and their mother smiled broadly.

No. No, no, no.

"Of course I understand, Mr. Forell. She's a wonderful girl." Mrs. Penchant looked gleefully at Lillian and backed away. "Come along, girls." She gave Melina a meaningful look and pulled her younger daughters along with her.

Melina spared Lillian a commiserating glance behind Mr. Forell's back and then hurried after her mother.

"*Mr. Forell,*" Lillian hissed, feeling an angry flush spread across her cheeks.

"Do you suppose I did that correctly?" he asked.

Lillian might have slapped him if he hadn't sounded so uncertain.

CHAPTER 11

Dan

Lady Ellstrom studied Dan critically before answering. "It would help if you smiled at her more often."

"Auntie," Miss Loraine fairly growled.

"And it's fortunate you started with that particular woman," Lady Ellstrom added, ignoring her niece. "Everyone here will know of your attachment in two minutes."

Dan ignored Miss Loraine's obvious irritation. It was for her own good if people thought he was interested.

"You would be more convincing too, if you found excuses to touch her," Lady Ellstrom advised unashamedly.

That didn't sound too bad.

Lillian glared at both of them and spun on the spot before storming off after her friend. He hesitated, but Lady Ellstrom jerked her head slightly to indicate he should follow. He wasn't *afraid*, but he couldn't shake an uncomfortable tightness in his chest as he hurried after her.

"Miss Loraine," he said as he caught up. He wanted to call her by her given name, but didn't think she actually wanted him to. "I should remind you that you were targeted by an assassin just a few days ago, and here in the open, you're an easy target for others. I would appreciate you taking particular care to—"

"*Mr. Forell,*" she interrupted huffily, though there was a smile plastered on her face, evidently for the benefit of the score of women watching them from a distance. "The only thing I particularly plan to do today is pretend you're not here, so I can enjoy the picnic and games. *You* can do as you like."

Dan narrowed his eyes at her, but she gave him a blank smile and spun away. The little...

He didn't get a chance to talk to her after that. She made sure she was busy with all the girls and women clamoring for her attention. She held small children and wrapped blankets around white-haired grandmothers, leaving a wake of smiles and laughter everywhere she went. She ran three-legged races with children half her size and came in third in one race only by bodily hauling the little girl along with her. Both fell down laughing across the finish line, and Dan found himself smiling like an idiot. How strange.

His good mood was short-lived. When Mrs. Penchant announced the obstacle course, he looked it over and cursed mentally. There were at least four places where the competitors would be out of view. A hundred ways she could come to harm or be killed flitted through his mind, making it difficult to breathe.

He quickly excused himself and strode over to Lady Ellstrom. "I don't want her to do the course," he muttered.

She sniffed. "Good luck keeping her from it."

"But—"

Lady Ellstrom interrupted. "You're the defender. *You* figure out how to keep her safe, and you'd better hurry. They're about to start."

Dan didn't reply, but jogged over to the starting line. Miss

Loraine was busy retying a hat onto a little girl who couldn't have been more than five.

"But I want to run," the little girl whimpered.

"Oh, Myra. I'm sorry. You have to be older than eight for this one," Lillian said soothingly.

"I'll take her through," Dan said quickly. It was a good excuse to be near Miss Loraine. The ingrate.

She'd glanced at him in irritation when he'd approached, but at his words, her expression softened. She almost smiled at him.

He would have smiled back if it wasn't for the surprisingly strong impact of a little girl trying to tackle his knees.

"Racers ready?" Lillian's friend, Melina, called.

Twenty young girls cheered from the line.

"Then go!"

Miss Loraine took off with surprising speed considering she wore a dress. Dan swung his little burden onto his back, firmly instructed her to hang on tight, and raced after her.

"We're going to catch her, Mr. Furl! Catch her!"

Dan might have laughed at her interpretation of his name if his air wasn't being choked out of him.

Miss Loraine vaulted over fallen logs, danced across balance beams, and hopped between wooden hoops set on the ground. She looked over her shoulder at the rest of the group, only to catch her foot and tumble onto the grass. Dan was there in an instant, scooping her off the ground and onto her feet, little Myra still hanging around his neck.

He tried to ask Miss Loraine if she was hurt, but the five-year-old didn't make a very good necklace, and he couldn't choke out the words.

Miss Loraine gasped out a laugh as other runners passed them. "Better hurry," she said as she sprinted after them.

He moved his little burden's hands from his neck to his shoulders, waited two seconds for the stars in his vision to clear, then followed.

The pack reached a small river, and Lillian ran down the bank and was lost to his view. Dan groaned and ran after her, urged on by cries of, "Hurry!" being squealed into his ear.

He quickly caught up to the girls waiting for their turns at stepping stones and simply waded through the water. The racers on the bank laughed and squealed, and Miss Loraine turned to look behind her as she reached the opposite bank. His very irrational thought at that moment was that he would have trudged through a hundred rivers for the smile she gave him. And then she was gone, disappearing into a stand of trees. Did she not consider her safety at all? Dan sprinted after her, hoping Myra's shrill screams wouldn't permanently damage his hearing. When he reached the trees, she was nowhere in sight. The path was straight, and it was impossible that she'd already reached the distant turn.

He paused, searching the trees as runners flew past him. Anxiety clutched at his heart. Where was she? He should never have let her out of his sight.

His little burden squealed again, and Dan set her down. "Miss Loraine is hiding, and I have to find her," he said quickly. "It's part of the game."

That brought about instant silence, and he spun in a circle, catching back choice words unfit for his running companion.

There, finally, a flash of white some distance off the path.

"Hide behind this tree and don't make a sound," he told Myra firmly before running toward his assignment.

"Let go of me this instant!" Miss Loraine said indignantly, her voice finally audible with the pack of girls farther away.

He drew his sword. The trees blocked sight of her captor until Dan was nearly upon them. The man stood with his back to a tree, facing away from Dan, his meaty hand gripping Lillian's wrist.

A new type of fury erupted in Dan's chest.

Someone had taken Lillian. A quick death might be too good for him.

Dan rode the tide of his battle rage as his blade moved forward with deadly precision.

Miss Loraine saw him and screamed, turning her head away and covering her face with her free hand.

At the last moment, it occurred to him she wouldn't like to have the man's blood on her dress.

~

Lillian

Lillian waited for the unfamiliar sounds of a man being decapitated. The moment drew out, and instead she heard a very shaky, "Don't hurt me. Please!"

She whipped her head back around to see Mr. Forell's blade had stopped an inch from Geoffrey's throat.

"I suggest you release the lady," Mr. Forell said tightly.

Lillian was hastily released, and she staggered back a few feet.

Geoffrey's stance was weak and his eyes terrified, but he hadn't been weak or terrified when he'd accosted her a minute before. He'd snagged her around the waist and clamped a hand over her mouth to keep her from screaming until she saw it was him, and then she hadn't wanted to scream and subject her young friends to a vulgar scene. Despite her efforts, he'd easily pulled her off the path. Until now Geoffrey's attentions had only been annoying, but this behavior was beyond inappropriate. If he wasn't Melina's brother, she might have actually tried to do him harm.

Now he stood pale and sweating, paralyzed at the point of her defender's blade. Lillian felt a giggle bubbling up inside, but she was too horrified to let it out.

"Would you like to tell me why you accosted the lady, or shall I slice the flesh from your bones?" Lillian had thought Dan looked angry when he'd found her in his room earlier that day. This was nothing like it—his narrowed gaze, the curl to his lip, his stance poised for the kill. He looked incensed, yes, but also incredibly lethal. She'd never realized such a thing could be attractive.

"I didn't mean anything by it. I'm sorry!"

"That's not good enough," Mr. Forell said quietly.

Geoffrey turned pleading eyes on Lillian.

"I believe Mr. Penchant has now realized his actions were terribly wrong," she said quickly. "And he'll never come near me again, will he?" Lillian almost felt sorry for him, but she wasn't about to miss the chance of shaking off his attentions.

"Are you going to kill him?" a curious voice interrupted before Geoffrey could answer.

Little Myra Bird, who'd been so happily perched on Mr. Forell's back during the race, now watched the scene with obvious curiosity.

"Of course he won't," Lillian said, striding forward to stand with Myra.

Mr. Forell's blade moved an inch farther from his target's neck, but Lillian still wasn't convinced he'd spare him.

"You are never to approach Miss Loraine again," he said quietly. "If I find you have..." He trailed off, but his eyes narrowed dangerously.

"What right have you to threaten me?" Geoffrey asked in a strangled whisper, apparently gaining some courage from the idea he might walk away from this encounter.

"Mr. Forell is her sweetheart," announced Myra suddenly. "Isn't he?" she asked, looking innocently up at Lillian.

Mr. Forell's eyes flashed to Lillian's, and her face heated.

"Yes. Yes, he is," she said hurriedly, disliking the lie.

Dan gave her an odd look, a strange softening to his features.

"Then I give my word I will not trouble you with my attentions, Miss Loraine," Geoffrey said, his face an unhealthy shade of purple.

Mr. Forell stepped back. "Leave now," he said quietly.

Geoffrey didn't need to be told twice. He stumbled off into the woods and was soon gone from sight.

"Did we lose the race?" Myra asked, apparently untroubled by the entire episode.

"One way to find out," Mr. Forell said with a smile for her. He sheathed his blade and swung Myra onto his back while she squealed gleefully. "We can at least beat Miss Loraine to the finish line."

He jogged back toward the path, and she followed, trying to shake off her distress. Dan moved slowly enough to keep her close, but kept far enough ahead to let Myra "win". Several women smirked in their direction, and she sighed over the likely gossip.

Somehow Lillian survived the rest of the picnic. Mr. Forell remained entirely too close, resulting in a palpable tension in her muscles and an odd awareness of his every move. By the time the last child had been given a pretty notion and most of the guests dispersed, Lillian was exhausted.

Before leaving, she had a very hurried and quiet conversation with Melina, whose eyes narrowed dangerously. "The idiot. How *dare* he?"

"It might be best not to tell your parents."

"I'll take care of tearing him down first, and *then* I'll hand him over to Mother."

"Mr. Forell gave him quite a fright already," Lillian said, smiling faintly.

"That is nothing compared to what I'm going to do to him, I assure you."

Lillian grinned at her friend and a few moments later, allowed Mr. Forell to hand her into the carriage. She quickly settled next to her aunt and as far away from him as the carriage allowed.

"What happened during the obstacle course?" Aunt Svea asked once the carriage was in motion.

Lillian didn't want Mr. Forell to give his version, so she quickly explained. "That boorish Geoffrey accosted me and made me lose the race. Horrid boy. And Mr. Forell very kindly came to my rescue."

"You don't think he could cause any further problems?" Mr. Forell asked seriously.

"That idiot," Aunt Svea said crossly. "He has the brains of a diseased chicken. If he was in cahoots with anyone more dangerous than the local drunk, I'd die of shock. No one smarter would trust him."

Mr. Forell grunted, and Lillian leaned deeper into the cushioned seat, trying to ignore him. He'd been so sweet and gentle with Myra. He made her day by taking her through the course, and it was a good thing he had. If Myra hadn't been there, Lillian was almost sure her defender would have killed Geoffrey.

She knew she ought to be afraid of Daniel Forell, and in a way, she was. She'd been pushed into a pretend relationship with him and was certainly afraid of what that would mean after two previous failed courtships. She dreaded the gossiping and smug looks.

As they pulled into their own drive, she decided she'd write to the coordinator, tell him she needed someone else, immediately. Her reputation would recover quickly enough if Dan left now. Her mind was completely made up.

Until he helped her from the carriage.

Instead of offering his firm open hand for support as he'd properly done before, he enclosed her entire hand in his. And once her feet met the ground, his free hand gripped her shoulder. "Are you sure you're all right?" he asked quietly.

His grey-blue eyes were startlingly intense, and his grip was... Her mind stumbled on that. She didn't know what to think of it, except that she knew she didn't want him to let go.

"It couldn't have been a pleasant experience for you," he added.

Lillian thought he meant Geoffrey, but he could have been alluding to her fib about him being her sweetheart. He was almost acting like one now.

"I'm fine. Only tired," she said, his concern making her smile. "And I've been remiss not to thank you for your timely intervention. It was very kind of you."

His eyes fell to her lips in a distracted sort of way before he shook himself and dropped her hand. His expression turned stiff as he stepped away. "Not at all. It was my job."

CHAPTER 12

Dan

Dan quickly paced away from Miss Loraine. What a fool he was, behaving like one of her pathetic admirers. He wished they would have covered these situations in his training. Did all defenders feel such rage against those who threatened their sorcerers, or was it simply that she was so defenseless, so sweet and innocent? Well, mostly innocent. She could be a terror when she wanted to be.

He had to keep his distance. Otherwise, what would happen to him when she managed to get a replacement? He would protect her. He'd be her defender, and he'd be successful at it. Then, when the replacement came, he'd be paired with a sorcerer dedicated to serving Kalmar.

The next day when Miss Loraine managed to keep her image of the royal couple perfect from behind a corner, he remembered his promise to himself. Instead of returning her grin, he only nodded once. He regretted it instantly. Her smile faltered, and she turned back to her work, unable to repeat the success for another hour.

"I'm going to go rest now," she finally announced.

He didn't press her, but followed her back to her room where she nodded in his direction and closed the door. He frowned and stood still a moment, listening. She hadn't looked tired, only...unhappy perhaps.

He closed himself in his own room, then pressed his ear to the door. Three minutes later her door clicked open and closed before her quiet footsteps receded down the hall.

He waited a moment more, then followed, keeping back so she wouldn't see him.

"Hello, dear," her aunt said from the parlor. "I hope you haven't come in here to hide with one of those horrid books."

"Hello, Aunt Svea. No, I only came to practice. May I join you?"

"Of course, dear. Just no creeping things near my chair, please."

Lillian laughed lightly, and Dan settled in a chair in the hallway, near enough that he could listen and guard without disrupting them.

After several minutes of silence, Lady Ellstrom asked, "Isn't her mole on the right side?"

"Oh, yes. I forgot. It's this mirror image thing. There."

"I think that's the best I've seen you do," Lady Ellstrom said thoughtfully.

"Thank you. I've been reading a book on theory. It's keeping me awake at night."

Dan held back a snort. It was much more likely her silly novels keeping her awake at night.

"Look at this paragraph here. Don't you think that would make things twice as convincing?"

"Why are you asking me, dear? I know much less about this than Mr. Forell does."

Miss Loraine sighed. "Never mind. I just thought it was interesting."

So she *was* reading his books.

A quiet hour followed, and Dan struggled to stay awake.

His head jerked up when Lady Ellstrom burst out laughing. "What a silly idea," she said.

He slowly eased himself around the doorway to see Lady Ellstrom and Sir Malick dancing spryly through the parlor. Sir Malick gazed adoringly at Lady Ellstrom, who smiled back.

"You know he wants to ask you," Lillian said. She stood to one side, smiling broadly.

"Now Mr. Forell. You'll be the judge," said Lady Ellstrom. "That doesn't look a thing like Sir Malick, does it?"

The dancing couple vanished. Across the room, sitting at a desk, Lady Ellstrom looked at him knowingly over the top of her spectacles.

"I couldn't say, Lady Ellstrom."

"Well, I'm glad you're here. Did you see how far Lillian has come with the image of the princess?"

"Oh, he's already seen, Aunt Svea, and I'm famished. It's past my snack time. Excuse me, won't you?"

She smiled for her aunt and moved past him in the doorway. He wanted to go with her, talk with her, but her aunt called him back.

"A word if you please, Mr. Forell. I'd like to discuss our upcoming journey." She motioned him to sit, and as soon as Lillian's footsteps faded away, asked, "How do you think she's progressing?"

"It's difficult to say," he said quietly. "Especially as she seems reluctant to work around me."

"Let me guess," she said wryly. "You stand watching, looking grim and critical."

Dan didn't know what to say.

"If she doesn't trust you to be pleasant, she's not going to confide in you or make herself vulnerable around you. Why should she?"

Dan frowned.

"If you're going to work with her, you'd better learn to like her. Be kind to her at least. She thrives on that. If you're harsh around her, you'll leach the energy and ability right out of her. That's just how she is."

Liking her was far too easy. "She'll have to toughen up if she wants to do serious work." The words were petty and defensive. He knew it as soon as they'd left his mouth.

"Will she? You don't think she could accomplish great things *now*, as she is? If you're in such a hurry to change her, perhaps you aren't the man for the job after all." She rose from her chair. "It's too bad. I'd had high hopes for you." She paced away, but at the door turned back. "You're a fool not to see how strong she is already, not to love her like the rest of us do."

$\approx$

Lillian

Lillian plucked nervously at her dress as Aunt Svea hurried to check the location of the royal couple. Daniel Forell stood nearby, methodically inspecting what seemed to be a hundred weapons hidden in his clothes. He occasionally peered around the corner of the enclave where they were hidden. "The carriage just pulled into the courtyard," he said after the third time.

To calm her nerves, Lillian pulled an image of the prince together in her mind and superimposed it over Dan. The prince was a little shorter, but had a similar shade of brown hair, so the transfiguration didn't take a lot of energy. She displaced the illusion by a few feet then practiced flipping it into a mirror image.

The prince, really Dan, nodded his encouragement, and Lillian's anxiety lessened by a degree. Dan had all but stopped frowning at her. He wasn't friendly exactly, unless they argued theory or law, topics over which he was surprisingly well read. Then he smiled and badgered her and taught her all kinds of things. He didn't like her yet, she was sure, but it was so much easier to work without his frowns.

Aunt Svea appeared in the doorway behind them. "They've just been escorted through one of the underground passageways. You can go now if you're ready."

Dan offered her his arm. Lillian shifted her own image forward and molded her appearance into that of the princess. She took Dan's arm, and a few feet in front of them, the princess copied the motion, latching on the arm of the illusionary prince.

"You can do this," Dan said in a low voice.

She nodded shakily as they walked into the courtyard, invisible behind the image of the royal couple. Once in the open carriage, Lillian carefully arranged the illusions of the prince and princess to sit facing forward, while she and Mr. Forell sat opposite them, providing the basis for the altered mirror images. The liveried driver faced forward, never looking back at them.

"That was perfect," Dan whispered.

The carriage jerked forward, and Lillian smiled and waved at the people gathered near the palace and then the people lining the streets of the capital. The princess mimicked her from across the carriage while the prince smiled and nodded in time to Mr. Forell's movements. Several soldiers surrounded the carriage, providing extra protection as the crowds cheered, unable to see Lillian and Mr. Forell at all. The carriage wound slowly through the streets for almost half an hour, but as they neared the city gates, a wagon pulled into the street ahead of them, blocking their way.

Dan swiveled his head back and forth, looking to the tops of the buildings on either side, and Lillian just managed to keep the prince from copying his movement.

"Archers," Dan whispered under his breath.

"*What?*"

"When the arrows come, try to make it look like they hit the prince and princess."

Lillian's throat constricted in panic, and she felt her control slipping. She was already tired from maintaining her illusion so long. Before the image could waver, Dan squeezed her hand gently. "You'll be fine. Press yourself back into the seat."

His encouragement was oddly calming, and she followed his instructions. He leaned sideways over her, covering her body, just as four arrows buried themselves in the leather carriage seat opposite her. She didn't have much time to respond, but thought she managed the illusion well. The couple across from her slumped forward onto the floor of the carriage, and the real arrows disappeared from view.

Shouting erupted around them as their guards located the assassins and aimed their own crossbows. The driver shouted at the horses and turned down a side street, gaining speed so that they nearly overturned at the next corner.

"You're too far forward. Move before you're hit," Lillian hissed in Dan's ear, but he shook his head and maintained his protective stance. She yanked him backward against her just before two more arrows thudded into the floor of the carriage.

"You see?" she added in a whisper, hoping she'd been fast enough to make the arrows appear to have sunk into the non-existent bodies at her feet.

He said nothing, but kept her pinned back against the cushioned seat, practically sitting in her lap as the carriage careened down the streets and eventually through the city gate. The deserted road was flanked by trees, and Dan finally moved to sit beside her.

The driver yelled the horses on, his whip cracking in the air above his head. The royal guards were nowhere in sight, and Lillian prayed they'd survived.

Dan bent his head to her ear. "When the carriage stops, we'll get down," he whispered. "The driver might be part of the assassination attempt. Can you keep the image intact until we're hidden?"

"I think so."

"Good." He dug in his pocket and produced a vial. "Ready for a couple drops?"

She nodded and took the dropper carefully, grimacing as the medicine hit her tongue. She handed it back to him, never taking her eyes off the bodies at her feet. She blinked moisture from her eyes, firmly reminding herself the figures were only figments of her own imagination.

The carriage slowed to a stop, and Dan timed his descent to the driver's, jumping down and holding out his arms for her. Instead of taking her hand, he encircled her waist and lifted her out so the carriage didn't shake. If she hadn't been so focused on keeping up her illusion, she might have been very disturbed by how easily and gently he gathered her to him. She managed to close the door without a click as the driver hurried toward the opposite side of the carriage. He jerked open the carriage door and reached for his sword.

Lillian's horrified gasp was covered by the sound of the driver's sword hitting the floor of the carriage. He'd aimed right for the prince's neck.

Dan tightened his hold on her waist in warning before letting go of her altogether. She hadn't realized until then how safe she'd felt with him holding her. Full comprehension of their situation seemed to hit her with a physical force. The image faltered, and Dan groaned lightly. With the carriage between them, the driver looked directly at Lillian, his eyes narrowing in understanding.

What had she done?

Before she could collect her thoughts enough to hide the pair of them, Dan drew a large knife from his side.

Lillian quickly closed her eyes, wishing she could block out the sound of the knife hitting its target.

"One moment more," Dan said quietly. She felt him stride past her, and she covered her ears with her hands.

CHAPTER 13

Dan

Dan took a few seconds to search the driver's body. He carried no identification, no obvious clues as to his motivation, but there'd been at least four archers working with him, and the attack had been orchestrated. Those behind it would be checking up on the driver soon. He tried to memorize the man's features before hurrying back to Lillian.

His assignment still stood with her eyes tightly shut, her hands clamped over her ears. Dan gently drew away one of her hands from her head, and her hazel eyes snapped open to regard him with…was it trust?

"We have to hide," he said quietly, pulling her toward the trees. "Can you hear the horses? Someone's coming." Her fingers tightened around his as they ran.

He pulled her behind a large tree as riders thundered up to the carriage.

Dan reluctantly released her hand as he leaned sideways for a better view.

"He's dead," one said. Was it a Kazat accent?

The next actually spoke in Kazatani, dispelling that question. Dan hadn't studied the language for some time, but he was almost certain he said, "Clean through the throat. Just like Carl. Where are the bodies?" The man leaned down from his horse to touch one of the arrows still imbedded in the back seat of the open carriage.

Two of the four men dismounted and pulled their dead friend over the back of a riderless horse before walking the perimeter of the wagon.

Dan swore mentally. They'd see their tracks. He'd have to run with Lillian. He might have chanced fighting them if he was certain she'd stay hidden, but she'd lost her concentration just minutes ago under stress, and he couldn't be sure she'd be safe. He turned back to indicate his plan, but she wasn't there.

Dan spun on the spot, still hidden behind the tree, his eyes combing the area. She was gone. His heart skipped a beat, but the surge of panic rising in his chest was suddenly halted when her frightened face appeared from the depths of a small fir tree a few paces away. She put a finger to her lips, then melted back into her hiding place. It took him a moment to realize she wasn't hiding *in* the tree. She *was* the tree, standing in the open without any cover aside from the illusion she had created. It was bad enough when she'd been in the open carriage. Then he'd known there was a *possible* danger. Now actual assassins, bowmen at that, stood only thirty paces away.

He peeked around the tree again, certain their trail had already been spotted, but one of the men pointed farther down the road. "I see someone, sir."

"Let's get them before the soldiers catch up," their leader said testily.

The two men on the ground mounted, and all four galloped off, the body of their dead comrade bouncing on a horse behind them.

The tree surrounding Lillian's form melted away, and she turned wide eyes on Dan.

Without thinking, he closed the distance between them and hugged her close. "You're all right?" He took her shoulders in his hands and pulled her to arm's length to study her face.

She looked surprised. And why shouldn't she, he thought in irritation, with him manhandling her? He released her and took a quick step back, her curious gaze following him. He had to get control of himself. "You're pale," he said, pulling a vial of medicine from his jacket and almost wincing when his voice cracked. Did he really have to make such a fool of himself in front of her? "You've done so much. Do you need a cookie? Or your medicine?"

"Actually," she said quietly, "it's too late. I think I'm going to be ill." She took in a slow shaky breath and blew it out.

His voice could have been gentler when he asked, "What were you thinking? Closing your eyes before the threat was neutralized, what if I hadn't been successful?"

She furrowed her brow before saying distractedly, "He didn't have a chance against you. I just couldn't bear to watch. Excuse me, please." She stumbled off into the trees.

He hurried after her, shaking his head. Her confidence in him was simultaneously gratifying and alarming.

He reached her just as she began to retch.

"You'll be fine in a minute, and then we'll give you your medicine," he said, praying he was right and that she wouldn't have another seizure. He rested his hand lightly on her shoulder. The few locks of hair that had escaped their knot began to swing forward, and he swiftly caught them back.

"You don't have to do this," she whispered after a moment. "I might get it on me. On you."

"So we'll take a bath," he said carelessly. *Oh.* "I mean, not together, of course."

She laughed shakily at his blunder, then retched again. A

minute later, she was done. She seemed about to apologize again, so he quickly changed the subject while scattering leaves and small branches to hide the evidence of her nausea. "You nearly gave me a heart attack when you moved out into the open. What if you'd lost your focus again? You could have had a Kazat arrow in you before you realized they'd seen you."

She gave herself a dose of her medication, made a face, and then answered tiredly, "I know, but I had to see them to describe them to the coordinator, and I had to hide our footprints."

"And give them someone to chase into the distance," he said, realizing the extent of what she'd done. Her power was incredible, but she only looked sad.

He took her hand. "You were amazing, Miss Loraine. Lillian." He waited for her to look up at him. When she did, he almost lost the ability to speak. Her eyes were so beautiful. "Truly amazing," he choked out. "You kept them from finding us. The prince and princess are safe. We'll both be able to describe the assassins to the coordinator. It couldn't have been much better." He took a small flask of water from his jacket pocket and pressed it into her hands.

She took a sip, smiling uncertainly. "A compliment, Dan?"

"Long overdue," he said with an uncomfortable shrug. "We need to hurry."

She nodded. "We shouldn't be here when the soldiers come."

"Let's get back to your aunt."

She still looked pale, so he handed her a cookie. As she took the first bite, a distant shout announced oncoming riders.

Dan put an arm around her shoulders, steering her farther away from the road and then back toward the city. He told himself that his instinct to be close to her was only part of his job, his duty to protect her, and had nothing to do with the softness of her hair or her breathtaking smile.

He was half-surprised she didn't pull away from him. It was even stranger that, when he did withdraw his arm several minutes later, he felt an undeniable pang of loss. Dan walked with Lillian in the cover of the trees for over an hour before he dared take her onto a main road. It gave him plenty of time to replay the events of the afternoon in his mind.

He'd done just what he should have. He identified the threat before the archers let their arrows loose, protected her body with his until they were out of harm's way, and killed the driver-assassin. But when he'd done those things, he wasn't thinking of his duty. He wasn't thinking at all. He'd only felt an all-encompassing terror that she might be harmed or killed. Was that how all defenders felt about their assignments?

Eventually they entered the city through a different gate, Lillian disguising them as an older couple. They wound their way back to their inn, and as they entered the parlor, Dan discovered his hand was at Lillian's waist. He snatched his hand back as Lady Ellstrom moved forward to fiercely embrace her niece. She raised an eyebrow over Lillian's shoulder, and the heat of a flush crept up his neck.

"The coordinator?" he asked.

"He's on his way," Lady Ellstrom said.

"I'll check the rooms and then wait outside." He needed some distance.

Once certain the area was safe, Dan walked back outside, shutting the door behind him. He slumped against the wall, his feelings so tangled he couldn't separate and identify them.

Lillian

"Are you all right, dear?" Aunt Svea asked.

"Yes, of course," Lillian said quickly.

She recounted the day's events to her aunt, who seemed to read more into the pauses than Lillian wanted her to. What did it matter that she'd gone from half-hysterical to completely calm when Dan had hugged her? That was a detail no one, including her aunt and Daniel Forell, should ever know.

Lillian fell asleep in her chair, exhausted by the day's events and her own use of magic, only waking when Coordinator Madsen arrived with flowers for Aunt Svea. Dan followed the coordinator into the parlor, then stood with his hands clasped behind his back as Lillian made an accounting of their adventure. He didn't bat an eye at her omission of being ill.

Madsen wrote notes in his personal code, occasionally grunting comments like, "four of them," and, "mirror images," and, "brilliant." When she finished, Madsen asked her for a description of the men they'd seen. Sneaking glances at Dan, Lillian created an image of the men around the empty carriage.

Dan's widened eyes, and the subtle part of his lips suggested he was impressed. He should be. It hadn't been easy to fix the faces of the men into her mind.

Madsen stood and approached the illusion, chuckling and shaking his head. "Miss Loraine. What I wouldn't give—" He glanced at her aunt and cut himself off.

"Oh. And the driver." Lillian added him to the side.

Madsen beckoned to Dan, who joined him in studying the images.

"Did she get them right, Forell?"

Lillian's indignation at the question was instantly dispelled when Dan gave the coordinator a cool glance. "Of course she did. They're perfect representations. She couldn't have done better today."

It was kind of him to overlook the time her image faltered, allowing the driver to see both of them.

Aunt Svea watched Dan with calculating approval.

Madsen pointed at the image. "These two work for Reznik," he said. "We've always known the man's half mad, but he's always targeted our sorcerers. This is the first time he's gone after Kalmarian royalty. Likely, his alliance with Commander Strihat is giving him more confidence."

"Are you sure the princess and her husband were the targets?" Aunt Svea asked. "Maybe they knew it was Lillian."

"If they'd known a sorceress was in the carriage, the attack would have been more sophisticated, likely with a few sorcerers involved. Reznik has a dozen working for him, including a man named Hessian Fast. They call him the Hound because he can detect magic, track it down. Octens believes he'll be sent here to scout out our sorcerers. We're not sure if he aims to win them to Reznik's employ or to eliminate them, probably the latter."

Dan gave the coordinator a hard look, but Madsen smiled at Lillian. "Nothing for you to worry about, my dear, I'm sure. Reznik wouldn't think to send him to a town so remote as Perch Harbor." He turned to Dan. "Anything else I should know?"

Dan looked a little uncomfortable. "I may have made a mistake," he admitted. "The attackers spoke of a man who'd been killed in the same manner as the driver. They may have meant the archer we met near Perch Harbor."

"So this man, Fast, has already been to Perch Harbor?" Lillian said, her stomach sinking.

"No," Madsen said with an abrupt shake of his head. "If they'd known about you, they would have kept trying." He turned to Dan. "And you never found the body?"

A muscle tightened in Dan's jaw. "His friends must have found him first, and now they suspect a connection."

They both looked speculatively at Lillian.

"So they *do* know about her, then?" Aunt Svea asked.

"More likely they suspect *you*," Madsen told her bluntly.

Aunt Svea gave a satisfied nod, but Lillian's fear escalated.

"Octens believes the Hound will come from Kazatania soon," Madsen continued. "Perhaps only weeks from now. Last time he was here, four of our most powerful sorcerers were found dead."

"You should have had him killed already," Dan said, glaring at the coordinator.

"Are you volunteering to be the next to try?" Madsen asked.

"I shouldn't go back home." The words felt dragged from Lillian's chest. "It would endanger Aunt Svea." She didn't want to leave home. She had nowhere else to go.

"I don't think that's necessary yet," Coordinator Madsen said thoughtfully. "We should explore options though, just in case. If Octens gets word Fast is coming, we'll need to move you."

Lillian nodded woodenly and was more than happy when the coordinator prepared to leave.

"Forell, walk out with me a moment, will you? I have news from army friends that will bore the ladies."

"Yes, sir."

Lillian waited a full ten seconds after the door shut on Madsen and Dan, then moved very quietly to the doorway, ignoring her aunt's questioning look.

Her eavesdropping was immediately rewarded.

"Was that as incredible as it sounded?"

"Much more so, sir." Lillian smiled at the hint of pride in her defender's voice. "Her illusions were perfect."

"Good. Whatever you've been doing with her, keep doing it. Whether we funnel her into the army sorcerers or into information gathering, it doesn't matter, as long as you can get her to choose one of them. We can't let her waste that talent."

Lillian held her breath, anger tightening her throat at Madsen's attitude. There was a pause before Dan said stiffly, "I'll do my best for her, sir."

There was another small pause that Lillian wished she could interpret. "Remember who you work for, my boy," Madsen said warningly. "It is a simple matter for me to replace you if I don't see progress."

"Yes, sir." Dan's answer was too fast for Lillian's comfort. "What about the Hound?" he asked. "He always finds his targets, Kazatani or Kalmarian, and I think—"

"You're the best, aren't you, Forell?" Madsen said tauntingly. "So there's nothing to worry about. And if you are smart, you'll do what I say, and find a way to make the girl do what I say."

Receding footsteps announced the conversation was over, and Lillian quickly moved to a chair near her aunt.

"I'm surprised you have to listen at the door." Aunt Svea's words were barely audible. "Can't you get information from him another way?"

"I haven't had many opportunities to feign exhaustion. I still can't believe you lied to him. I've never had any trouble remembering what happens after I work big magic, and you know it."

Aunt Svea smirked. "You're welcome, dear."

Lillian simply shook her head. Aunt Svea insisted she eat dinner, but Lillian had little appetite. Madsen planned to use Dan to push her to work in the army or as a spy. She had done good work today, and she had to admit that a little of that was due to her desire to impress Daniel Forell. She wanted to kick herself. Was he truly only Madsen's puppet? She'd melted in his embrace, but he might only be trying to control her.

Lillian felt hot tears of anger forming and quickly ate a few more bites to appease Aunt Svea before saying, "I'm too exhausted to finish. I'm going to bed."

Her aunt eyed her with concern and didn't protest, for which Lillian was grateful. Before she could reach her door, Dan appeared next to her. She hadn't even heard him come back into the apartment. He passed by her with a murmured, "One moment, please."

He quickly searched her room, securing the window before coming back into the parlor. "Miss Loraine," he said, almost curtly. He bowed stiffly and turned away without meeting her eye.

If he was supposed to be manipulating her, he was too resentful of his instructions to try it. Mr. Forell wanted reassignment as much as she did.

She slipped into her room and shut the door before allowing her tears to spill over. She always cried when she was angry. She fell asleep telling herself that was the only emotion she felt. Almost instantly she found herself at the seaside, her parents on either side of her, infusing her with love and support. The pain slowly dissolved, though she knew some of it would surely resurface in the morning.

CHAPTER 14

Dan

Three weeks after the attack on the princess and her husband, Dan found himself at yet another ball hosted by Lady Ellstrom. When he'd taken dance lessons at the academy, he'd never dreamed he'd actually need them. The army defenders never danced at social events, never had to hide half a dozen weapons in finely tailored clothing.

He eyed his assignment from a few paces away. She was surrounded by no less than ten people, all of whom hung on her every word. Perhaps they were as affected by her smile as he was.

"What are you thinking about so seriously, Daniel?" Lady Ellstrom asked quietly from beside him.

He gave her a wry smile. "I was wondering if your niece would consent to hiding weapons in her skirts. She has abundant room to hide things while my uniform for the occasion is sadly lacking in pockets."

Lady Ellstrom nodded thoughtfully. "There may be something to that idea."

Dan had only been joking, but it was good for Lillian's aunt to think of something else. She watched him too closely these days, and her constant scrutiny made his difficult balancing act even worse. He helped Lillian without giving too much advice, praised her regularly but not as much as he wanted to, kept close enough to her to keep her safe but not close enough to gather her into his arms as he wished he could. Trickiest of all was trying to thwart the coordinator without thwarting Lillian's best interests.

He'd wanted to plant his fist in Madsen's face when he suggested Dan manipulate Lillian. She already took on enough dangerous assignments for someone so inexperienced, and with her rapid progress, she'd be ready to join the army sorcerers by the end of the year, especially if she stopped wasting time on romance novels. Madsen would be thrilled with all she'd done, but Dan's assignment was not to make Madsen happy. It was to keep Lillian Loraine safe. Even if Madsen threatened him with reassignment, he wouldn't push Lillian faster than might be good for her. She wanted a replacement when one came available anyway, so Madsen's threat had been empty.

Dan looked at her again and caught back a sigh. She was smiling at something one of her friends said, and her dimples were in full force. If he watched her for too long when she smiled like that, he sometimes felt strange pains in his chest. He had a suspicion, one he hardly dared voice even in his mind, that when it came time for him to give up this assignment, that odd little pain would become acutely unbearable.

The music began in the hall, and the men surrounding Lillian glanced at each other, obviously evaluating the competition. She met his eye, and he hoped he understood the look she sent him. He strode to her side. "Is this our dance, Miss Loraine?" he asked with a small bow.

"Of course, Mr. Forell."

Dan took her hand in his and led her to the dance floor.

"Your timing is excellent," she whispered. "And I appreciate your willingness to sacrifice your time this way."

"Nonsense," he said with a faint smile. "I just triumphed over every man in the room." They joined the swirling couples. The usual combination of tension and peacefulness gripped him as soon as she was in his arms, making it difficult for him to feel anything else.

"Don't belittle the favor you're doing me. My friends are very sweet, but it is best not to dance with some of them." Her lips quirked up in a wry little smile.

"I have to apologize for the way I talked about it last," Dan said quietly, getting caught in her gaze. "But if it is more convenient for you to have me appear as a suitor, I don't mind it." The words were out before his mind caught up and verified the truth of it. "I know it's your aunt's idea, not yours, and I don't want you to be uncomfortable."

She searched his eyes before giving her head a tiny shake. "You mean like trouncing me at pins last night? My humiliation might be interpreted as discomfort."

He couldn't help his smile. "You beat me twice before that."

"As to appearances, Aunt Svea is already telling everyone we're attached, so I think it might be too late to get that under control."

That shouldn't make him so happy. "But how do you feel about that?"

Her lips twisted into a bitter line for a moment before she said flippantly, "Well, it isn't as though I already have a suitor, is it?"

He ignored a pang of disappointment. What had he expected her to say?

They danced quietly a minute before she added, "She's watching us, you know."

"Your aunt?"

"Mm-hmm. She wants you to act interested in me."

"But what do you want, Lillian?"

She stared at him a moment before saying, "Could you dance with some of the girls who don't get asked often and watch to see if I need you to rescue me again?"

"I think I could manage that."

And he did. It wasn't as bad as it could have been, and he kept Lillian in sight as much as possible. The only thing that dampened his mood was the appearance of the coordinator halfway into the evening. Madsen pulled Dan aside, and with a jovial laugh asked him how things were progressing.

"She's doing amazingly well." It wasn't a lie.

"And she trusts you now?"

"More than before." That wasn't saying much. They'd come to the point of enjoying each other's company, but she always held something back. It was evident in her eyes, and in the way she sometimes retreated from him, physically and in conversation. It pained Dan for reasons that had nothing to do with the coordinator.

"Good. Because you're going to have to run with her."

He was so lost in his own thoughts that he wondered if he'd heard Madsen correctly. "What?"

"Hessian Fast, the Hound."

"Yes?"

"He's coming this way. Traveling down the coast. We think he's headed here."

Dan's heart felt leaden. The Hound was after Lillian.

~

Lillian

"Sorry I'm late," Melina said, appearing next to Lillian. "I'm glad Bennet and I won't miss the dancing."

"You look disgustingly beautiful and well-rested," Lillian

said, embracing her friend. They moved away from the musicians so they could hear each other.

"Your dress is divine, Lillian, and if you didn't stay up reading those horrible books half the night, you'd feel well-rested too," Melina said as she scanned the ballroom. "He's watching you again," she added.

"What do you mean? Who?"

"He's *always* watched you," Melina said with a smirk. "Since the first day he came here."

"You're being silly."

"No. It's true." She lowered her voice. "Neither of the others looked at you like that."

"Like what?"

"Like that."

Lillian turned to look at her defender and gulped, unable to tear her eyes from his. She'd been sure Mr. Forell was simply irritated with the coordinator when she'd first snuck glances their way a few minutes ago, but that had changed, his irritation now replaced by a fiery intensity.

Dan shook his head at something the coordinator said, then stalked toward Lillian, people melting out of his path. She stepped forward to meet him and, without a word spoken by either, she was in his arms and whirling out onto the dance floor.

He pulled her close, stretching the bounds of propriety as he murmured in her ear, "we have to leave, have to get you out of here."

Lillian had difficulty focusing on the words. His mouth was almost touching her hair.

"Do you have relatives you want to visit?" His voice was hypnotic. "Or perhaps you'd like to see the mountains? Soon. Tomorrow maybe."

"Tomorrow?" she said breathlessly. Over his shoulder she saw Madsen deep in conversation with Aunt Svea. Under a polite expression her aunt's eyes were alarmed, and that finally brought Lillian out of her defender-induced stupor. "What do you mean? What's happening?"

"I just found out…" He didn't get to finish his sentence. The song ended, and Aunt Svea motioned to her guests. The room quieted, and Lillian wished her aunt would have waited a few more minutes to announce dinner. Her anxiety over Dan's words was growing, but out of habit, she began mentally reviewing the seating arrangements for their guests. Madsen had requested a seat by Dan, but Lillian didn't want the two together.

"My dear friends," Aunt Svea began. "You've all met the special guest staying in our home."

Lillian wondered if she could convince Sir Malick to trade seats with one of the Miss Mitters.

"So I'm sure you will not be surprised to hear…"

Then Madsen would be distracted by Malick, and she could still sit by Dan.

"…that my niece, Miss Lillian Loraine…"

Wait. What?

"…has accepted Mr. Daniel Forell's proposal of marriage."

What?

The applause almost drowned out Mr. Forell's whispered, "I should have seen that coming."

Lillian couldn't draw breath.

Mr. Forell's hand found hers and squeezed her fingers gently.

A sea of people turned to look at them, but their faces blurred as Lillian grew dizzy.

"Breathe," Mr. Forell instructed under his breath.

She inhaled mechanically.

"They will be married this winter after Lillian has had a chance to meet his family," Aunt Svea said. "They leave tomorrow on their journey."

Lillian gulped a breath and looked up at her defender, who murmured, "It's all going to be fine. She must be trying to give us an excuse to leave, but we'll fix this. Do you want a mask?"

Of course she did. She carefully placed a smiling Lillian's face over her own and turned each direction to show her creation to the guests applauding them.

Dan squeezed her hand again. "Your aunt's motioning us forward. She'll want us to say something."

"I don't think I can. I had no idea she'd do this. I'm so, so sorry."

"My dear Lillian," he murmured with a flirtatious wink. "Don't you realize half the men in the room are desperate to be in my shoes?"

Lillian was glad the illusion of her smile was carefully intact as he led her forward. She couldn't make her real mouth do anything but gape open in surprise.

Dan led Lillian to her aunt, then turned to address the crowd gathered close by.

"Thank you all for your kind wishes," he said with a bright smile.

Even in her state of shock, Lillian couldn't help noticing how attractive he was.

"You can't imagine my astonishment at finding myself so fortunate."

Lillian caught back a hysterical laugh.

He looked slyly at Aunt Svea. "I'm sure you all know our hostess well enough to guess she had a hand in our engagement."

Everyone laughed, and Aunt Svea didn't look guilty at all, more smug really.

Sir Malick barked out, "Well, aren't you going to kiss her?"

Oh, no.

Dan smiled with a glint of humor in his eyes and leaned closer to Lillian.

"Mr. Forell," she whispered from behind her mask. "Dan. Really." A terrifying blend of anticipation and panic froze her in her place as he moved closer still.

"I hope you appreciate my extreme self-control in this moment, Lillian," he breathed. He gazed deeply into her eyes, and her heart took off at a mad gallop.

Whatever he said, he was going to kiss her. The intent was plain in his eyes. He leaned close enough that his forehead was almost touching hers. Curiosity battled her panic, but he didn't lean forward to kiss her mouth. Instead, he raised her hand to his face. Despite an unfounded feeling of disappointment, her hand still trembled in his, and his grip tightened. At the last moment, he turned her hand over and pressed his lips to her palm. Shivers traveled down her spine as heat flooded her face.

Lillian's friends laughed and cheered, and she was quickly pulled away to be hugged and congratulated by dozens of people. Dan was busy shaking everyone's hand, but she knew he watched her.

Melina threw her arms around Lillian. "How could you not tell me? I'm so happy for you." She stepped back to take Lillian's hand, turning it this way and that. "But let me see."

"What?"

"Just checking for scorch marks. I've never seen a kiss on a hand with that much heat."

CHAPTER 15

Dan

Dan wished Lillian would come rescue him from Melina's mother. Mrs. Penchant seemed determined to tell Dan every detail of Lillian's past. Normally he'd have been very interested, but he was desperate to talk to Lillian.

"It is so good to see her happy now."

He tried to break in and excuse himself, but she added, "Especially after, you know…"

Maybe everyone would leave if he feigned food poisoning. "After what?" he asked distractedly.

"Well, the two… you know."

He finally tore his eyes away from Lillian and looked at Melina's mother.

She fidgeted nervously while he waited for her to speak. "Her two… disappointments, I mean."

Now she had his attention. "Disappointments?"

"Well, one engagement and almost another before she found you. We're all very anxious to see her with the right man."

Two engagements?

"You already know about her lack of title, and none of us know why the second left last year, but I'm sure you won't share his idiocy."

"Of course not, ma'am."

Dan made his escape, his mind in shock. Lillian had been engaged twice, and both men left her. Surely there couldn't be *two* men that stupid. And the last was a year ago, when Lillian had begun taking on more work. She must have given up on love. He felt the simultaneous impulses to thank the unnamed strangers and to beat them senseless.

Lillian met his gaze again from amidst a group of older women, all apparently congratulating her. She smiled, but it had to be a mask. A fake fiancé after two failed engagements.

Lady Ellstrom wisely kept herself at a careful distance from her niece, but after dinner when he danced with Lillian again, Dan found it difficult to keep himself at any distance at all. He told himself it was only because she was in danger and that he felt protective, but the way she smelled and the feel of her smooth fingers in his contradicted the lies in his mind every few seconds.

At the end of the dance, under the noise of gentle applause, he whispered, "Madsen thinks the Hound is after you, that your life is in danger."

She didn't answer, and he hesitantly suggested, "Once everyone is gone, can we go to the library and talk? I want to look at some maps with you, so we can plan what to do next."

The smiling Lillian nodded once and moved toward the door to bid her guests good night.

An hour later she met him in the library.

"You can drop the illusion," he told her quietly. "I know you can't be happy about this."

Her smile instantly dissolved. "Oh, Dan," she whispered, her eyes wide. "I promise I had nothing to do…"

Dan strode quickly forward, taking her shoulders in his

hands and looking directly into her troubled hazel eyes. "Lillian," he said earnestly. "None of this is your fault. It can't hurt me at all. You're the only one who could suffer from this. I don't know whether it was Madsen's idea or your aunt's, but I swear I'll make it right for you. When you get the defender you want, we can fake my death or do whatever we have to. Please, don't let it worry you."

It suddenly occurred to Dan that his face was only an inch from Lillian's. The temptation to kiss her was almost overwhelming, but it wouldn't help the situation at all, wouldn't help *her* at all. He slowly eased back, taking a deep breath.

"It will be all right," he said.

She nodded in agreement, though she didn't look much more convinced than he felt. "You said the magic tracker is coming?"

He briefly outlined as much as he knew, trying to be truthful about the danger without scaring her.

"So I *do* need to leave?" she said.

"I'm afraid so."

"Where do you think we should go?"

"Madsen suggested we visit the army sorcerers, and it would be a safe place for you. Hardly anyone would realize you are a sorceress. They'd only see you as my guest. And Hessian Fast wouldn't dare track you there, even if he did suspect your abilities. But Madsen wants to push you into joining the army sorcerers. What you want is more important, so let's go somewhere else." He frowned and added, "As long as it's safe."

Lillian considered a moment. "That is where *you'd* like to go though, isn't it?"

Dan shrugged uncomfortably. "It is a familiar place, but look here." He pointed to the map. "No one would be surprised if a girl of your beaut—" He caught himself. "That is, a girl like you, were to go to the capital. The social scene is livelier there, and there'd be plenty to keep you occupied, though we'd need to be careful about which invitations you accepted."

"Aunt Svea told everyone we're going to visit your family. Where do they live?"

Lillian had drawn so close to him, he could smell her hair soap. An odd buoyancy filled his chest, and he had no intention of examining it. "My parents are both cartographers and live out of the country most of the year. I doubt we could find them if we tried. Between their work and my time at the academy, we aren't the closest of families." Her eyes were sad, so he quickly continued. "Besides that, I only have a brother. Well, he's actually my cousin, but we grew up together."

"Where does he live?"

Dan closed his eyes and admitted, "Oliver's a defender to one of the army sorcerers."

"Madsen planned well," Lillian said dryly.

"I'm afraid so."

"I'd rather not introduce you to my acquaintances at the capital," she said slowly. "The fewer people that see us together..."

"The fewer explanations to make when we need to end it."

She nodded. "The army base, then."

"Really?" Dan asked, trying not to let his relief show. "You don't have to. We can think of something else."

Lillian sighed. "I can't think of any better options."

"You might actually like it," he said, his hope growing. "The sorcerers could teach you so much more than I ever learned at the academy, and you'll like them." He considered a moment. "Well, some of them, but I love it there. You might too."

Lillian

H is expression was so akin to a hopeful puppy that Lillian couldn't help laughing at him. "I can see you're devastated about us going."

He smiled sheepishly. "I've been trying not to influence your decision."

"Why?" she asked, curious.

"Madsen wants to control you." He shrugged. "Be sure your next defender isn't under his thumb either."

Why should she feel a pang of discontent over the thought of a new defender? "There are other ways to get around Madsen," she said.

He raised his eyebrows expectantly.

A bee appeared, flying around Dan's head and then landing on his sleeve. A large spider lowered itself to dangle before Dan's face. And when he took a step back, he realized a paper was stuck to the bottom of his foot. He shook it before chuckling.

"Now I know how your poor governess felt," he said.

Lillian stared a moment before snapping her mouth shut. Dan was shockingly handsome when he smiled. "Oh, no," she assured him. "She was actually *very* mean. She called Liv and Aunt Svea names behind their backs, so she got wolves watching her from the woods and armies of ants crawling toward her across the porch steps, bird droppings on her skirt..."

He was laughing in earnest now. "Remind me never to irritate you."

"I'll do that," Lillian said, trying to crush the giddiness induced by his laugh.

They stayed up late planning, and then Lillian stayed up even later packing, so that in the morning when she'd hugged her aunt goodbye and climbed into the carriage, she was more than ready to go back to sleep.

"You aren't angry with her?" Dan asked, looking back at Aunt Svea.

"Of course I am," Lillian said with a shrug. "But why dwell on it? What if something happens to me, or to her?" Either was likely, but Dan wouldn't understand. He probably already considered her too passive and dull.

"It's not just that. You're *happy*, different than last night."

She gave a half-smile as the carriage jerked forward. "I have nice dreams. It's difficult to stay angry afterward." She wasn't ready to tell him that her dead parents visited her in her sleep to make her feel better, especially since she didn't know how they did it.

He studied her for a moment, then let the matter drop.

She changed the subject. "I read that chapter on meditation and intent yesterday, and I want to experiment."

"In the carriage?"

"What carriage?"

He laughed as their cushioned benches shifted into large rocks, the floor at their feet into sand, and walls of the carriage into an ocean view. "Very good," he said with a grin. "But how does it look from different perspectives?"

"Try it."

Dan immediately began moving around in the carriage, shifting in his seat, leaning down to look up at the ceiling, and finally dropping onto the seat next to her. "It's perfect," he said.

Lillian shrugged carelessly, trying to ignore his nearness as his gaze flitted between her eyes.

"Lillian, I—" He shook himself. "What else besides oceans?"

Too late, she realized her hand had reached toward him, and she gave it a careless wave to cover up her blunder. "How's this?"

They sat in a dimly lit forest, then in a shadowy cave, and then by a fountain in a bustling town square.

"Here," he breathed, handing her a vial of her medicine and

studying the people moving in what appeared to be a distant shop. "The detail is amazing. I didn't know you could do this." He blinked at her a few times, then sprang back to his side of the carriage. "I suppose we can get a lot of work done in the two-and-a-half days we'll be stuck in here."

Lillian rolled her eyes. "You mean *I'll* get a lot of work done."

He laughed again, and Lillian grinned at the sound. For the rest of the day, Dan stayed on his side of the carriage, but he smiled his approval as she worked more complex images and angles. At his insistence, she rested and ate regularly, and if she wasn't working or napping, she had her books to distract her from the way his smile made her breath catch. At least, she tried to distract herself with them. Whenever she pulled one out of her satchel, Dan pressed his lips together and looked away. He seemed to disapprove of them almost as much as Aunt Svea did, but Lillian wasn't about to give them up.

That night they slept at an inn with a closed door between their two rooms, an imaginary chaperone accompanying Lillian everywhere outside the carriage. Their driver was one of Madsen's men, and he never flinched at the sudden appearance of another woman. The next day they traveled almost continuously through forest. Lillian took the opportunity to practice larger images. Keeping a watch out for other travelers ahead and behind them, and making sure to hide what she was doing from their driver, she transformed the landscape as they passed.

Dan leaned out the window in his excitement to critique her work. "No shadows," he pointed out when the trees turned to a cliff face. She corrected it, and he shook his head with a grin. "The angle is perfect. How do you manage that? And that bear lumbering along next to us is so real. Can the driver see it?"

"What bear?" Lillian asked, forcing her eyes wide.

Dan turned a startled gaze on her before doubling over with laughter. It was better than a hundred doses of her medicine, but she couldn't bring herself to tell him that. Trusting him was still new, and she found herself uncharacteristically shy.

If she wasn't so sick of the carriage, Lillian wouldn't have wanted the journey to end. They argued magical theory, she badgered him with questions about the army sorcerers and the base, and every time he smiled at her, Lillian's heart rose a little inside her chest.

"Which sorcerers do you like best?" she asked him.

"I suppose I know Sir Mendine better than most of the others. And Sir Hollis, who works with my cousin, Oliver. But I think you'll like Lady Teresa. She's from Guasave, but came to Kalmar with her husband decades ago. She joined the army sorcerers after he died."

That sparked another fifty questions about the sorcerers, and Lillian committed as much as she could to memory.

That evening, she transformed the inside of the carriage to a spacious ballroom, with people moving on every side of them. Dan's reaction didn't disappoint. He turned every direction in his seat as people passed between and around them. "Have you ever kept so many angles, so many moving figures, going before?" he asked, handing her a cookie.

"No." She took a bite and swallowed. "But notice how I'm cheating. All the women have Melina's face, and all the men look like her fiancé, Bennet." Even despite the cookie, she had to let go of the image. She slept almost immediately, not waking until Dan shook her gently to tell her they'd arrived at another inn.

The following evening they reached the army base, a hideous, unwelcoming, and very utilitarian garrison. Dan's face lit up when it came into sight, so she made an effort not to look as apprehensive as she felt. She found her fingers drumming nervously on the seat. What was wrong with her? She never worried about meeting people. That was what she was best at. Wasn't it?

When a soldier approached the door, Dan called out a greeting, and the man slapped his knee, laughing loudly.

"Ah, Forell. We knew you couldn't stand to be away for long. We've had a bet going when you'd be back."

"I'm just back for a visit, Ferlman. I brought my fiancée to meet everyone." The lie sounded natural, but it was still a lie. Only the sorcerers were to know of her ability, and even they would be told Dan was her fiancé.

Lillian was immediately handed out of the carriage to meet the men at the gate. She almost forgot to wave to her "attendant" whom, they told anyone who asked, was driving on to another destination after the carriage was unloaded. Lillian was introduced to what seemed like hundreds of men as they made their way inside. Most of the soldiers were sweet and polite, but some looked her over in a very ungentlemanly manner. One in particular, a man named Williams, sent his eyes over her from head to toe with such an unpleasant leer that she wanted to completely disappear. The crowd was so tight around them, she never could have done it. Dan was distracted by his friends and didn't seem to notice.

Once inside, they found an imposing officer waiting for them.

"General Adams," Dan said, saluting the much shorter man. The general returned the gesture, then turned his piercing blue eyes on Lillian, who had no idea what kind of curtsy to make.

"Miss Loraine," he said gruffly with a bow.

She settled on a respectful version of a curtsy to an older person. She was a sorceress, yes, but the man was old enough to be her grandfather.

"Lady Teresa will be pleased to have another woman at the fort, I'm sure," he said, not sounding pleased at all. He motioned them to follow, and Lillian allowed Dan to thread her arm through his as they walked in the general's wake.

"I'll take you to meet Lady Teresa and the others first," General Adams said over his shoulder.

"Are we really going to meet them now?" Lillian whispered to Dan, tiny prickles of panic stinging her insides.

"Of course," he said. "Why not?"

Men. "I should change my attire, of course," she said.

"Why would you want to do that?" he asked, his eyebrows knit together.

Lillian took a calming breath and was about to try to make him understand when the general said, "Here we are."

The small crowd that followed them had melted away, and Lillian looked about for an excuse to delay. She must have looked scared, because Dan gave her a reassuring smile before propelling her into the room with a whispered, "You'll be fine."

Lillian shook her head, but it was too late. If she changed her appearance now, people would notice.

She soon realized she needn't have worried. The unkempt men lounging in what could only be described as a den couldn't be offended by her appearance. Most of them were unshaven, their uniforms showing the wear of the day. She moved into the room, trying not to let her skirt touch anything.

CHAPTER 16

Dan

Lillian was nervous, but Dan seriously doubted anyone else would see it, and surely being in such a comfortable sitting room after all their travels would make her happy. At their arrival, the sorcerers looked up from their respective books, maps, and entertainments, and the general ushered Lillian forward.

"This is Miss Loraine. You've already been told why she's here. I'm sure there is much she can learn from you." The general left immediately, and Dan was glad to be able to stay with Lillian. A surge of pride swelled in his chest, not just because he was a defender to a powerful sorceress, but because she was brilliant and sweet. The army sorcerers would likely be learning some things from her too.

Unfortunately, it was Sir Pescall, the animal expert, who sat closest. Dan would have preferred one of the more polished sorcerers greet her first. Sir Pescall stood, his expression surly and resentful. He gave the barest nod to Lillian, and Dan had never been so aware of the animal hair clinging to the man's clothes.

Lillian was her usual self. She smiled brightly, as though meeting Sir Pescall was a sincere pleasure. "Some time when it's convenient, I'd love to talk with you about the way you differentiate the feeling in your mind between species in the same family," she said with interest.

Pescall looked too startled to say anything. It was just as well. His teeth and breath usually weren't appealing.

Next was the healer, Sir Carlos Vidal. He was known for his abrupt nature, but his understanding of magical theory was unparalleled. At least he murmured a somewhat polite greeting and inclined his head in her direction, displaying the white streaks in his black hair. Lillian remembered to express her interest in his library, and Dan was grateful she'd asked so many questions about him on their journey.

"Of course, Miss Loraine. At your disposal." Sir Carlos immediately turned back to his book. Lillian didn't seem to notice the slight, but turned with a smile to the next sorcerer.

And so it went on. The dozen sorcerers in the room each had a polite, but disinterested word or two to say. Dan bristled inwardly as he realized they were underestimating her because she was pretty and pleasant.

Isn't that what you *did?* whispered a voice in the back of his mind. Well, regardless, they were going to be surprised when they saw how powerful she was. He had to remind himself three separate times that his position was only temporary and that he shouldn't become too accustomed to his pride over being her defender.

"And your gift is...?" the fire starter, Sir Drake, asked bluntly. He was one of the youngest of the group, despite his short white hair and beard.

"I'm learning to make illusions," Lillian said placidly.

"Learning, you say? Madsen led us to believe you'd shown some promise already."

"Don't we develop our gifts for decades before we truly master them?" she asked innocently.

Dan nearly laughed at Drake's scowl. He had only discovered his gift five years ago.

Sir Carlos smiled into his book. The healer had often badgered Drake to study magical theory, and if Drake had even cracked a book, he wouldn't have allowed himself such a blunder.

The last of the sorcerers was the individual Dan was most anxious for Lillian to meet. Lady Teresa Juárez, the only female among the group, would surely be able to convince Lillian she belonged with the army sorcerers.

Lillian curtsied politely at their introduction, and Lady Teresa studied her with calculating brown eyes. In comparison to Lillian's sweet countenance, Dan now saw the grim lines of cynicism in Lady Teresa's face. How had he never noticed?

"I hope you learn enough to stay alive, and that *he*," she said, jerking her steel grey head in Dan's direction, "is as good a fighter as everyone says."

With that, Lady Teresa turned her back and walked away, crushing Dan's hopes into a wilted little heap inside his chest.

"Thank you for introducing me to everyone," Lillian said. "I should see to my things."

He didn't try to convince her to stay. There was no point. She was going to hate it here, and there was nothing he could do. He escorted Lillian back into the corridor.

At least he could get her some pink roses as an apology. Sir Mendine owed him a favor, and the plant sorcerer could easily grow roses from any shrub. No one ever teased Sir Mendine for his talent with flowers, likely because he towered over almost everyone and was strong as an ox, not to mention his life-long reputation as a hot-headed fighter.

"I didn't meet your brother," Lillian said questioningly once the door shut behind them.

Dan shrugged. "His sorcerer isn't very social."

"You said he guarded a...distance walker?"

"Yes," Dan said, only to be polite. He didn't feel like talking. The sorcerers were so blind. "He can step many miles at a time, but you'll likely get fewer words out of him than you did out of the others."

"Why?"

"He has a difficult time with speech."

Lillian frowned and looked about to question him further but instead gave a startled shriek as two figures suddenly appeared in front of them.

Dan gave a short laugh and stepped forward to shake hands with Oliver, who clapped him on the shoulder. Oliver's brown hair was a little longer than he usually kept it, but his smirk hadn't changed.

"Couldn't stay away, could you?" he asked.

Sir Hollis looked on as though not quite sure what to make of the pair. He stood, as though it cost him some effort, which it likely did, his short and very slender frame bent slightly to the side.

Dan turned to look for Lillian, who for some odd reason had stepped behind him. "Miss Loraine, may I introduce Sir Hollis and my dimwit cousin, Oliver."

Oliver looked Lillian up and down. "I was told your assignment was a child," he said with a laugh. "I can see that is *not* the case."

Lillian didn't smile. She actually looked... uncomfortable?

Sir Hollis gave a startled grunt, stepping jerkily toward Lillian. She gamely stood her ground, and Dan wasn't sure if he should intercept the man or not. He glanced at Oliver, who only looked confused at his assignment's behavior.

Sir Hollis reached out, his movements uncoordinated as

usual, to touch Lillian's shoulder. It likely didn't cost him extra difficulty because their heights were similar. "Bianca," he said reverently but in drawn-out painful syllables. "Bianca?"

"Pardon Sir Hollis, please," said Oliver. "What he lacks in wit he certainly makes up for in talent."

Lillian cast Oliver a cool look before turning back to Sir Hollis. "I look like someone you know?"

"He grew up with a sister," Oliver said. "She went missing almost twenty years ago, a few years before he found his gift."

Lillian gently took hold of the hand still touching her shoulder. "I am not your sister," she said softly. "But I can tell she loved you very much to leave such an impression."

Sir Hollis gave her a wry but still astonished smile.

"Women do end up loving the strangest men," Oliver said with a wink for Lillian.

Dan cleared his throat meaningfully. "On that note, I should tell you that Miss Loraine is not just my assignment. She is also my fiancée." How strange that he didn't tire of saying it aloud.

Lillian

Lillian repressed the urge to hide behind Dan again. His cousin Oliver was the worst type of man: self-important and smug, not to mention the way he looked at her made her skin crawl. Oliver's hair was a lighter brown than Dan's, and his eyes a lighter blue. Some would have thought Oliver the handsomer of the two, with his broader shoulders and wide smile, but the unkindness in his face was extremely unattractive, and worst of all was the way he treated the man he was supposed to be guarding. She wished Dan was more convincing in his role of fiancé.

Oliver looked incredulously back and forth between them. "You're engaged? That's impossible. You only like work."

"Things change," Dan said shortly. He turned to Sir Hollis, a man with expressive and young eyes, despite the grey sprinkled through his dark brown hair. "If you'll excuse us, we've had a long journey. It's good to see you again, sir."

Sir Hollis' answering smile, just a subtle upturn of his mouth, was so oddly familiar to Lillian. She'd thought she imagined it moments ago, but there was no mistaking it now. She knew that smile. If not for Oliver, she would have found an excuse to stay and talk to Sir Hollis about his gift, but as it was, she only swept him a polite curtsy, the same one she'd given the other sorcerers. Then she gave the slightest of nods to his defender and took Dan's proffered arm.

He sighed as they walked away.

"Disappointed?" she asked.

"I thought you would be."

Lillian smiled carefully. "It's too early to tell, and I'm too tired to think."

"Of course."

They passed a window overlooking some practice courts, and Dan eyed a nearby group fighting with wooden swords.

"You'll want to be out there practicing in the morning?" Lillian asked as innocently as she could. "Perhaps you could leave me with the sorcerers."

"You want to..." He trailed away, obviously confused.

"I'd like some time alone with them. They didn't all have defenders with them tonight."

"No. They often don't when they aren't on assignment."

"Well, then," she said, feigning confidence.

Dan's answering smile was worth the anxiety.

The next morning when he dropped Lillian off at the door to *the den*, Dan turned to her worriedly. "If anything makes you feel uncomfortable, you'll be able to see me from the window, so put something in my line of vision, and I'll come back for you."

She smiled at the concern in his voice and nodded with more cheerfulness than she felt. She took a deep breath, drawing on the courage brought on by dreams of her parents the previous night, and slowly pushed the door open.

It was just as bad as she remembered: dark, dingy, the sorcerers all in their own little corners, no conversation, no discussion. She started off by borrowing a book from Sir Carlos. He was willing enough to share, just not talkative, and she chose a seat in a corner where she could see Dan out the window and still observe the sorcerers. There were only two or three defenders for the eight sorcerers in the room. No, nine.

Sir Hollis had arrived. The door never opened. He just appeared, as he had last night, but this time, he didn't have his defender with him. He gave Lillian a pleased smile, and the next second, he appeared before her.

"Good morning, Sir Hollis," she said, happy to talk to anyone who recognized her existence. "Won't you sit down?"

She immediately realized that might have been the wrong thing to say. He looked at the seat she indicated and frowned for a moment. He made an awkward shuffling attempt to get into it before starting to fall. Lillian jumped up to help him, but he disappeared and reappeared in the chair almost instantly, looking sheepish.

Lillian grinned at him, but Sir Carlos called from several tables away, "You need the exercise, Hollis. You know you can't stop moving entirely."

Sir Hollis' expression contorted with effort as he slowly said, "I. Know. I. Would've. Fallen."

Lillian longed to ask Sir Hollis about his physical difficulties and if they were a byproduct of his gift. The intelligence in his eyes suggested there was nothing wrong with his mind, but she didn't want to offend him.

Sir Carlos went back to his book, and Sir Hollis shrugged a little uncomfortably. "You're. Happier." The words were drawn out, as though he fought with his mouth to form them.

Lillian grinned. "I have good dreams at night sometimes. You're happier too." She lowered her voice. "Is it because you don't have your defender with you?"

Sir Hollis laughed aloud.

A few of the other sorcerers looked over, and he turned his head away from them to hide a smile. "We. Tolerate. Each. Other. But. Are. Happier. Apart. I. Have. Good. Dreams. Too."

She snickered. "I'm surprised you stay with him. I'd think you'd want someone with a more developed sense of humor."

He smiled again. "Accustomed," he said slowly.

Lillian already wanted a new defender for Sir Hollis, and she hardly knew him.

He seemed to understand what she was thinking. "No. Defenders. Are. Fun."

She laughed again. "Not any of them? Maybe you have to surprise them into it." She added conspiratorially, "That's what I did with mine. We should think of ways to surprise yours."

She ignored the stares of the other sorcerers as Sir Hollis laughed again. He grew serious and looked intently at her a moment. With a sad sigh, he said, "Bianca."

"Do I really look like her?"

He nodded slowly, his eyes beginning to mist.

Lillian touched his hand gently. "I hope someday you'll tell me about her. When you feel like it. Right now I wish you'd tell me how you manage not to leave important things like your liver behind when you transport yourself. Have you ever done that?"

His smile came back. It was uncoordinated, like the rest of his movements, but beautiful, and it pricked her memory again. The sorcerers must not have been used to it. They watched Lillian and Sir Hollis openly. She tried to ignore them as she listened to him slowly describe the sensations of transportation.

After a minute, she forgot about the others. The things Sir Hollis casually inferred about time and space jarred her understanding.

"You must have already read Bleak's treatise," she said.

"Don't. Read. Much. It's. Hard. To. Turn. Pages."

"I'll have to find a copy and show you a few parts I've always disagreed with. I want to know what you think."

Sir Carlos broke in. "I have the volume in my room. You can borrow it."

Lillian barely managed to hold back her smile. She nodded gratefully at Sir Carlos as though he'd been a part of the conversation from the beginning. "Thank you. That would be wonderful."

"Benson, do you mind?" Sir Carlos said, addressing a giant of a man wearing a soldier's uniform. The defender looked suspiciously at Lillian before he turned on his heel and strode from the room.

"Now it will take ages, Carlos," Lady Teresa complained. "You should have gone yourself. You know how he despises being sent on errands."

Lillian felt her confidence growing. They weren't stones. They were real people. And that meant she would be fine with them.

CHAPTER 17

Dan

Dan worked an hour in the practice courts, trying to ignore the nagging anxiety over what trouble his assignment may have found. She was in a room surrounded by the most dangerous people in the kingdom. They would keep her safe from any threat that could arise, except possibly from themselves. He drove back an attack from Lars Williams and wiped the sweat from his eyes. He couldn't help a glance toward the window to the sorcerers' study.

"What's the matter, Forell?" Williams asked, panting a little. "Can't get your mind off that pretty little morsel you brought with you?"

"Exactly," Dan said with a lazy smile. He wanted to punch Williams in the face for his tone. He'd only accepted a match with him because Williams was the next best swordsman at the garrison, and Dan needed the practice. They'd never been friends exactly, and now Dan understood why. "I *was* thinking about my fiancée," he said.

Williams smirked unpleasantly.

"And how her swordplay is better than yours," Dan added. "Though that's not saying much."

Williams' smirk faded. He eyed Dan appraisingly and gave a mocking little bow.

Dan pretended nonchalance, but he knew what was coming.

Williams suddenly sprang forward, attacking with unchecked ferocity.

Ten seconds later it was over. Williams lay in the dirt with Dan's sword tip at his throat.

"I yield," he grunted angrily.

Dan whipped his blade away and walked off. "Thanks for the match, Williams," he said calmly over his shoulder.

He shouldn't have let Williams irritate him, but he was growing frantic over Lillian and wanted to end the match anyway. As he neared the sorcerers' study, he quickened his pace at the new sounds issuing from the room. Yelling, arguing, and…laughing?

At the threshold, he stopped short.

There Lillian sat, surrounded by almost every sorcerer from the base. It appeared he'd walked into an animated discussion, with several conversations going on at once.

"It is no different than walking," Sir Adivino, the future teller, said heatedly, his mop of dark hair falling into his eyes. "A simple distortion of space. Linking the—"

"Don't be an idiot," said Sir Drake. Tendrils of smoke rose from his shirtsleeves, as they often did when he was upset. "There's nothing simple about it. You cannot disappear from one place and reappear in another without altering time. It is an aberration of nature."

Lillian's gaze slid around the room. He knew she saw him, but she didn't make eye contact. She did, however, flash the tiniest smile at the wall near him. The little minx.

"And what you do isn't?" Sir Adivino retorted.

Sir Carlos was gesticulating toward his own abdomen. "The

pressure alone, squeezing through the nothingness between spaces. Why, it should rupture bowels, like deep divers off the March islands rupturing their eardrums, and one man is said to have collapsed his lung on three different occasions. It's a miracle anyone survives."

"That defender, Oliver," Sir Pescall said. "He's the only one idiotic enough to risk it time and again."

Lillian seemed to be listening raptly to three different conversations, but at these words a cloud passed over her expression. "Why, Sir Pescall, do you mean to tell me that *none* of you have traveled with Sir Hollis?"

There was an uncomfortable silence. Lady Teresa watched Lillian shrewdly, but none of the others seemed to think there was anything premeditated about her question.

"Won't you tell us?" she asked, turning to Sir Hollis. "You already know what it feels like. We can only guess."

He looked uncomfortably at the group, but when he turned back to Lillian, he gave another difficult smile. "Fly."

"It really feels like flying? Do you hold your breath?"

"Show. You?"

Dan found himself ten feet in the room before he realized it. "No. Absolutely not. It's not safe." Hadn't Oliver told him that fifty times?

Lillian's left eyebrow rose the tiniest fraction before she turned to Sir Adivino and shared a commiserating smile. Sir Adivino's defender was famous for being bossy and overprotective. How could she know that already?

She turned back to Sir Hollis. "Is it safe?" she asked earnestly.

Sir Hollis dipped his head once, and Lillian laughed. "Wonderful. I can't wait. Can you show me your favorite places?"

Slowly and jerkily he extended his hand to her, and she deliberately reached out and gripped it, but somewhere in Dan's mind it registered that her hand wasn't quite as beautiful, her fingers not quite as smooth. Her smile was in place, but it wasn't as radiant as usual.

She was faking it. It was just an image. She didn't feel confident about going. He launched himself toward her, but it was too late. She was gone.

He stared at the sorcerers. They looked as surprised as he felt. A moment later, Oliver burst into the room.

It took over fifteen minutes to convince Oliver that nothing bad had happened to Sir Hollis. Just as Oliver's worry was replaced by anger, Lillian and Sir Hollis reappeared in the middle of the room.

If Lillian's laugh was a little shrill, no one else seemed to notice. "That was the most incredible thing I've ever done," she exclaimed breathlessly. "It *is* like flying."

The sorcerers crowded around them both, peppering them with questions.

"How do you not materialize on top of anyone?"

"How does your destination appear in your mind?"

"Could I try it?" Sir Adivino said, his request instantly echoed by at least three others. They were likely emboldened by the fact that Sir Adivino had already seen his own death by heart attack a few decades in the future. If Sir Adivino was going to survive it, they could too.

While it was evident Sir Hollis wasn't used to the attention, the constant upward tilt of his usual frown suggested he was enjoying himself, at least until he saw Oliver. The moment Sir Hollis saw his defender, his countenance fell.

Oliver spoke up quickly. "It's obvious Sir Hollis is tired and should go rest until—"

Lillian cut him off with a sympathetic little clucking noise. "Oh, I am so sorry. Did a few minutes carrying me with you cause you to overexert yourself?" Her smile grew mischievous. "Or is your defender trying to keep the fun all for himself?"

Oliver spluttered, and Hollis smiled at Lillian again. "Not. Tired. Carry. Him. All. Day."

"And he's twice as big as I am." Lillian laughed good-naturedly. "He *is* trying to steal all the fun."

The other sorcerers laughed boisterously, and requests were repeated. Hollis slowly moved his hand out toward Sir Adivino, who took it quickly, as though worried he'd change his mind. The two were gone in an instant.

Oliver's stony glare transformed into a sneer as he stalked toward Lillian.

Lillian

Lillian held her breath, wondering if Oliver would strike her. She almost hoped he would. She'd read enough of Dan's books to know that if he did, he would forfeit his position as defender, and Sir Hollis would be safe from him. She kept her eyes on Sir Drake, who was questioning her about her experience traveling with Sir Hollis. Her attention, however, was trained on Dan's cousin. She was a little afraid of him, but nothing could be as terrifying as traveling with Sir Hollis, not that she'd admit it.

Oliver was close enough for her to feel the disturbance of his movement in the air, before two things happened that stopped him in his tracks.

Dan appeared out of nowhere to block his cousin, just as a wall of fire ascended next to Lillian. She leapt aside with a little squeak, stumbling into the wiry Sir Iloh, a handsome sorcerer with a touch of grey at his temples. He caught her elbow and watched the fire grimly.

Dan looked over his shoulder to give a respectful nod to Sir Drake.

The fire died instantly, leaving only the tiniest soot mark on the rug.

"Perhaps you ought to go cool off somewhere, Oliver," Dan said tightly. "It seemed you intended to be less than respectful to a sorceress."

The cousins glared at each other, and it occurred to Lillian that only now, when they looked close to blows, did they really seem related. They carried the same sort of dangerous confidence.

"Who also happens to be my fiancée," Dan added through clenched teeth.

Oliver straightened, pushing Dan a little back as he did. "My apologies if I seemed at all disrespectful." He stalked from the room.

Lillian turned to Sir Drake. "That was very gallant of you, sir."

"Not at all, dear girl," Sir Iloh said with a mischievous glance at Sir Drake. "We love to take any opportunity to show off around each other." Lillian wished Sir Iloh had been present the previous night. His kind words had been much needed.

Sir Drake harrumphed but gave her a small smile. "Just reminding the boy of the circumstances."

Lillian bent a little light so she could see Dan behind her. He didn't look angry, but he must have known she'd purposefully provoked Oliver. She allowed herself to be drawn back into conversation by Sir Drake and Sir Iloh, who asked about Sir Hollis. She forced a smile and spoke enthusiastically, but inwardly she was still ill and trembling. The jerking motion involved in each landing was terrifying. Sir Hollis had been right—the entire experience *had* been like flying. She had simply discovered she didn't enjoy flying. *At all.*

She surveyed the group. It had taken time to get them talking, but they were surprisingly delightful people. Well, most of them. Lady Teresa still hadn't joined in. She sat in a chair and watched them sedately but without much interest. Every time Lillian met her eye, she was certain the woman was appraising her, but it was only her second time in the same room, so there was still hope they might be friends. Dan had certainly taken longer than two days to stop glaring at her.

Dan. She wanted so much to know what he was thinking. She spied on him shamelessly with her gift. He usually watched her with an unreadable expression or studied the room for threats. The other defenders were much the same. She couldn't detect any significant differences other than that Dan seemed sterner than the others.

She talked and laughed with the sorcerers, and even Sir Pescall found her after his turn traveling with Sir Hollis to tell her gruffly, "Decent of you to show us what we were missing. He's a good fellow."

Lillian had to check herself from hugging the man. At least one of the sorcerers so far had figured it out.

Sir Hollis materialized again a few minutes later, holding onto a gasping Sir Carlos. "You people enjoy that sort of thing? That was terrifying!"

Dan gave Lillian a sharp look.

A few of the sorcerers laughed, and the line waiting to travel with Sir Hollis didn't shorten at all.

Sir Carlos staggered over and collapsed into a chair next to Lillian, a sheen of sweat across the light brown skin of his forehead. "You can't tell me you actually enjoyed that."

"Where did you go?"

"To my family's home on the coast. I nearly scared the lights out of my niece."

Lillian laughed. "He took me through different points in the air in fast succession. We literally flew to the mountains and back."

"And you are still nauseated."

"Yes," Lillian said, surprised. But of course, he would know. He was a healer.

Dan glared at Sir Carlos.

Silly man. It wasn't the healer's fault.

"Was it worth it?" Sir Carlos asked.

Sir Hollis popped back into being, holding onto another laughing sorcerer and smiling brightly. He met Lillian's eye, and his smile deepened.

"Of course it was."

Sir Carlos frowned at her a moment, and Lillian's nausea dwindled to almost nothing.

She gave him a grateful smile just before Sir Hollis reappeared next to Lady Teresa. "Your. Turn?"

The sorceress smiled fondly. A smile. She wasn't immune to *all* other humans. "I wouldn't dream of taking your time when there are so many desperate for your attention, but I believe Miss Loraine was hoping for another opportunity."

Why, the devious…

Sir Carlos chuckled under his breath just as Sir Hollis reappeared next to Lillian, holding out his hand to her.

"Where?"

Lillian glanced back at Lady Teresa, who smirked into her book.

"Would you show me where you grew up?" Lillian said with as much enthusiasm as she could manage.

He smiled, and with a jolt, the sorcerers' study disappeared. It felt as though someone had pushed her off a cliff, and she couldn't breathe while she was falling. Her hand was in Sir Hollis', but she only knew because she felt it. Her eyes refused to open.

A few moments later she stood near the summit of a mountain, looking down into a beautiful, green valley. The air felt different, and Lillian's breathing sped up. Sir Hollis didn't seem to notice any difference. He let go of Lillian's hand and leaned against a tree, looking down at a village and surrounding fields.

Despite the discomfort of the altitude, she wasn't in a hurry to repeat the experience she'd just had. Her body trembled almost as violently as her stomach. "Sir Hollis. You said you have good dreams at night. I hope you don't mind me asking, but do you dream of your sister?"

"Yes. When. Sad."

"I dream of my mother when I'm sad," Lillian said. "I want to show you what she looks like. I would appreciate it if you wouldn't tell the others what I can do. There are so few people who I trust with it."

Sir Hollis looked properly impressed and curious. Lillian sighed, hoping she knew what she was doing. She pulled together a life-sized image of her mother, who stood with her brown hair shining in the sunlight and her dimples flashing as she smiled in the direction of Sir Hollis.

He nearly fell over, instead disappearing and reappearing before the image. "Bianca," he breathed.

"She was your sister," Lillian whispered. "I have family." She hiccupped a sob, her smile mirrored in her uncle's. That was where she'd seen his smile. It was hers.

CHAPTER 18

Dan

Dan paced the room in agitation. She'd left again so quickly, not even checking with him first. She could be halfway around the world for all he knew. The other defenders left him alone. They understood the situation he was in. If only sorcerers thought of the importance of their own lives rather than simply running after every reckless scheme that popped into their heads.

Dan's irritation turned quickly to anger, then full-blown panic. She could have been separated from Sir Hollis. What if she hadn't been able to hold onto him? What if they'd materialized inside a mountain? Was she even alive?

Thirty minutes later, when she popped into existence only a few feet away, he didn't waste time closing the distance between them. He couldn't decide if he should lecture her or kiss her first. His hand closed around her upper arm, just to be sure she was real. She looked up at him with a sweet smile. He definitely wanted to kiss her first.

Then oddly, for the tiniest moment, her form blurred and

resumed focus into two versions of herself. One Lillian slumped against him, and the other stood straight and calm, her hand resting on his arm. She was allowing him to see herself and her illusion simultaneously. With some effort, he hid his astonishment. The image was perfect. No one else noticed her distress.

"Thank you so much, Sir Hollis. You are a delightful traveling companion," she said.

Sir Hollis smiled, but his eyes were misty, and he looked at Lillian like she was a treasured gift.

"I'm afraid I need to rest," Lillian said. "I haven't quite caught up on sleep after the drive here."

This time when Lillian left, every man in the room stood respectfully, and Lady Teresa nodded in their direction.

Lillian's image smiled at everyone, and oddly enough, everyone smiled back. Even the sternest defenders betrayed hints of pleasantness toward her.

"Are you all right?" Dan asked anxiously once the door had closed behind them.

She nodded tiredly as the extra image of herself disappeared. "It's just that flying feels a lot like falling." Her eyes were wet.

"Did Sir Hollis say something to upset you?"

"Of course not." Lillian smiled strangely and strode forward. "He's a dear. I like him very much."

Dan followed after her, but she turned suddenly. "Did you—"

The impact of their collision didn't hurt him at all, but she stumbled back, almost falling before he snagged her around the waist and pulled her to him.

He stared into her hazel eyes before taking a shaky breath and stepping away from her. She immediately swayed on her feet, and he quickly gathered her to his side, fumbling in his pocket and producing her medicine. He pulled the stopper, and she took it from his proffered hand, making a face as she gave herself a dose.

He held her to his side as they walked toward her room. "Oh, Lillian. Why did you overdo it?"

She gave him a tired smile. "I didn't. This is how I keep you from yelling at me."

"I've never yelled at you."

"You want to. You're furious with me, but I had to do it."

He grunted in disbelief.

"It was so horrible traveling that way, but they aren't afraid of him anymore."

"Afraid of him? What on earth are you talking about?"

She leaned closer into him and looped her arms around his waist, holding onto him weakly as they walked. She couldn't know how much he wanted to keep her right there.

"Don't pretend you can't see it." She wrinkled her nose. "And did you know you smell?"

She'd already passed into her honest phase.

Dan grunted, suddenly more thoughtful of his odor than he ever had been in his life.

"You never want to touch me," she said conversationally as they continued down the corridor. "I don't think I've ever been this close to a man before. It's nice, isn't it?"

"Take your medicine again," Dan instructed tonelessly, though he was horrified and elated by her bluntness.

"I don't want to. I want a cookie."

"Have you been a good girl?" he asked wryly.

"The others think so, but you never do," she said, her voice accusatory. "Even Sir Pescall likes me, and Sir Iloh says he doesn't like anyone."

"Of course he likes you," said Dan, not ready to admit to her what he felt, even if she wasn't going to remember it. "He loves you. Everyone does. How do you do that?"

"I'll tell you when it works on you," she promised, stopping to pat his cheek.

"How do you know it hasn't?"

"Oh, Dan, that's sweet." She reached up on her toes and kissed him lightly on the cheek. "But I would know if it did." She took his arm again and walked on, apparently oblivious to Dan's astonishment. She'd kissed him. It didn't mean anything. It couldn't.

How he wished it did.

~

Lillian

L illian waited for Dan to say something, but he didn't seem inclined to talk. What was the point of exaggerating her fatigue if she wasn't going to learn anything? He seemed completely unaffected by her affection.

She was tired enough to be excessively annoyed by that. The emotional whirl of discovering Sir Hollis was her mother's brother had been exhausting. In less than an hour's time, they'd traded life stories, pieced together facts about her parents' deaths, and shared as much as they could about them. Mostly that involved Sir Hollis answering Lillian's rapid questions as best he could. Worried about tiring him, she'd insisted they go back to the sorcerers' study. Also, she could barely breathe on the top of that mountain.

Her uncle's answers had only given her a thousand more questions to ask when next they spoke. But she knew her parents' names now, and that alone buoyed up her heart in a way she'd never guessed it could. They'd both been sorcerers, her mother with a gift for planting ideas in people's minds, causing those ideas to resurface when they slept. Her father manipulated plant productivity. They'd met when her mother had just discovered her gift at age thirty-five, very young for a sorceress, and they'd married shortly after. Once her mother's gift had been added to their majesty's registry, the assassination attempts had begun. The spy, Octens, had caught the traitor who leaked the information to the Kazats, but it was too late. Eventually her parents had gone into hiding, and that was the last her uncle had seen of them. Bianca had been pregnant at the time. Uncle Hollis hadn't discovered his gift until five years later, and his self-reproach for not being there for his sister tore at Lillian's heart.

To distract herself from the painful blend of grief and happiness warring in her chest, she focused on her defender. If a kiss on his cheek didn't get his attention, perhaps it was time for a round of wheedling. Before she could start, General Adams appeared at the opposite end of the corridor.

Dan immediately loosed her, then grasped her around the waist again as she stumbled. He groaned quietly and closed his eyes.

"You don't want to be seen holding onto me?" she whispered irritably. "I thought we were engaged?"

"He knows the truth. Madsen told him. It will just look like I'm…"

"Oh, quit worrying, Dan," she said under her breath as they neared the general. "Do you think I would let anyone see me like this?"

He turned and saw an illusion of her standing properly beside him. The general bowed to Lillian and nodded at Dan. "You should probably know your friends are throwing a surprise party for you tonight, Forell."

"A party, sir?"

Lillian almost laughed at the look of revulsion on Dan's face.

"To celebrate your engagement."

"Oh."

Lillian kept back a snicker. Perhaps he thought he'd escaped parties when they left Perch Harbor.

"I thought I should warn you. Be sure you play the parts convincingly. Madsen insists the façade be maintained."

"Yes, sir."

"And three of Madsen's men have spotted Hessian Fast ten miles north of Umea. It looks like he's still working his way down the coast. We've tried to kill him four times already, but we keep missing him. We haven't found any dead sorcerers, though, so we don't really know what he's doing. At the rate he's going, he should be to Perch Harbor in less than two weeks."

The general took his leave, and Dan pulled Lillian back against his side. "Only two weeks," he said reassuringly.

It was an eternity, though less so since she knew about her uncle.

"I'm sorry about the party," Dan said. "I should have guessed they'd do it."

"What are you worried about? Just get me back to my room, and you can go back to fighting someone while I sleep off the dizziness."

"I can't be that far away from you," Dan said matter-of-factly. "I'll practice in my room, and we can leave the door between it and your room unlocked, in case you need anything."

Once the door was closed between them, Lillian noticed a large vase of pink roses on her nightstand table. They were the most beautiful she'd ever seen. The garrison couldn't be all bad if the occupants were given fresh flowers. She softly caressed a few velvety petals. Perhaps Uncle Hollis had brought them.

She buried herself in her blankets, listening to Dan's footfalls in the next room. She hardly had time to wonder if he'd discarded his shirt before sleep claimed her.

She might have slept the rest of the day if there wasn't a party to attend. When she was almost ready, she made a few noises that Dan would surely hear. He knocked on their shared door seconds later.

"Yes?"

Dan opened the door and took a few steps into her room. "Do you need anything?"

"I'm almost ready," Lillian said. "Could you please tell me about your friends?" She fished a bracelet out of her jewelry case.

"What do you want to know?"

"Anything. What are their interests?"

"Sword play, archery, and warfare tactics."

Lillian gave him a sharp look. He held a serious expression a full second before grinning widely.

"You *are* teasing me," she said, missing the catch on her bracelet. She tried again.

"They will all love you," he said with an exasperated smile. "Hold still." He strode forward and grasped her hand, turning it over to help her with the bracelet.

She caught back a shiver, not wanting him to see the way his touch affected her.

"You could charm the devil himself if you felt like it, Lillian." His tone was distracted as his fingers fumbled with the clasp.

She needed to say something. She considered a snide comment about not wanting to charm his cousin, but she didn't think he'd appreciate the joke. Instead she raised her wrist up to his eye level so he could see it better.

He was so close that she could feel his breath on her forearm. His hair begged her to sink her hands into it, and his scent was clean and soapy, not like after he practiced, though she didn't actually mind the smell of his sweat.

"Not very cooperative, is it? I thought it was only because you were doing it one-handed." He drew even closer, concentrating on the beaded bauble and not apparently realizing his foot touched hers.

She studied him intently as his fingers struggled with the clasp. How had she not realized from the beginning how beautiful his grey-blue eyes were?

"There. I've got it," he said with a mildly triumphant smile. He met her eyes, and the triumph faltered, quickly replaced by an intensity she didn't recognize. He froze a long moment before his eyes flickered to her mouth. Hoping she didn't misunderstand, and wondering only a tiny bit if she'd lost her senses, Lillian tipped her face up to her defender.

"Lillian," he breathed out, almost a warning in his voice.

Just as she reached her hand up to trace his jaw, a footstep in the hall startled her. They stepped apart from each other, and she crushed a strong surge of disappointment.

A rap sounded on the door between Dan's room and the corridor. He gave her an inscrutable look before retreating back to his own room, silently shutting the door between them.

Lillian flew to finish readying herself but was still slipping on her shoes when someone knocked at her other door.

She opened it to find Dan. His wide eyes contradicted his calm voice. "Lillian, you remember Sam? He came to walk with us to dinner."

"Oh, how nice of you, Sergeant Nillson," she said pleasantly, proud of herself for remembering his surname and for stringing words together coherently when her heart pounded so furiously.

Sam didn't seem to notice their agitation, insisting they all hurry to dinner. When they arrived at a large room where fifty people suddenly called out good wishes, Lillian feigned surprise and allowed herself to be swept inside.

The few women present soon clustered around her. Dan stood only a few paces away, and Lillian reveled in the fact that his eyes rarely strayed far from her, no matter who he spoke to. Of course, he was her defender, so it was his job, but he never used to look at her like that.

The only thing that dampened her mood was the appearance of Oliver, Dan's cousin, who arrived with the revolting man she'd met during her first few minutes at the garrison. Oliver clapped Dan on the arm as though nothing was amiss and gave Lillian a smile that looked a lot like bared fangs. After intro-

ducing his companion as Williams, he asked with mock innocence, "How did you meet your fiancée, Dan? I thought you
went away to become a defender."

The snake. Only the sorcerers and defenders knew about her
gift. He just wanted to watch Dan squirm or have to lie.

Dan smiled lazily, but Lillian detected a hint of uncertainty.
She willed him not to fumble the answer.

"Things never go quite how you plan," Dan said with a smile.
"I went looking for a sorcerer, and found something much
better. You'll excuse me?"

He left Oliver's side and strode to Lillian, offering her
his arm.

She smiled coyly at him and under her breath, whispered,
"He's making them doubt."

They mingled a few more minutes before Dan led her to the
terrace. "Too blasted hot in there," he murmured, "and my
cousin is an idiot."

"You did well for being put on the spot," she said distractedly. It was hard to concentrate when he held her hand. It felt
nice and comfortable, but at the same time...tingly. She looked
down at their clasped hands, and Dan's eyes followed hers, his
gaze softening in a way that caught Lillian's breath.

CHAPTER 19

Dan

Dan had never realized that hazel was the most fascinating eye color. The light from the setting sun caught gold glints within the green and brown, and Dan couldn't think about anything else, that is, until he noticed her lips. Was it possible they were as soft as they looked?

It had been so difficult not to kiss her an hour earlier, but he'd been in *her* room. With no chaperone. He was her defender and had no business kissing her. But now, with a dozen people probably watching through the window, not to mention a fake engagement to maintain, things were different. His heart rate increased with his resolve.

"Please don't slap me, Lillian. They're watching," he murmured as he pulled her closer.

He half expected her to jerk away, but she simply clutched his upper arms and looked up at him with wide eyes. A few wisps of honey-toned hair framed her face, and Dan gave in to the temptation to trace a few silken strands with his fingertips, his hand coming to rest at her jaw.

"I'd like to kiss you, Lillian," he said honestly.

"All right," she whispered back.

He wanted to tell her it had nothing to do with their audience, but he didn't dare.

He lowered his head, his heart accelerating. Her tightening grip on his arms was almost as maddening as the scent of roses in her hair, but he didn't want to scare her, so he leaned forward slowly, giving her time to back away if she wished. When his lips were only an inch from hers, his hand trembled against her jaw. Hoping she hadn't noticed, he closed the slight distance between them and gently pressed a tender kiss to her lips.

He'd imagined kissing her more times than he'd ever admit, but he never could have guessed the overwhelming reaction he'd have to her closeness, the feel of her lips, and the sound of her breath catching. Dan had shared a few kisses with girls before, and they'd been very calm experiences. This was completely different. Kissing Lillian was powerful and instinctive. It felt like coming home by jumping off a cliff.

His lips moved against hers a little more forcefully, then broke away to explore her face and jaw. He didn't have to hold her so tight. He didn't have to let his breathing betray his emotion, but she felt so good in his arms. Her skin was so soft.

He felt suddenly faint and abruptly pulled away, though he couldn't let go of her entirely. He took some deep breaths, trying to steady himself as he gauged her reaction.

The skin around her mouth was tinted red where the shadow of his beard had scratched her, and her cheeks were several shades darker than before, but what did she *think*? He met her gaze with some trepidation.

Her eyes were wide, assessing. He couldn't read the emotion in them, so he began to loosen his hold on her.

"Are they still watching?" she whispered.

"Probably."

Instead of commenting, she moved her hands around his

shoulders and stretched up on her toes to press a lingering kiss to his mouth. The gesture was so sweet, with so much innocence and trust, that Dan checked himself from responding as aggressively as he wanted. Instead he gently pulled her closer while his free hand traced her jaw and neck.

She clutched him tighter, and his lips met hers again, just as a shout of good-humored laughter and a few whistles came from the window. Lillian immediately turned her face away, blushing madly. They walked back to the party, where she was quickly pulled into a circle of his friends.

He followed, nervous to have anyone between them, his mind and heart still reeling from her kiss.

She'd kissed him back. That had to mean something.

Oliver intercepted him. "People certainly like her," he said, nodding toward the group surrounding Lillian.

"What? Yes. I suppose so," Dan said, trying to move around his cousin.

Oliver blocked his way. "Is that her gift?"

Dan shrugged. "It is a gift of sorts. You'll see how talented she is if the games are ever played while we're here." Let Oliver wonder what she could do. It was good for him.

"I'll have to be sure they are."

Dan eyed his cousin. "Since when do you get to decide?"

"The general has always relied on my advice," Oliver said smugly, and Dan snorted. General Adams didn't ask anyone's advice.

"You were too busy admiring your honors from the academy to notice," Oliver added.

"Shut up." Dan shifted around Oliver to keep Lillian in his line of sight.

Oliver only smirked at him.

It seemed hours before Dan could drag his friends away from Lillian. The entire room called goodbyes to her when he threaded her arm through his and led her toward the door.

"Oliver thinks your gift is making people like you," he said as they walked back to her room.

Lillian smiled tiredly. "It doesn't work on him."

"You don't want it to."

"Hmm. Until very recently, it didn't work on you either."

"It's always worked on me," Dan said. "To my condemnation."

"That's ridiculous," Lillian said with a heart-stopping smile. He wished he could kiss her again, but she patted his hand and pulled out her key.

Dan searched her room before going to his own and beginning his evening exercises. After a few minutes, Lillian tapped on his door. He sprang to open it, a lightness in his step he didn't recognize.

"Are you practicing?" Lillian asked, glancing behind him into his room.

"Yes. Is the noise disturbing you?"

"No, but how do you practice all by yourself?"

"Forms, mostly. It isn't the best practice, but it's better than nothing." He focused on her eyes so he wouldn't look at her lips.

She considered him a moment, then asked hesitantly, "Would you like help?"

For one ridiculous moment, he thought she was offering to be his opponent. He covered his snort with a cough.

Lillian arched a delicate eyebrow at him, then inclined her head back toward his room. Dan spun to see three men with swords striding toward him. Battle energy hit him, and he leapt toward them, his sword passing through two of them before he realized what Lillian had done. He turned to her while the last attacker jumped around him, brandishing his sword erratically. Dan fought it for a full three seconds before he chuckled.

"Yes, I could use your help," he said. "But first let me show you how to hold a sword."

Lillian's fighters grew increasingly more skilled over the

next half-hour, until at last he convinced her to go to bed. She gifted him with a beautiful, sleepy smile before retreating back into her own room and shutting the door between them.

He washed and settled down into his bed, only to find that his face was sore. His muscles were used to the exertion of a work out, but he'd never smiled so much in his life.

The next day General Adams met Lillian and Dan at the door to the sorcerers' study. "Games today," he said curtly as he passed them.

"Wait," Dan said in surprise. "Excuse me, sir, but why today?"

"Because your cousin cheats at cards," he said, glaring at Dan. "And I can't catch him at it. He wagered a round of the games. I'll be back to start them as soon as I've seen that everyone else in the garrison is safely away from the area."

Dan waited until the general was out of earshot before allowing a chuckle.

"What kind of games?" Lillian demanded nervously.

Dan quickly explained.

"So the sorcerers pair off with their defender to try to capture the object?" she asked. "Before any of the other sorcerers? And there are no other rules?"

"Well, it's expected that you won't kill anyone, and your defenders aren't supposed to hurt the other defenders, no more than Sir Carlos can fix anyway. The games have been a little more intense in the last several months. Oliver and Sir Hollis have won more than half the time, and Oliver has become the champion of these games."

"Oliver?"

Dan nodded as he began to size up the crowd already gathered in the room.

"And not Uncle Hollis?"

"Uncle?"

Lillian shrugged delicately. "We found out we're related. I'll tell you about it later. But why?"

"Excuse me?" Dan had lost track of their conversation at Lillian's pronouncement.

"Why isn't Sir Hollis considered the champion of the games?"

"I…" Dan didn't know quite how to answer that. Sir Hollis never really seemed to care about the outcome.

After a few seconds of expectant waiting, Lillian's gaze hardened. "Well, I like games."

What? "You can't play."

"Why not?"

"You might get hurt."

"But not more than Sir Carlos can fix."

Dan stared at his assignment. She wouldn't purposefully put herself in harm's way. She must be teasing him. On the other hand, she'd traveled with Sir Hollis without hesitating. And she didn't actually look as beautiful as usual, but it may have been something to do with the glare she gave him and not that she was projecting a mask on herself. Either way, he needed to stop underestimating her.

Lillian was quickly welcomed into a group of sorcerers arguing over theory. Oliver took her place at Dan's side.

"Now you see who controls the games?"

"Gambling, Oliver? What would Mother and Father say?"

"They wouldn't say anything. I was always their favorite."

It stung a little that he was right, but growing up with a cousin was better than growing up alone.

Sir Drake clapped his hands. "All right, then, it's decided. No defenders for this round."

No! Why was Lillian trying to keep him from helping her?

"What?" Oliver hissed.

Dan looked to Lillian. Angelic innocence infused her features.

"I can't allow that," Oliver burst out. Two dozen surprised and disapproving faces turned in his direction. Dan realized with a jolt what Lillian had done. She wasn't trying to block *him* from helping her. She was blocking *Oliver*, taking away his importance in the room. In all other pairs, the sorcerer gave the orders. There were varying levels of give and take, but only with Sir Hollis and Oliver did the defender lead.

"I apologize, but I am very worried for Sir Hollis," Oliver said sincerely. "I don't want him to need Sir Carlos' attention."

The frowns of disapproval turned to shrugs of understanding.

"I'm. Fine. Don't. Worry."

A cheer went up, and several hands clapped Sir Hollis gently on the back.

Oliver was ignored.

Dan thought quickly over the work Oliver had accomplished with Sir Hollis. Of course he wouldn't want his assignment in harm's way. That was all. Dan was still glad Oliver didn't know it was Lillian who had introduced the change.

Lillian

It only took a few well-placed questions to get the sorcerers to change the rules for the games.

"Shouldn't we be working to *complement* each other's gifts, rather than defeat them?" she finally asked with a careful mixture of curiosity and naiveté.

One minute later the issue was decided, and she watched in satisfaction as Sir Hollis once more became the center of attention. Her uncle had the most amazing gift in the room, and she'd never let him be treated like that horrid man's burdensome charge ever again.

She actually had to use a touch of her gift to hide her smirk over Oliver's outburst. He'd be replaced before she went home to Perch Harbor. She only needed to find a new defender for her uncle first, one that was smart enough to see how brilliant he was, and careful enough to keep him from getting hurt.

From among the six sorcerers vying to be his partner, Uncle Hollis looked to her, a question in his eyes. She smiled and shook her head, thrilled he thought of her first. He closed his eyes and pointed blindly into the crowd. Sir Adivino cackled with triumph.

Lillian allowed herself the tiniest breath of a laugh, and Lady Teresa gave her a shrewd look. Could the woman read her mind? What was her gift? Dan had never said.

Several sorcerers kindly applied to be Lillian's partner.

"Thank you, Sir Iloh," she said sweetly. He'd been first to ask. "I'm afraid you've doomed yourself. You know I've never played before, and I'm so new to *everything*."

She ignored Dan's sharp look. There was no reason for the rest of them to know she'd been working with her gift since she was a child.

The game was short, but brutal. General Adams showed them a book of poetry before leaving the room to hide it. She shamelessly used her gift to refract light through the open window and around the corner into other windows in the fort. The general mingled with a large crowd of soldiers before going to the kitchen and placing the book in a plain wooden box. He carried the box to a room with his own nameplate at the door. Unfortunately, he shut the door and closed the curtains, so Lillian couldn't see exactly where he placed it.

"I know where it is," Lillian whispered to her partner. Sir Iloh nodded and glanced furtively to Lady Teresa, who smiled lazily, pushing a strand of steel-colored hair back into her tight knot of hair.

"We'll have to run to get there before they do."

"They?"

"I'll explain as we go."

Using her gift to hide it, she peeked at Dan. His eyes were wide, and he watched her with a clenched jaw and a tense stance. There was something very satisfying about having a strong, handsome man wanting her to be safe, even if he was grumpy about it.

General Adams reappeared in the doorway. "Begin," he said, before hastily retreating.

"Run," Sir Iloh yelled.

Fire erupted at the doors and windows, and Lillian held back a scream. Ice smothered the fire, and Sir Iloh gripped her hand to pull her through the steaming doorway. Sir Carlos and Sir Drake were far ahead of everyone, but they were going in the wrong direction. Sir Hollis and Sir Adivino were nowhere to be seen.

"Lady Teresa's gift is hearing," explained Sir Iloh. "So don't say where we're going. Just lead. I'll keep the others off us."

Lillian lifted the hem of her skirt and raced ahead, nearly screaming when several rats appeared in front of her.

"Pescall's controlling them. Just go."

The rats all scampered toward Sir Iloh, whose way was suddenly covered in ice. The rats slid across, thumping against the wall, while Sir Iloh sprinted on. "Notice he didn't send them after you," he said, not even out of breath. Lillian was already panting from their mad dash and didn't answer. "He's still mad at me for turning a skunk into an ice block years ago. The thing was about to spray me, but he won't let it go."

Lillian raced on, stifling a half-hysterical giggle.

Several other impediments met them before they reached the general's room, including an entire tree erupting through a window ahead of them, courtesy of Sir Mendine. Sir Iloh made a staircase of ice for her to walk over it.

"There," Lillian said, pointing. "That room."

Lady Teresa and Sir Mendine appeared at the other end of the hall, much closer to the general's room. Lady Teresa rushed for the door as a wall of flames shot toward the ceiling several feet in front of Lillian and Sir Iloh. That meant Sir Drake was close by as well.

Ice and fire battled through the hall as Lillian battled inwardly. She didn't want anyone to know how well she cast images, but she knew who needed to win the game, and it wasn't Lady Teresa.

The sorceress reached the door and grabbed at the handle and missed, and missed again, her hand passing right through the metal.

"What?" She pressed both hands to the wall and began feeling quickly along for the doorway. She gasped and pulled her hands back as the wall turned to ice.

Muttering, she bundled both hands in the folds of her skirts and resumed her search, but at that moment, two more pairs of sorcerers appeared behind her. Mayhem erupted, and Lillian was suddenly jerked backward off her feet, a half-second before a wall disintegrated into a pile of rubble just where she'd been standing.

"Oh," Lillian said breathlessly as her defender righted her. "Thank you, Dan." She should have known he'd break the rules to follow her and keep her safe.

He glared across the hall at one of the sorcerers. "Reckless idiot."

Lillian fought to keep from throwing herself into his arms and kissing him soundly. The effort caused her to lose her concentration entirely. Lady Teresa took the opportunity to seize the real door handle. She pulled the door open only to find Sir Hollis and Sir Adivino standing in front of her, both smiling broadly. Sir Hollis held the book tucked against his side.

"What a shameful mess you've all made," Sir Adivino said delightedly.

Lillian grinned. Sir Adivino's glimpses of the future weren't very clear, and he'd collected a lot of criticism for predicting a large attack from Kazatania without being able to say when it would happen, but he'd apparently known right where the general would hide the book.

The noise instantly settled, and General Adams stepped into the corridor, frowning. "I had thought the destruction would have decreased by more than this without your defenders," he said with a frown.

"That was less?" Lillian whispered to Dan, who nodded curtly.

"I'm never playing cards with Oliver again," the general grumbled half-heartedly.

The sorcerers immediately began putting things to rights, all of them calling out congratulations to her uncle and Sir Adivino.

From a distance, Lady Teresa met Lillian's eye, nodding once and giving her a slow smile. Lillian grinned, and to add to her satisfaction, Oliver appeared on the scene with his face a shade of purple that didn't suit him at all. He left before Uncle Hollis explained to the group how he and Lillian were related.

That evening when Coordinator Madsen arrived for a visit, Lillian pressed her lips into a firm line. It was time he stop underestimating her uncle. She made sure he was watching before she took Uncle Hollis' arm. "I want you to tell me all about the coordinator," she whispered. In a carrying voice, she added, "Please, won't you explain Boetius' position on elevation and gravity again? I'm still having trouble with it."

From the corner of her eye, she watched Madsen's head snap in their direction. She hoped he'd studied enough physics to know what she meant.

Predictably, Dan started forward with a worried look on his face.

"We're only going to discuss theory. We won't travel anywhere. Besides," she added sweetly, "who could possibly keep me safer than Uncle Hollis can?" She didn't wait for that to sink in before walking away, though she bent some light to see over her shoulder.

Dan nodded thoughtfully, but Madsen's look was priceless, as though someone had hit him over the head with a bouquet of daisies and dead fish. He immediately turned to the sorcerers near him and demanded to know what she meant. He received several simultaneous reports on the sorcerers' travels and competition with Sir Hollis. Lillian wished she had Lady Teresa's gift for listening but knew she'd have to make do with lip reading. She roughly knew what the sorcerers would say anyway, so she took the opportunity to ask a question that had been on her mind for some time.

"Uncle Hollis, do you mind telling me, is the weakness in your muscles caused by your gift? Does using your gift eat away at your body like mine does at my blood sugar?"

He frowned a little, and she hurried to add, "But of course, you don't need to tell me. It is personal."

He shook his head, his eyes thoughtful. "Started. Ten. Years. Before. Bianca. Left. My. Gift. Halted. It. Oster. Said. It. Would. Be. Worse. By. Now." His lips twitched in a wry smile. "Big. Magic. Makes. Me. Lose. Taste. And. Hearing. Sunshine. Helps. I. Go. To. My. Mountain."

"Of course. You'd be closer to the sun. That makes perfect sense. There, look at Madsen. He's just realized how stupid he's been with you. Maybe he'll want to give you a better defender. As long as it's any defender but mine."

Her uncle snorted a laugh.

"I hope I didn't make your life harder. I just hate the idea of them underestimating you."

He shook his head, but failed to suppress his smile. "You. Are. Just. Like. Bianca."

Lillian grinned. "She was this smart too?" she teased before nodding toward the coordinator. "Good thing I can lip read. If they make horrible plans for us, we can get away."

CHAPTER 20

Dan

Dan wished he could overhear Lillian and Sir Hollis, sure they were planning another trip just to scare him to death.

"Well, it's about time, Oliver," Madsen said, bringing Dan back to the present. "I thought you'd never convince Sir Hollis to travel with others."

A very faint blush gave Oliver away. "I had nothing to do with it, sir."

"Is he willing to fight yet?" Madsen asked.

"He hasn't said."

"Well, keep working on him."

Dan hadn't known Oliver was trying to convince Sir Hollis to travel with others, and fighting was the only thing Dan had ever known Sir Hollis to refuse. It was even written into his contract with the army. It wasn't Madsen's place to push him, and it certainly wasn't Oliver's, but Oliver only nodded. "Yes, sir."

Madsen raised his voice to address the room. "We need to

clear out a group of bandits the army has been unsuccessful in rooting out. We've lost a lot of men to this group, but it should be an easy day's work for all of you. The general will have more details for you this week."

Afterward, he pulled Dan aside. "You two are welcome to go along if you'd like. Perhaps it would inspire her if she saw how the sorcerers work."

"Yes, sir."

"And I hear she participated in the competition. Good work."

Dan was on the verge of telling him he had nothing to do with it and would strongly be discouraging it in the future, when Madsen turned away to talk to Sir Adivino about the premonitions he'd had in the last week.

"The visions are getting closer together," said Sir Adivino seriously. "I can't see where yet, but there are a lot of Kazat soldiers involved. And the terrain always looks different. Sometimes the sea, sometimes land."

"Multiple attacks at once?" Madsen asked.

"Or a long campaign. And…" Sir Adivino faltered.

"Yes?" Madsen asked sharply.

"Nothing," the sorcerer said, a red flush infusing his face. "I had some nightmares mixed in, I suppose. I saw some horrifying things, unnatural things that…well, never mind."

Sir Adivino's premonitions were often vague and rarely time specific. Five years ago, he'd dreamed a sorceress would save the entire country from invasion by making a tornado of water, and two years before that, he'd woken in the night claiming Kovan Reznik, the clan leader's son, would slice up the only person who could bring peace between Kalmar and Kazatania. There was no guarantee when any of his predictions would come about, or even *if* they would, though Dan never remembered Adivino to doubt himself.

"What about Hessian Fast, sir?" Dan broke in. They could be speculating for hours, and this was more urgent.

"The Hound?" Adivino asked. "I've only had a focus on him once, and that was a vision of him at a party in Kazatania when he's much older. Not much use."

"Nonsense," Madsen said. "It tells us that he'll escape us. Fast was spotted this week along the coast. He dodged the men following him, and the trail went cold."

"He could be anywhere," Dan said through gritted teeth. "The idiots shouldn't have lost him."

Madsen gave him a cool look. "Those idiots are the best trackers in the country. We're lucky they spotted him at all. The man is a genius at tracking and escape. He always finds what he's looking for."

Dan turned away in irritation, looking past the coordinator to the far end of the room where Lillian sat talking earnestly with Sir Hollis. She laughed delightedly at something he said, and Dan's chest lightened in an odd way.

As the coordinator's words sunk in, the feeling turned to lead. Not her. Fast wouldn't find Lillian.

Dan excused himself and strode across the room to where Lillian and Sir Hollis spoke.

Sir Mendine beat him there, his broad form blocking the way. "Ah, Lillian, my dear. As promised." He set down a satchel on the table before her. "Some of them are written in Kazatani, but sort through and see which you want to borrow."

Lillian grinned and clasped her hands together. "I want to borrow them all. I'm so happy to find someone with similar reading tastes."

Sir Mendine left, smiling over his shoulder at Lillian as he went. She immediately loosed the drawstring of the satchel and traced her fingers along the spines of the books inside. Some were rather worn, and the titles difficult to make out. Lillian closed the satchel, and Dan turned to stare in bewilderment at the sorcerer's retreating back. He never would have guessed. The man was a ferocious fighter, even before he could control plants. Recently he'd used seaweed to sink pirate ships and trees to launch instantly-made spears into advancing armies.

And he read romance novels.

Mendine's special gift with roses suddenly made sense. Dan snapped his mouth shut and shook his head. Even *he* knew that Kazat romance novels had a reputation for over-dramatization and sometimes lewdness. Sir Mendine had no business sharing them with Lillian. It was a good thing they were written in a different language.

"Hello, Dan," Lillian said, pulling him out of his astonished silence.

He bowed politely. "The sorcerers are going into the mountains to capture a pocket of bandits." He turned to Sir Hollis. "Madsen wants Lillian there. If she goes, can you stay close to her? Take her far away if there's danger?"

Lillian studied Dan's face a moment, then smiled softly. "See? I told you, Uncle Hollis. My defender really is a darling, even if he hides it behind that frown."

"I. Won't. Be. There. Madsen. Gave. Me. A. Different. Assignment," he said worriedly.

Dan nodded in acceptance and turned to Lillian. "I don't think you should go," he said, just as she said,

"I'm definitely going."

"No. It could be very dangerous, and without Sir Hollis there—"

"But you'll be there, and the other sorcerers. Besides, I should learn how the army sorcerers work, and I know you want to go."

"What does that matter?"

Sir Hollis watched them in turn, his eyes thoughtful.

"I can help the others," she said.

"Absolutely not." She didn't have enough experience to be around fighting. She was *not* going.

· · ·

A week later, Dan found himself riding with Lillian and most of the other sorcerers through a desert mountain pass a few days from the garrison. General Adams rode at the front with Sir Drake. The fire sorcerer could be a little pompous, but as a fighter, he was perhaps the most lethal of the group. The others ranged in a line next to their defenders, with Lillian and Dan in the middle of the column. The other sorcerers often found reasons to get out of line to come speak with Lillian, who treated the entire occasion as though it was a picnic. She hadn't batted an eye over sleeping in a tent or riding a horse most of each day. Luckily, Sir Carlos took care of the worst of her discomfort, but Dan often caught her looking a little less beautiful than usual, the lack of brightness in her eyes contradicting her lively chatter.

He was torn between scolding her for her mask and appreciating her humility. It didn't seem possible for her not to realize how beautiful she was, but it was plain every time she disguised her expression. He cringed inwardly, knowing she did it to keep anyone from worrying. She did so much to make others happy, but bringing her on this excursion did *not* make him happy. He thought of a hundred ways this was bad for her. Even at a distance, she would hear the sounds of the bandits' screams as they died or were incapacitated, and what if one of them got near enough to put her in harm's way? The anxiety clawing up his insides was a relatively new feeling. He found he didn't care for it.

Sir Iloh guided his mount up to Lillian's other side. He'd never caused Dan particular unease in the past, though he'd seen him freeze an assassin's blood in his veins from thirty feet away, but lately an irrational annoyance seized Dan anytime the man came near Lillian.

"Are you well enough in this heat, my dear?"

A few of the sorcerers called her by such familiar terms. Dan didn't want to hit things when the others did it, but Sir Iloh didn't look at Lillian the way the others did. He was the youngest of all the army sorcerers, only forty-five, and despite the fine manners and clothing, he often gazed at Lillian in a decidedly Geoffrey-like way. Dan had seen the same expression on other men. It was a longing for acquisition, and Dan knew, though he didn't care to examine it closely, that Sir Iloh was not the man for Lillian.

And you are? His own thoughts mocked him.

"I'm very well," Lillian said, "with you cooling the air around me."

Sir Iloh waved his hand dismissively. "I do it for Lady Teresa whenever we travel in the summer."

"It is too bad she couldn't come," Lillian said sincerely.

"She is devoted to her family."

"I thought it was her defender who needed to go home for an emergency."

Sir Iloh flashed his perfect teeth. "One and the same in their case. Her defender is her late husband's grand-nephew."

"Oh, how nice to be with family."

Would Lillian now want an extended family member to replace him? Dan scowled as his eyes raked the hills to either side of them. Without Lady Teresa there to listen for people in the surrounding area, the group was far more vulnerable to attack. Aside from the occasional snake, mouse, or lizard, Sir Pescall wasn't able to contact any animals. Dan wished for the hundredth time that Lillian had stayed at the garrison.

"What's the matter?" Lillian murmured when Sir Iloh finally moved away.

"Something feels wrong," he admitted tightly, not expecting her to understand, and certainly not expecting her to know he alluded to Sir Iloh as well as possible dangers.

"Do you want me to look somewhere for you?"

It took a moment for the meaning of her words to sink in.

He met her earnest gaze and lost track of his thoughts. She was so beautiful, so good. She didn't belong here. He shook himself and reached in his pocket for her medicine.

"Would you mind?" he asked, offering her the vial. "I wish it was a cookie."

Her answering smile had him thinking all sorts of things a defender had no right to think about his assignment.

"I'll make sure you get the recipe when we get home. I should look ahead?"

"Yes, and over the hillsides." It was so easy to forget how powerful she really was.

Her eyes went a little unfocused. "Hills, dirt, more hills. Ahead, dirt, sand, and…" Her eyebrows contracted. "Something on the hills."

Dan hardly drew breath as she spoke.

"Men. There are men on the hills."

"What?" he hissed urgently.

"They've dug up some sort of sand-piles in front of themselves."

"What?" he said, more loudly.

The column of riders slowed as everyone turned to stare at him. Dan beckoned to General Adams.

He came, clearly annoyed. "Forell, we need to make better time if we're going to be there before nightfall." He frowned at Lillian as though she'd interrupted something important.

"Lady Loraine has important information for you," Dan said.

The sorcerers crowded closer, forming a tight circle around Lillian and Dan.

She hesitated.

"Please show them," Dan said. "It's the fastest way."

She nodded nervously and looked around the circle of sorcerers. "I would ask all of you to never tell anyone what I can do."

The sorcerers agreed, mild curiosity and good humor plain on their features.

Lillian's illusion appeared and expanded in the air before her. "I don't know what they are doing," she said quietly, "but this is a quarter mile up the road."

The sorcerers' eyes bulged, looking back and forth between Lillian and the image she maintained for them. Dan's heart swelled with pride and something else he didn't dare name.

General Adams whispered hoarsely, "You're sure there aren't any others?"

Lillian shook her head. "Dan felt something might be wrong, so I looked around us first."

"Longbows," Adams said in a low voice. "And thirty men."

"I wouldn't see where to send fire before I had an arrow in my chest," Sir Drake growled.

"I'd be dead long before I could freeze their blood," Sir Iloh said.

"No horses," said Sir Pescall. "A couple snakes in calling range. That's all I have."

"No plants around aside from a few tiny shrubs," Sir Mendine said grimly. "I'd only be able to kill a handful of them."

"I wasn't watching for anything like this," Sir Adivino said, full of self-reproach.

Sir Carlos' jaw almost creaked when he unclenched it. "I'd never be able to heal everyone fast enough, even if I didn't take an arrow myself."

All eyes turned to General Adams, who smiled faintly. "A dozen sorcerers and their defenders against thirty assassins. The poor scum don't stand a chance."

An ominous rumble of low chuckles drowned out Dan's murmur of agreement.

∼

Lillian

illian tried to ignore the shouts of the ambushers, the clash of metal on metal. General Adams watched her thoughtfully but didn't say anything. She closed her eyes against the temptation to check on Dan. He'd assured her he wasn't in real danger, and she'd believed him, mostly. Helping him practice swordplay at night had become a routine, and even when Lillian had finally managed a hundred imaginary attackers at a time, Dan had fought them with amazing skill. But the men in sand-colored clothing weren't imaginary, and Dan now led the group of sorcerers and defenders sent to neutralize them.

The general had wanted her to help too. When they'd hastily made up their plan of attack, the general had immediately requested she maintain an image so he could see what happened. Dan took a hasty look at her and turned to face the general. "That is not something she will do, and you don't need it, sir," he'd said flatly and with complete authority.

Lillian could have hugged him. The thought of watching a battle made her stomach roil.

When the general began to protest, Dan lifted his chin and looked down several inches at him. "Lady Loraine has no obligation to you and is not under your command. She's already saved every life present. Her part is done." He quickly changed the subject. "How many survivors would you like?"

The general had reddened at Dan's words but nodded curtly. "At least five. Anything after that is a bonus."

"I have enough sedative to keep them all quiet until we make it back to the garrison," Sir Carlos said.

The worst part was watching Dan walk away with some of the sorcerers and most of the defenders. And now, with him away from her and actually in a fight, Lillian had to keep reminding herself to breathe. The remaining sorcerers stood in a circle around her, which was exceptionally sweet of them.

When Dan came back, helping to herd over a dozen men in plain, sand-colored clothing, Lillian's heart leapt a little in her chest. He met her gaze at a distance and nodded in greeting, his mouth lifting at one corner.

Sir Iloh gave her an odd look, and she realized she was beaming. She quickly slipped a mask over her features.

The interrogation didn't take as long as she'd expected. Sir Drake made a show of starting a few twigs on fire near the prisoners' feet and allowing a couple pant legs to smolder. Lillian stayed far from the questioning, and though he eyed the group longingly, Dan insisted on staying by her side.

Once General Adams was satisfied with their information and the prisoners succumbed to Sir Carlos' sedative, Sir Mendine broke from the group and strode to Dan. "Kazats, all of them," he said. "Reznik sent them to kill as many sorcerers as they could, and it sounds like they were more than willing to take the assignment."

"But they had to have been working with someone *here*," Dan said, scowling at the horizon. "They seemed to know which sorcerers were coming and chose the terrain and weapons to fit."

"Good thing they didn't know about you, Lillian." Sir Mendine smiled and nodded his head in her direction before moving back toward the group of sorcerers surrounding the prisoners.

Lillian waited till he was out of earshot. "Dan?" she said quietly. "Why do the Kazats hate Kalmarian sorcerers?"

"Because they don't know *you*, Lillian," he said immediately.

She made a face at him. "No, truthfully."

"They are…encouraged…to believe our sorcerers are wicked, baby-eating monsters."

"Why?"

"The clan leaders, and back before they assassinated all their kings and queens, the royal family, all encouraged the belief.

The Kazats are extremely superstitious. Their leaders use it to keep the lower classes in check."

Lillian nodded thoughtfully. "I guess I should have known that already. Their books are so much more frightening than ours. Of course, it makes them so much better. Thank goodness Aunt Svea taught me Kazatani, because so many of their works aren't translated. It makes reading slower, but—"

Dan spluttered something unintelligible, staring at her as though she'd sprouted horns, and she would have asked him what the matter was, but they were interrupted by Sir Iloh. "Lillian, my dear, it's unanimous," he called from within a pack of sorcerers a short distance away.

"What's unanimous?" she asked.

"We will all be your devoted servants forever."

Lillian giggled. "That's ridiculous." Some of them looked a little crestfallen, and she quickly added, "But if any of you are feeling indebted, I've been wanting a game of Merrels for ages, and I'll trade a lifetime of your servitude for anyone who can match me."

Sir Iloh grinned and strode forward to take her hand. "My dear, I would love to be your match. Name the date."

Lillian laughed at the joke, but Dan was suddenly next to her, his hand at her waist. "The horses are ready," he said stiffly. He gave Sir Iloh a cold look, but it was Dan's hand at her side that made her shiver. As appropriate as the gesture would be if they were actually engaged, his touch unsettled her, probably because she craved it. She could be honest enough with herself to admit it.

They rode in relative silence back through the little canyon. The prisoners drowsed in the supply wagon under the watchful eye of Sir Carlos.

"Lillian?" Dan murmured after some time, too low to be heard by any of their companions.

She looked at him, but he didn't meet her eye. Was he blushing?

"You speak Kazatani? Their language?" He still didn't look at her.

"No. I read it fairly well, though rather slowly, but my accent is atrocious. Why? You don't wish for me to help question them?"

"No," he said quickly. "Certainly not. It's just that, well, the books you read, you said some of them are in Kazatani."

"Yes."

"You said...they are frightening?"

What on earth was he worrying over? "The one I have now is about a town over-run by upira. It nearly scared me to death. I had to skip to the last few pages and finish it before I could even go to sleep last night."

"Upira?"

"Oh." She bit her lip, thinking of how to explain. "They're like vampires to the Kazats, only with an insatiable appetite, and they can transfer their spirits to reanimate the bodies of the dead, and...Dan? Are you all right?"

He'd turned an alarming color of red and seemed to be choking a little.

He cleared his throat. "Your books," he said. "They're about monsters? They're ghost stories?"

"Well, if ghosts drink the blood of their host victim and then blood of anyone around them, then, yes. You could call them ghost stories."

"I never realized." He sent a slightly guilty glance her way.

"What do you mean? You've seen me reading over a dozen of those books. What did you think they were?"

He didn't answer but turned a deeper shade of scarlet.

The obvious answer clicked into place. "Daniel Forell," she hissed. "Do you mean to tell me that all this time you thought I was addicted to *questionable* novels?"

"You were always hiding them," he defended himself in a whisper. "Your aunt said they were inappropriate, so I assumed..." He let his answer trail away, his eyes roving the terrain, looking everywhere but at her.

Lillian knew she ought to give him a piece of her mind, but after staring at him in shock for a full five seconds, she burst out laughing.

"Don't fall off your horse," Dan grumbled, but he laughed too, a low throaty chuckle that had Lillian's heart soaring.

Then she remembered. "At the garrison. Sir Mendine. That's why you gave him such a strange look when he loaned me his books."

At that, they both laughed harder, until their entire party was staring at them, some turning almost fully around in their saddles to see what was going on.

General Adams caught up to them. "Really, Forell. Show a little decorum." But even *he* smiled at Lillian. "I'm afraid you will get the wrong impression of defenders, Lady Loraine."

"On the contrary, General Adams. I'm finally realizing they aren't so bad." She grinned at Sir Drake's defender, a hardened soldier with a reputation for only smiling in battle. He gave her a small lift at the corner of his mouth. Another victory.

Once Sir Mendine heard the story, he favored Dan with a long look before barking a laugh. "That's rich, Forell, but there *are* plenty of men who read romance novels. Nothing wrong with it." He winked at Lillian. "Besides, our little rescuer assured me she needed practice with her Kazatani. I only knew a few words until I started reading their books. It helped my studies immensely."

"What words did you know before you began studying?" she asked.

"'Retreat', mostly, and some swear words. Those were the things they always yelled when they saw me."

Lillian laughed and begged him to teach her how to say

retreat. Dan went back to studying the terrain, but she was sure he listened as well.

A festive atmosphere followed them the rest of the day, despite the terrifying fate they'd narrowly avoided. The sorcerers joked with each other and taught Lillian more about magic than she'd learned in years on her own. Even better, Dan smiled almost continuously. It was such an attractive sight that Lillian had to force herself to take breaks from watching him so the others wouldn't notice her gawking.

And on top of everything else, they were even going to stay in a town instead of tents that night because they would detour to Rosenlen to have the prisoners questioned by a truth-teller. The thought of a real bed, and perhaps some time to talk with Dan without dozens of people listening, lifted her spirits even further.

That evening when Dan checked her room for her, Lillian snuck in behind him and shut the door. He immediately looked around, a guilty twist to his features.

Oh, dear. He was going to be difficult.

"Lillian, we can't be—"

"Shhhh. I want to talk to you without everyone else around," she said quickly, crossing over to where he stood. "I'm worried."

His face relaxed. How insulting. What did he think she wanted behind a closed door?

"About what?"

"Today, of course. Who do you think the Kazats were working with at the garrison?"

Dan shook his head, and Lillian restrained the impulse to reach up and smooth the lines between his eyebrows. "It could be almost anyone, but since they waited until Lady Teresa wasn't there to warn everyone, it must have been someone who was at the base in the last week. No one else would've known she'd gone, but that only narrows it down to about three hundred people."

"Will the truth-teller come to the garrison?" She took a tentative step forward.

His eyes locked on hers, and his words came more slowly. "Almost certainly, but the closest is here, and he won't come until he's had enough time to question each of the prisoners extensively." His voice trailed away at the last, and he stared down at Lillian, his expression softening.

Lillian's heart leapt a few inches in her chest. Did she imagine the hunger in his eyes?

CHAPTER 21

Dan

Dan forgot what he was saying when Lillian turned the full force of her hazel eyes on him. It didn't seem possible that someone with such power and deviousness could also be so angelically sweet... with such perfectly formed lips. He knew he was staring, but he couldn't stop thinking about the kiss they'd shared only a week ago at their surprise party. He'd hardly stopped thinking about it in the days since, but now, alone with her, he remembered the softness of her lips, the subtle fragrance of her hair. The desire to close the last several inches between them was almost overwhelming.

"You were amazing today." He meant to say it steadily, but it came out only a whisper. "You saved us all."

She stared back at him. "Oh," she finally said, giving her head a little shake. "I'm glad they didn't know about me."

Had he moved closer, or had she? A scant few inches separated them now.

"But no one has anything to fear from me," she whispered distractedly. "So I wouldn't be targeted anyway."

Unbidden, a vision of a blade flying through an image of Blevin Octens sprang into his mind. He perfectly remembered the surprise flickering across Lillian's face as the knife sliced her arm, the scarlet of the blood soaking her dress.

A sharp pressure filled his chest, and now his breathing wasn't erratic because of how attractive she was. It came instead from the increasingly familiar panic as he thought of all the ways she could be harmed.

Looking into her beautiful hazel eyes, he knew why his concern for her eclipsed the concern he'd felt for any other person he'd ever known. It had nothing to do with him being her defender.

She was so close now, her face upturned. It would take almost no effort to gather her close. Instead he staggered back.

Her eyes reflected the pain he felt.

"Lillian," he said hoarsely. "You will *always* be a target."

Her hurt expression dissolved instantly, though he couldn't tell if it was because she understood or because she was wearing a mask.

"I was a fool to bring you here. I'm so sorry."

"What do you mean?" She reached out a hand as though to touch his shoulder, but he stepped back from her, knowing he had to put some distance between them. He had to think.

"Excuse me, please, Miss Loraine. I find my thoughts are disorganized. May we speak in the morning?"

"Of course, Dan," she said with a gentle smile that tore at his heart. "Sleep well."

Dan fled the room, closing the door behind him. He leaned his head against the wall of the empty corridor.

The other defenders slept in the same room as their assignments. They were their shadows. Even Lady Teresa's great-nephew always managed to get a partitioned area of her room when they traveled. He hated that a door always separated him at night from Lillian, hated having her out of his sight.

How had he let himself fall so hopelessly in love with her? He turned his back to the wall and slid down to sit in a pathetic heap on the floor. There was no way this could end well. He would lose her. She'd wanted a different defender from the day she'd met him, and if by some miracle she decided to keep him, he'd lose his dream of working with the army sorcerers.

They were the most exposed and targeted sorcerers in the country, the most endangered. She couldn't work with them. He had to keep her safe, not just because it was his duty, but because she was infinitely precious. The coordinator didn't understand that. General Adams wouldn't either, but Dan felt it acutely.

He remained slumped against the wall another hour in a dazed stupor, wondering how he could have let this all happen. His mind took him through a thousand scenarios in which she could be harmed or killed by working with the army sorcerers.

No one but a maid saw him in such an undignified state. She probably took him for drunk, because she skirted him as widely as the hall allowed.

Just as he decided to fetch a pillow to ease the discomfort of sleeping on the floor in the hall, Lillian's door creaked open. He was immediately beside her, taking in her large, frightened eyes and the nervous way she clutched her dressing gown. "What's the matter?" he demanded, his eyes darting beyond her into the empty, candle-lit room.

"Oh, Dan," she whispered. "I'm so frightened."

And then she stepped into his arms, clutching him around the waist and burying her face in his chest.

His arm instinctively went around her as he moved into her room, pulling her with him. It was empty.

"What's the matter, Lillian?" he asked in a low whisper. "What's happened?"

She gave a tiny laugh that was almost a sob. "I was so stupid to think I could handle it."

"What do you mean?" He rubbed her back. "What is it, Lil?"

"I'm not sure if you can help with this problem," she muttered into his shirt.

He gave a wry smile she couldn't see, and said truthfully, "I'd do anything to help you."

"I feel so silly. Sir Mendine warned me, but I didn't see how it could be this bad. I know if I just fall asleep, I'll be fine."

"A ghost story?" Dan didn't even try to keep the relief out of his voice.

"Not just a ghost story," Lillian contradicted indignantly, though she shivered and clutched him more tightly. "It was Sir Mendine's book about the psoglav by a gifted Kazat writer. Now I hear them all around the inn."

"Psoglav?"

"Demonic dogs. They feed on fears for an appetizer and then on the flesh of humans. If you have no fear, they leave you alone, but Dan, there must be an animal outside. I hear something moving below my window, and I can't help being afraid and…. What are you laughing at?"

Dan leaned back to look into her beautiful, but now angry, eyes.

"Lillian, you're a delight." He softly brushed her loosened hair away from her face. "And you certainly know how to give a man a heart attack."

"You said you would help me," she accused in a whisper.

"I will. Anything you need." It may have sounded light, but Dan meant it as an oath. "It's just a relief that it's psoglav you are afraid of and not something that can actually hurt you."

"But I can't sleep alone in this big room now. I never should have started that book."

"Lillian, there aren't any women around that I would trust enough to stay with you."

"I don't want someone else. I want *you* to sleep in here with me."

Dan gulped and gently disentangled himself from her. "Now Lillian—"

"Don't take that tone of voice with me, Daniel Forell," she said, crossing her arms in front of her chest and glaring at him. "I'm not trying to steal your virtue, but I've scared myself silly and can't be alone. If Aunt Svea was here, I'd sneak into her room and sleep on her sofa, but she's not, and you're all I've got." Her imperial tone turned pleading at the end.

"Do you have any idea how bad it would look if someone knew I stayed in your room?"

"There's a sofa in here. It's plenty long enough for me to sleep on. You can have the bed," she said primly. "You're tall as a house, so it's the only place you'd fit. Once I'm asleep, I'm fine, but I can't fall asleep when I'm this frightened."

"Lillian, I'm not going to take your bed. I'll sleep on the sofa. It's better than the floor in the hallway anyway."

"Why would you sleep in the hallway? Don't you have a room?"

"Of course, but it's two doors away from you, and if you needed me..."

She looked deeply into his eyes a moment, her expression unreadable. "So you'll stay?"

Dan smiled wryly. "Yes, I'll stay. Now read the last few pages while I check this window."

For a brief, oddly hopeful second, Dan thought she might throw herself into his arms again. Instead she said, "Thank you," in a solemn sort of voice before snatching up a book from the chair and perching on the end of her bed, close to the candles.

Dan shook his head as he secured the window latch and drew the curtains more carefully. Then he secured the door and slumped onto the sofa, stretching out his legs in front of him.

"I'm almost done," Lillian said, her eyes wide as they darted back and forth across the page. "Then I'll put out the candles."

Dan allowed himself to watch her longer than he should

have. She was distracted and wouldn't notice, and she was so beautiful. He couldn't help studying the way her teeth worried her lip. In fact, her lips held his attention far too much lately.

Lillian

The psoglov were finally defeated by the sacrifice of three brave villagers who drove the beasts off a mountain but were carried down to their deaths also. Lillian shivered as she read, but the ending was not as gripping as it should have been, mostly because Dan watched her. She could feel his eyes on her, and her curiosity got the better of her. She very carefully held an image over her eyes so it would appear she was still reading. His expression was unguarded, and she couldn't resist.

She'd half-expected him to resent her for dragging him into her room, but his eyes weren't resentful or critical, only thoughtful. His brows contracted once, and he sighed. It drove her wild with curiosity.

Lillian finally closed the book and set it carefully on the bedside table. "Thank you, Dan. I think I can sleep now." She eyed the various weapons he pulled from his belt and inside his clothing to lay in a heap next to the sofa. "Do you want to practice tonight?" She could give him fifty opponents without even needing her medicine now.

"I should, and you could use more practice with the angles, but I can't keep the noise of my footfalls silent, and I don't want to attract attention to your room."

"All right." She quickly slid under her covers, exhaustion finally overpowering her fear.

"Lillian?"

"Hmm?"

"What do you mean, you're fine once you fall asleep? Don't you have nightmares after reading those books?"

"Oh, I never have nightmares," she said sleepily. "She wouldn't allow it."

"Who?"

Lillian wasn't even sure she was awake anymore. She was so exhausted from all the traveling. "My mother, of course," she mumbled. "If I fall asleep worried, her love fills my dreams until I feel better. She does the same thing for Uncle Hollis."

She didn't hear Dan's response. She was already asleep.

When she woke the next morning, she immediately looked to the sofa. Dan was gone. She took a mental inventory of her appearance. Her hair had mostly fallen from its braid last night and lay swirled around her head. She was well-covered by her blankets and dressing gown, but one of her feet was exposed, her leg bared half-way to her knee. Perhaps he'd left as soon as she'd fallen asleep. That would be like him. She sighed and dragged herself from bed. She'd probably slept later than anyone else again. Military men woke at such unholy hours.

She had just dressed when Dan knocked at her door. "Lillian?"

A smile crossed her features, and she immediately pushed it away. She'd practically forced herself into his arms last night, and he hadn't done a thing about it, hadn't wanted her there. She couldn't appear too enamored with him. It might drive him away.

She opened the door and beckoned him in. He bore a breakfast tray and a wary expression. She barely managed to not roll her eyes. "Will you update me on the general's plans while I finish getting ready?" She moved as far away from him as the room allowed and sat down at a small vanity. "Sit down, please," she added.

He sat on the sofa, his back perfectly straight. "The general feels we should leave within the hour rather than waiting for any more of the truth-teller's report. The prisoners were questioned most of the night and…" His voice trailed away as Lillian finished pulling her braid apart.

Dan's eyes widened, and his frown deepened. He almost looked the tiniest bit afraid.

She picked up a brush, enjoying his discomfort. There was nothing particularly immodest about a woman wearing her hair completely down, but it wasn't typically done in public, and he'd never seen her hair this way before.

She was so constantly vulnerable around him. He knew all about her lack of bravery, her fears. They'd developed a friendship, certainly, but he held himself back sometimes, and his aloofness hurt.

"Yes? Go on." She ran her brush slowly though her brown hair. Aunt Svea told her that she had nice hair, glossy and thick, but she'd always wished for Liv's light blonde. The distracted expression on Dan's face was enough to make her reconsider.

Dan's eyes followed the movement, but after a couple seconds, her words seemed to sink in, because he inhaled a deep breath and snapped back into full speech. Lillian slowly eased an image over herself and peeked at him from behind it. To his view, she faced the window, nodding her head occasionally as he described the travel plans for the day. Behind her mask, she watched him carefully, trying to discern his thoughts.

CHAPTER 22

Dan

Fifteen minutes prior

Dan woke after a restless sleep and immediately looked to his assignment. Lillian was perfectly serene in sleep, her expression unguarded. Her coverlet had slipped off her foot, and he stared in fascination at the small gap between her first and second toes. It was absolutely adorable.

He stood, disgusted with himself. He had no right to drool over her. At the door he paused and glanced back, wondering how he'd let himself fall in love with someone so completely unattainable.

After talking with General Adams and flagging down a maid to get breakfast, he found Lillian almost ready. He sat reluctantly on her sofa, updating her on the plans for the day, but stuttered to a halt when she loosened her hair.

He couldn't help staring. Lillian was so beautiful, and he'd always loved her hair. It seemed to glow, and he leaned forward, wishing he could reach out and touch it. She ran her brush through the shining strands and said something—he wasn't sure what—but it reminded him he was being pathetic.

He sat up straight. "You'd better eat your breakfast before it gets cold."

"Oh, I will. Just one moment more." She twisted her hair into a complicated knot at the back of her head. "Do you see my box of hair-pins?"

"These?" he asked, snatching them up from the table beside him and striding forward.

At the same moment, she said, "I remember," and still holding her hair in place with one hand, Lillian popped up from her chair. She spun right into Dan's chest, the collision knocking her off balance. Dan grasped her elbows and righted her gently. She'd let go of her hair when she collided with him, and it tumbled freely over her shoulders. She laughed a little breathlessly. "Thank you," she said. "I should have looked where I..." Her words trailed away as she stared up at him.

What was it about her eyes that made his defenses dissolve so quickly? Dan drank in the sight of her. He slowly released one of her arms to run his hand down her hair. Her eyes were wide and trusting. Heaven help him. He'd wanted to kiss her for so long, really kiss her, not just trick her into kissing him because someone was watching. His hand traced her jaw and tilted up her chin. His heart pounded frantically against his ribs as her eyes slid closed and his head bent toward hers.

Only a fraction of an inch separated them when they both jumped at a knock on Lillian's door.

"Lady Lillian? It is almost time to leave." It was Sir Iloh.

Dan's immediate surge of anger toward the sorcerer helped clear his mind. He wasn't behaving honorably, trying to steal a kiss from his assignment, the person whose best interests were supposed to supersede his. He wanted to kiss her more than he could remember wanting anything else in his life, but he didn't want it more than he wanted her to be happy, and that would probably *not* make her happy.

"Thank you. I'll be there in two minutes," Lillian called back. Her eyes searched Dan's.

"I'll get the hairpins," he said quietly. "You'd better eat. You might need to save all our necks again today."

She smiled on a sigh and nodded, turning away from him and breaking the spell of her hazel eyes.

The ride back was punctuated by Lillian's practice. Various illusions, some of them as large as mountains, appeared on the surrounding landscape as the sorcerers took turns coaching her. Dan wished they had juice with them, but at least he had two vials of her medicine, on top of what she carried.

By the time they made it back to the garrison that evening, the entire group was exhausted. After dinner, Sir Hollis made a short appearance, quickly leaving again to learn what he could of the Kazat prisoners in Rosenlen.

"No, not you, Forell," the general said. Dan looked up, but General Adams was talking to Oliver. "He doesn't need you, and I have questions for you."

Oliver sat back down, his expression stormy. He wasn't happy about not going, and Dan didn't blame him. It was beyond frustrating to be kept from doing your job. Dan turned back to his own assignment to see Lillian watching Oliver closely. He wished they liked each other better.

After dinner, Dan practiced knife-throwing with a few of the defenders while Lillian enjoyed her popularity with the sorcerers. When she secluded herself across the room with Sir Iloh, however, Dan found he couldn't keep his mind on target practice.

He wandered closer under the pretense of getting a book from some tall shelves behind Lillian.

"Has there been a problem with him?" Sir Iloh was asking in tones of curiosity.

"Oh, that's not important," Lillian said quietly. "What I really want to understand is the *process* for exchanging defenders."

What?

"Do you have to go through Madsen?" she asked. "Can you present yourself at the academy to negotiate with a new one? What is the fastest way to make it happen?" Her words were earnest, urgent.

He must have scared her that morning after all. Or perhaps she'd never considered keeping him for her defender.

Sir Iloh glanced up and noticed Dan. The pity in his eyes was enough to make Lillian's words real.

She didn't want him.

Keeping his features blank, Dan chose a book at random and moved slowly away, never looking back over his shoulder or even letting a flicker of his panic cross his face. He spent the rest of the evening moving his eyes from one side of the page to the other, never looking up, never joining in conversation.

Lillian wanted to be rid of him. He was sick with the pain of it, and nearly didn't notice when Sir Hollis appeared in the parlor at General Adam's side. It was the noise of all the defenders and sorcerers hurrying to hear the news that finally jerked him from his paralyzing despondency.

The general accepted an envelope from Sir Hollis, tore it open, and quickly read aloud. "The Kazats were coordinating with someone at the garrison. They don't know his name, and only one of them ever saw him in person. Description: brown hair, medium to tall height. The truth-teller and several soldiers will escort that prisoner here so he can identify him." The general lowered the letter. "That will take another day at least, and we have the cavalry training expedition on the schedule for tomorrow. It means we'll have to wait two days or delay the training."

"I. Can. Get. Them. Now," Sir Hollis said slowly.

"Respectfully, General Adams, I must protest," Oliver broke

in. "Sir Hollis is tired. I think we should delay the training tomorrow and wait here for the prisoner."

"I can't deny I'm tired too," the general said, lightly clapping Sir Hollis on the shoulder. "Let's have you bring us the prisoner tomorrow night, eh? Or, if you came with us tomorrow, we could have the prisoner identify the man during the training exercises."

Sir Hollis reluctantly nodded, and the defenders and sorcerers slowly left the parlor, each of them bowing to Lillian as they went. Oliver watched them with narrowed eyes, obviously not understanding their respect for her. He still didn't know what Lillian could do. Dan had been looking forward to Oliver's expression when he first saw Lillian's real power. Now that she was getting rid of him, he'd probably never get the chance.

Dan searched Lillian's room quickly before bidding her a hasty goodnight. He couldn't bear to look at her. In the morning she slept through breakfast and halfway to lunch. He was beginning to worry about her when she knocked hesitantly on the door that separated them. Dan dragged himself to the door, knowing that at any moment she was going to dismiss him.

Lillian smiled tentatively at him, and his heart thudded painfully.

"May I come in a moment, Dan? I need to talk to you about something."

He followed her back into his room, but only a few steps in, she spun to face him. "Dan, hear me out. I know you're not going to believe me, but at least think about it."

"About what?" he asked quietly. He already knew what she was going to say.

"I think Oliver is involved in the Kazat attack."

Oh. He *didn't* know what she was going to say. Her bizarre statement brought an unexpected smile to his mouth. "Why on earth would you think that?"

"A hundred small things. The way he treats Uncle Hollis, how nervous he was when the general spoke of bringing the prisoner here to identify the traitor. Dan, he's the exact description they gave."

"So am I. So are about a hundred other men at the garrison."

"Oh, Dan, please don't be angry. You know I can't bear it." Her eyes pled with him for understanding. "I'm really worried. I don't think he's trustworthy."

But Dan *couldn't* understand. She thought him so worthless that she planned to replace him, and now she was accusing his only family on the continent of treason.

"Oh, admit it, Lillian. Just because he doesn't roll over and beg you to scratch his belly like every other man you've ever met—"

"Well, there's no need to be vulgar. I only—"

"The real problem here is that you're used to getting your own way." His voice grew unintentionally louder, and he took a step closer. "For some reason, you've taken a dislike to my cousin, and I cannot agree with you on this."

"But—" She tried to break in gently, but he overrode her, taking another step forward until they were almost toe to toe.

"You are *wrong*." He crossed his arms and looked down at her. "And I would appreciate it if you wouldn't tell anyone else about your childish and unfounded suspicions."

She flinched away at the last, and Dan immediately regretted his outburst. Lillian looked down a moment more, then looked up at him serenely. Her eyes were less bright, her skin slightly dull. "I suppose I'll see you at lunch, then." Her voice was steady and polite, but only a whisper.

She spun on her heel, and less than two seconds later, was back in her room, closing the door between them. Dan stood with his mouth open, gulping for air as though she had taken it all with her when she left.

He'd hurt her feelings, or she wouldn't have masked her features. Guilt tore at his chest. He was such an idiot.

He crossed to the door and knocked twice. There was no answer, but a tiny little sniff from the next room told him all he needed to know. Cursing his temper and stupidity, he paused, pulling together his courage. He couldn't bear it when she cried. He slowly turned the knob. She hadn't locked it. That was good. "Lillian, I'm coming in." He waited a moment more, but there was no answer. He pushed the door open. "I'm so sorry," he said, stepping into the room. But she wasn't there. Or was she? It was impossible to know.

"Lillian? Are you in here? I'm so sorry for behaving that way. I was upset about something else, and I never should have taken it out on you. Let's talk about what worries you, and I can check into it." He paused, listening. The room was silent, not even the sound of her breathing.

She was gone.

And they still didn't know who in the garrison was trying to kill Kalmarian sorcerers.

Cursing under his breath, he ran back to his own room, pulled on his boots, and bolted into the corridor.

Lillian

Why did she give him power to hurt her? It was completely stupid of her to care for him so much. He obviously didn't return her affection, and now she was sniveling like a baby.

Lillian dried her face on a handkerchief just as Dan knocked on the door that separated their rooms. She quickly slipped out the other door and into the corridor, placing a tear-free image over herself. She hated it when anyone knew she was crying, and Dan worst of all. It was clear that the soldier in him found tears offensive, and she couldn't deal with any more criticism from him.

Before she could decide which way to go, a soldier passed by, pausing to bow politely. Her smiling image nodded, and he moved on.

Dan's door handle jostled, and Lillian melted her image into the walls. On a snap decision, she gave the retreating soldier's back her own dress and hair.

"Lillian, wait," Dan said in a low, urgent voice that tore at her heart. He set off at a jog to catch up with the soldier, who helpfully disappeared around a corner ahead. Dan was probably only afraid she would complain to someone about him.

Well, he was wrong. She didn't want to talk to anyone. She just wanted to go somewhere she could be totally alone, somewhere her defender wouldn't bother her. She rematerialized and set off in the opposite direction, running on her toes to muffle the sound of her footfalls.

After several turns, Lillian passed a promising-looking door near the kitchen. She knocked twice, just in case, before trying the door. Inside she found a half-empty storage room, lit dimly by a very small window. She quietly closed the door behind her and walked to the far wall where she leaned her head against a wooden beam. She wished Uncle Hollis would come take her somewhere else, anywhere else, far from her defender and his hateful cousin. A pang of homesickness constricted her throat, and her tears fell unrestrained, just as she heard footsteps outside the room. Would she never know a moment's peace in this foul place?

She glanced around quickly at the bags of grain and barrels of dried meats. She sighed. It wasn't very dignified, but it was better than having to face anyone.

Lillian stepped behind a barrel and assumed the shape of

another bag of grain. Hopefully whoever it was would get what they wanted and leave her in peace.

The door opened. "In here, quickly," Oliver Forell muttered, ushering several men into the room. He repeated himself, but in Kazatani, and Lillian watched him open-mouthed. Oliver spoke Kazatani?

He pushed past the assembled men to stand in the center of the storage room. "Plans have changed," he began as someone closed the door.

A soldier stepped forward. "There should only be two sorcerers left, and yet, all are still here, very much alive." His accent was thick, but his anger was clear.

"We'll get rid of them," Oliver said tightly. "I'm arranging it."

The man broke into another string of arguments in such rapid Kazatani that Lillian couldn't follow it. She set about memorizing the men's faces.

"It's not our fault," an angry voice growled from near the door. "The sorcerers knew they were there even without their listener."

Williams, Oliver's unpleasant friend, turned to glare at the man. "It's not our fault that your friends set up a shoddy ambush."

The Kazats glared back. She quickly counted them. Five, aside from Williams and Oliver. One of them was so close, she feared he'd hear her breathing.

"I told you I'll take care of the sorcerers once the healer is gone." Oliver patted a bulge in his shirt pocket. "You'll only have to witness it. Then you can all go home. You'll never even need to bloody your swords. Now get back to your drills. You're supposed to be the new recruits I'm training, remember?"

The Kazats exchanged meaningful glances, then filed out the door, pausing only when Oliver murmured tightly, "Remember not to speak to anyone, not one word."

Williams watched them go, then glared after them. "You sure

you don't want to poison the lot of them along with the sorcerers?"

Lillian caught back a gasp.

"I'd rather not. I need them to take the story back home that I did as we planned, though as confident in me as Reznik seemed, he might not even wait for confirmation."

"It better be worth it," Williams grunted.

"An earldom is worth the risk. Not having to play nursemaid to a cripple is worth it. And you, with the gold you'll have, you might as well be an earl."

"Well, when you put it that way," Williams said with an unkind smile, "I guess I can go put the new recruits through their paces. All the practice fields are empty with the men gone."

He followed the Kazats, and Lillian hardly dared breathe in the silence. Oliver turned in a circle, looking around the storage room, and Lillian prayed her image was flawless. If he found her here, he'd kill her, and no one would ever know. She had no way to cast an image where Dan could see it. She didn't even know where he was.

Oliver strode once around the storage room, studying the contents of the shelves and barrels. Lillian held her breath when he paused, inches away from her. Her heart thudded painfully. Surely he'd hear it pounding, but after several seconds, he pulled a flagon from a shelf next to her and strode briskly from the room, closing the door behind him. Lillian waited to a count of one hundred before she released her image and tiptoed to the door. She eased it open and angled her vision around corners in each direction. There was no sign of Oliver or anyone else.

Lillian hurried breathlessly down corridors, searching for Dan, or a sorcerer, or even General Adams, but she only passed a few strangers, men in uniform who bowed to her politely. Any of them could be a Kazat. She raced around a corner near her room and almost collided with Dan.

"I've been looking for you everywhere," he exclaimed quietly. "Don't you know it's dangerous to—"

He stopped suddenly when she threw herself into his arms and buried her face in his chest.

"Now hold on," he said, though he wrapped his arms around her. He leaned his head down to rest on hers. "What's the matter? You're trembling. What's happened?" His face pressed the top of her head. Before she could decide if he'd kissed her hair, he pulled away to look into her eyes. She hadn't even thought to mask her expression, and he quickly pulled out a handkerchief. "Lillian, I'm so sorry. I was such a fool. Please forgive me."

Lillian hiccupped a sob and buried her face in his chest again.

"Come on," he said, pulling her into her room and shutting the door behind them. "Something's happened aside from your defender behaving like a complete jack—" He cleared his throat. "What's going on?"

"Oh, Dan. I'm so sorry. It will make you so unhappy, but we have to do something."

"What do we have to do?"

"The Kazats. They're here. The sorcerers are in danger. Oliver said—"

"You don't still think Oliver is—"

"Oh, Dan. Just look." Lillian conjured up the image of the men in the storage room. Some of the Kazats' faces were indistinct. She couldn't remember all of them. "Oliver was with that man, Windon or whatever his name was, and these other men are Kazatani. I heard them talking. Oliver said he's been offered an earldom if he can kill all the sorcerers at the garrison, and that the Kazats are here to help him and make sure it gets done. He said something about poison."

Dan's face was unreadable. "Go on, but slower, all right?"

"Windon—"

"Williams?"

"Yes, that's his name. He said the Kazats were pretending to be new recruits. The Kazats were unhappy that the sorcerers weren't killed in the mountains. Oliver said he was going to take care of it while most of the men at the garrison are out with General Adams. He said he was waiting for the healer to leave. He must mean Sir Carlos. He's already left, hasn't he? And Lady Teresa isn't back yet, so she wouldn't have heard any of their conversations. So no one knows there are Kazats here."

Dan frowned at her, and she trailed off, feeling uncertain.

"Lillian, there must be some mistake." He held up a hand. "I believe you saw and heard all of that, but Oliver could be trying to trick the Kazats."

Lillian rolled her eyes, but he didn't notice. He was frowning at his hand. She looked down to see he was holding her own. When had that happened? Hopefully he wouldn't stop.

He stopped.

"We need to find the sorcerers and their defenders," he said. "And we need to get you out of here."

"Don't be silly. I'm not leaving without you." Lillian wiped her nose fiercely.

"You can't stay. It's not safe for you."

"But you have to come with me. You're my defender."

"I wasn't thinking of leaving you without protection."

"That's not what I was worried about," she said indignantly.

Dan seemed not to have heard. "Come on. Let's check their study."

They almost ran through the halls, Lillian checking around corners before they reached them.

The sorcerers' study was empty, and Lillian's panic rose another notch. "Dan, we have to find them. Before they're hurt."

They turned back to the door and found their way blocked.

CHAPTER 23

Dan

Dan's sword was half-drawn before he realized it was Sir Hollis standing in their path.

"Uncle Hollis," Lillian cried, relief saturating her voice. "I've been so worried for you." She hurried forward and grasped his hand.

Dan bowed. "I'm very glad to see you, sir. It appears Kazats have infiltrated the garrison, and the sorcerers are at risk."

"How?" Sir Hollis' eyebrows contracted as he patted Lillian's hand haltingly.

"We aren't sure yet. Oliver is involved somehow. I've got to find him, but I don't dare risk Lillian. Can you take her somewhere safe? Somewhere far away? Maybe her home?"

Sir Hollis nodded, just as Lillian cried out, "No!"

He wanted to clasp her close and promise her it would be all right, but Sir Hollis was there. Dan was certain he knew about the fake engagement. "Oliver's my cousin," Dan said. "I've got to either prove him innocent or stop him. I feel responsible to see this through. Once she is safe, if you could fetch Sir Carlos? He's gone with most of the men from the garrison on a training expedition."

"I'm not leaving," Lillian said firmly.

"Please get her out of here, Sir Hollis," Dan pled fervently. "She's not safe here."

Sir Hollis gave Lillian a troubled look, and they both disappeared, just as Lillian tried to protest.

A familiar heavy knot formed immediately in Dan's stomach. It was always the same when she was out of sight. He highly doubted he would feel the same way about his next assignment.

Dan hurried through the nearly-empty garrison. The sorcerers would be going to lunch soon. He had to delay them while he spoke to Oliver, but a few minutes later, he rounded a corner to find Oliver coming from the kitchen.

His cousin grinned. "There you are. Your pretty little assignment taken care of for the moment?" A small bulge in his shirt pocket caught Dan's eye. "Come walk with me," Oliver said, gesturing back the way Dan had come. "I meant to ask you how she fared on your trip with the sorcerers. All anyone has told me is that you caught a pack of Kazats on your trip."

Dan frowned at Oliver, who laughed openly.

"You're too protective of the girl, Dan. I bet you hovered over her the entire journey and acted like a complete ninny."

"Of course I didn't," Dan said, falling into step with his cousin and watching him sideways. "And I wish you'd be a little more diplomatic around her, even if you don't like her."

Oliver chuckled again. Anyone who didn't know him well would think Oliver was in the best of spirits, but there was something wrong with his laugh, a subtle change in the pitch. "Just because I find her a pain in the..." He caught Dan's eye and coughed a laugh. "That doesn't mean I don't like her. I admire her tremendously. She's pretty, she keeps you out of my way, and her figure. I think half the men at the garrison dream—"

His speech halted abruptly when Dan's sword materialized several inches from his nose.

"Neither you, nor anyone else, is allowed to dream about Miss Loraine. She is a lady, not to mention my fiancée and my assignment. I will not allow her to be discussed by vermin."

A look of hate flashed across Oliver's features so quickly, Dan couldn't be sure it was ever there. Then Oliver grinned. "You really *like* her, don't you?" he asked, ignoring the blade. "I never would have guessed. I thought Madsen was making you marry her."

Dan glared at his cousin and sheathed his blade. "Of course I want to marry her," he said, relieved to be able to say it aloud. "Only an idiot wouldn't."

"Huh. Dan Forell in love. I never thought I'd see the day." As he moved forward again, his shirt stretched over the object in his pocket.

"Where's *your* assignment?" Dan asked abruptly, wondering how closely Oliver kept track of Sir Hollis.

"Who knows?" Oliver said with a shrug and a trace of annoyance. "He could be anywhere in the world right now. I used to think he could help your parents. Think how quickly they could make accurate maps if travel didn't take so long, but I'm not sure how much longer he'll live."

"What makes you say that?"

"He's a cripple, isn't he? I thought he'd die years ago."

Oliver *had* changed. When he'd first become a defender, he'd been annoyingly proud of his work.

"What will you do when he's gone?"

"Oh, I'm always planning for the future." Oliver gestured toward an empty practice room. "Come see my training schedule for the new recruits."

"Since when do you train new soldiers?" Dan asked, reluctantly following Oliver through the arched entryway. His distrust, so long in coming, was now escalating swiftly.

"Well, my assignment's been feeling pretty independent lately, thanks to your fiancée. He pops in and out all day, so I've got more time on my hands." Again the tightness around the eyes. He was lying. "Now tell me about your trip into the mountains. There must be more to that story than I've heard."

"I'm sure you've heard it all." Dan turned to face his cousin, wishing desperately his answer would give him confidence again. "Why do you think the Kazats were so well-prepared to attack us, Oliver?"

"How should I know? They have spies everywhere." He didn't meet Dan's eyes.

"And Oliver?"

"What?" Oliver's eyes darted behind Dan and then around the room.

Dan nodded at Oliver's chest. "What's in your pocket?"

Oliver shook his head, looking pityingly at Dan. "You really are the most interfering simpleton."

Something struck Dan from behind, and all went dark.

Lillian

After a few nauseating seconds, Lillian once again stood on firm ground. Sir Hollis had brought them directly to Perch Harbor.

"Where. Is. Your. Home?" Uncle Hollis asked with his usual effort.

"There." Lillian pointed at the large house overlooking the bay. "But Uncle Hollis—"

Time and space lurched, and they stood at the front doors.

"We have to go back," Lillian finished. "Dan is in danger, and so are Sir Pescall, and Sir Iloh, and Sir Drake. All of them."

"I'll. Go." His eyes were troubled.

"Lillian? Is that you?" Aunt Svea walked briskly toward them from the north gardens, a basket of greenery in one hand. "How did you get here?" She looked around, as though a carriage would materialize on the driveway.

Lillian groaned and said quickly under her breath, "Please, Uncle Hollis. I've told you how far I've come, the things I can do. I can help. I can keep myself safe, and I love him. He's going to get himself killed without me there. He trusts Oliver, but it's Oliver that brought the Kazats."

"My dear, where is Mr. Forell?" Aunt Svea said as she neared them. "And aren't you going to introduce me to your friend?" She quickly embraced Lillian, who was almost too distracted to hug her back.

"Aunt Svea, this is Uncle Hollis. My mother's brother."

"What? How wonderful! How did you know?"

"He thought I was my mother. We look a lot alike," Lillian said in a rush. "And he dreams of her too. Uncle Hollis, this is my Aunt Svea. You're going to love each other, but right now we have to go rescue my ridiculous defender."

Uncle Hollis shook his head sadly.

She groaned. "Oh, Uncle Hollis. I don't know what I would do without him. And look." She turned invisible. "See? I'll be in no danger at all." She winked back into view.

She'd told him she could do it, but his mouth still dropped open, and his eyes widened.

"Dear, you know that is a disturbing thing to see," Aunt Svea said reproachfully. "So you've got to save the boy, eh? You'd better get a move on." Her smile was a little too smug.

Lillian turned back to her uncle. "Please?" she begged, allowing her tears to run down her cheeks. It was a low trick. Lillian could hide her tears if she wanted, but this was a desperate situation.

Uncle Hollis sighed, and Lillian's heart leapt in relief. Her uncle bowed haltingly to Aunt Svea, then took Lillian's hand.

With the familiar jolt, their surroundings disappeared, and Lillian caught back a scream as she felt herself flying sideways.

The stone walls of the garrison corridor were a welcome sight. Her room was only a few feet away.

"I'll. Help. You," Uncle Hollis said while Lillian waited for her stomach to settle.

"Thank you," Lillian said quickly. "But we'll need Sir Carlos. What if one of the sorcerers has already been hurt?"

She smiled at Uncle Hollis' reluctance. "I promise I'll be just fine."

He frowned at her, obviously about to do something against his better judgement. "Don't. Be. Seen."

"I won't," Lillian assured him as she threw her arms gently around his neck and kissed his cheek.

He shook his head but looked pleased. A moment later he was gone.

Her courage disappeared with him. What had she been thinking? Half a dozen Kazats, plus Williams, not to mention Oliver Forell, a defender. She had no chance against all of them. She had to find Dan.

He wasn't in his room or hers. She hurried through the corridors, searching for him. Twice she passed soldiers she didn't recognize and simply melted into walls, waiting for them to move by. After many minutes, she heard muffled voices ahead and slowly inched forward, cloaking herself in invisibility as she neared a stone archway.

It led to a practice room full of weapons and straw dummies, and beyond that was another archway where a uniformed man stood guard. Behind him came the sound of Kazat accents. She eased back around the corner and gave herself a few moments to think. She didn't know much about Kazats. She'd never studied their military training and had no idea what to expect from them.

She looked back around the archway to see the guard leave his post and hurry into the next room.

Invisible again, she quickly sneaked through the practice room and hovered where the guard had been standing. Another corner blocked the speakers from view, but she angled the light to see where the guard had gone. He stood with three uniformed soldiers just around the corner. She recognized them from the storage room where they'd plotted the murder of her friends. Her breathing came more rapidly, and she felt faint. She needed help, but Uncle Hollis might not be able to bring reinforcements soon.

She angled more light to look further and finally saw Dan. He was gagged tightly and tied to a wooden chair at the far end of the room. Her anxiety escalated as she looked him over. Blood saturated the back of his head, but his eyes were alert, and he watched his captors with absolute loathing.

Two more Kazats stood nearby, and among them was Williams, a disgusting smile twisting his features. "A shame you didn't bring your fiancée, Forell," he said. "We could have had some fun with her while we wait for the sorcerers to take their medicine. Then you could have died together. That would have been sweet."

"Shut up, Williams," another familiar voice said. Lillian angled more light to see Oliver leaning against the far wall. He gave Dan a considering look. "It wasn't supposed to be this way, Dan. That Kazat assassin sent after you to Perch Harbor? I offered him double if he could kill your sorcerer without harming you. I never wanted you to die, but I'm afraid I can't think of a way to keep you alive, and time has run out. I regret it." He drew his sword.

They were going to kill him. She couldn't wait for Uncle Hollis to come back with help. She stood from her hiding place and walked around the corner. She really only knew one thing about Kazats. Hopefully it would be enough.

CHAPTER 24

Dan

Dan worked his bonds without notable progress. Oliver had always been good with knots, and all Dan had to show for his efforts were bleeding wrists. He called himself several different types of idiot. How could he have trusted Oliver and not seen the way he'd changed? He ignored Williams' taunts as he focused on finding a way out, a way that involved catching or killing all the men in the room.

Then Oliver drew his sword, and Dan defiantly locked eyes with his cousin and one-time brother. At least Lillian was miles away from the filthy snake. She wouldn't see Dan die, wouldn't be in danger. That was his only consolation. Lillian was safe.

A second later, something happened to drive every thought from his mind. Lillian, wearing a pretty white party gown, stepped into the room. A dark red splash stained her abdomen. She was bleeding. A sharp stabbing in his lungs kept him from drawing breath.

Her wide eyes immediately turned to Dan, then glanced around at the other men.

"I don't know who did this to you," Oliver said grimly, "but you shouldn't have come here." He ripped a crossbow from the arms of the Kazat nearest him and leveled it at Lillian.

Dan's strangled cry of warning and despair muffled the sound of the impact. The arrow buried itself deep in Lillian's chest. Blood immediately soaked the front of her dress, running down to join her other wound. Her eyes were shocked as she slumped back against the nearest wall.

Time stopped for Dan. Agony like he'd never known ripped through his entire body. The grief and rage were all-encompassing. He wished they'd kill him too. He couldn't stand it. Tears immediately streamed from his eyes, and he fought against his restraints with every shred of energy he had. He'd kill all of them. He'd find a way.

Her eyes met his, and they didn't seem pained. More... curious.

Lillian's fingers wrapped around the shaft of the arrow protruding from her heart. Her eyes slowly traveled down to regard it with fascination. Then, with one quick, wrenching motion and a gasp, she ripped the arrow from her body. A generous amount of blood dripped from the point of the arrow, and the bodice of her dress was now saturated. Dan watched her, unable to look away. The room was quiet, aside from Dan's own frantic breathing around his gag, so he knew Oliver and his men watched her too.

Lillian carefully brought the arrow point to her face, and then, to Dan's confusion, and the surprised murmurs of the Kazat men, she slowly licked the blood from the point of the arrow. The whites of her eyes flashed bright red and a slow, pleased smile spread across her face.

If she still hadn't been in such danger, Dan would have laughed in relief. She was playing them. His worry lessened, but only by a degree.

"Hers *does* taste good," she said, a sultry note in her voice. No one seemed to notice her voice came from a little to the left. "But I've had enough from her already, and I've always been one for a variety of tastes." She looked hungrily between Oliver and his men.

"Upira," choked out one of the men, pointing at her.

Oliver put another arrow to his bow and let it fly, but with inhuman speed and agility, Lillian dodged it.

The Kazats yelled out to each other, covering any sound she was making. He joined them with his muffled yells as Lillian turned with a flirtatious grin to the Kazat nearest the door. He held a large knife in his hand but actually cried out with fear as she stalked toward him. The man bolted, but she was faster. Just as he reached the door, she caught up to him, lifting and bending his knife hand so that he plunged the blade into his own throat. His body crumpled to his knees as his friends cried out in horror. Dan thought he heard the distant sound of boots running away. She'd let the man go.

Oliver let loose another arrow and Dan yelled through his gag to muffle the sound of the arrow hitting whatever was behind Lillian's image. To the Kazats' eyes, the arrow buried itself in the image of the victim's chest. He fell to the floor, and the Kazats yelled at Oliver in fear and anger. Lillian gave him a gracious nod of thanks as she knelt gracefully, bending over to touch her lips to the dying man's throat. A moment later, she straightened, blood running from her mouth as she smiled evilly.

Oliver's men panicked. They eyed each other, as though wondering who should try to get past her first.

"There are no such things as upira," Oliver snarled as he drew his sword. He raised the blade above his head and ran at Lillian.

Dan thrashed to get loose. She wouldn't be far away from her image. Oliver still might hit her, but the eyes of Lillian's image turned red again, and she smiled at Oliver, desire and longing evident on her blood-stained features. She raced directly toward him, her speed too fast to be real, the sound of her footfalls masked by the hammering of Oliver's boots on the flagstone floor.

As they drew close, Lillian darted right through his defenses and jumped up to clamp her mouth onto his neck. He went down with a large thud and a clatter. His hands fluttered uselessly, and Dan heard another distinctive thud and grunt before Oliver lay still.

Lillian sat up, wiped her mouth on her sleeve and smiled at the horror-frozen men around the room. "So kind of him to volunteer, and his blood is so much stronger than hers." She frowned thoughtfully. "I think it would be easier to help the rest of you sleep if I just…." She gave a little moan of pleasure, and her skin shuddered. Lillian's body collapsed next to Oliver, who immediately sat up, the whites of his eyes blood red. He leered at his men and stood, scooping up his sword from the ground as he went.

The Kazats fled in terror, Williams far ahead of them, their screams echoing through the hallways as they raced away.

Immediately Dan felt Lillian working at the ropes around his hands. He sagged against the chair, wondering if he might die of pure joy. She was alive.

"Sit forward, Dan," she hissed. "You weigh a ton, and I've got to hurry. He's going to come around any second." The panic in her voice shook him to his senses, and he turned his wrists so she could get at his bonds.

Seconds later, his hands were free. He removed the gag in his mouth and helped her untie his feet.

When Oliver groaned in pain, Dan was ready.

Oliver turned and retched, emptying his stomach onto the heavy club Lillian must have hit him with. Dan let him finish before slamming the hilt of his own sword to Oliver's head and watching clinically as his cousin collapsed again. "That ought to do it for a while longer." Half a minute later, Oliver was trussed in knots as merciless as his own had been.

Dan jumped up, panting a little, and turned to Lillian, who stood pale and trembling next to him.

"Thank you," she said weakly. "I couldn't hit him quite hard enough."

She moved to take a step but stumbled, and he gathered her into his arms, holding her tightly. "For the record, I am *so* angry with you," he said, pressing his lips to her hair over and over.

"Why?" she asked weakly.

"It wasn't safe. What were you thinking by coming back?" he demanded.

She reached up to pat his face sleepily. "Silly. I could never leave you there. I love you too much, Dan," she breathed before going limp in his arms.

Something strange was happening in the general vicinity of his heart, something to do with her words, but it was foolishness. She couldn't have known what she said. He supported her with one arm and pulled her medication from inside his jacket with the other. He whipped the stopper free and dripped her medicine into her mouth.

"Please don't seize, please don't seize," he chanted under his breath as he lifted her into his arms and carried her toward the door. An arrow was embedded in the wall where her image had first entered the room. Another was stuck against a different wall near the floor. The body of the man she'd first taken down was missing. She had let him run away. Dan moved through the halls on high alert, considering what to do if the men came back. He stopped every minute to drip more medicine into Lillian's mouth.

"Forell." Sir Carlos waved at him from a distance after the second pause.

"What happened?" Dan asked, hefting Lillian in his arms again.

"Hollis brought me back," Sir Carlos said darkly. "He's gone for reinforcements. What has happened here?" He reached a hand toward Lillian as he approached, then smiled in relief. "She's only sleeping."

"You don't think she'll have a seizure?"

Carlos gave him a startled look and put a hand to Lillian's forehead before shaking his head. "No. She'll be fine."

"The other sorcerers are in danger," Dan blurted out. "They may have already been poisoned," Dan said. "Lillian incapacitated Oliver."

"Oliver?"

"And she chased off the Kazats working with him."

Carlos eyed Lillian's limp form with respect.

Dan added grimly, "And she saved my life." It hurt to admit that she had to rescue her defender, but he was tired of people underestimating her.

The healer gave him a sympathetic look and touched the back of Dan's head. The sharp pain from Williams' blow dwindled. Dan nodded his thanks before hurrying with Carlos to the dining hall. He wanted to take Lillian to her room. She deserved rest, but he couldn't leave her alone at a time like this, so instead he carried her along. They found the sorcerers still at their meals.

"Stop!" roared Carlos. He ran to the table and sniffed at different dishes while his peers watched him curiously. "The wine and the meat are both poisoned," he announced after a moment.

There was a general outcry from the sorcerers and an even louder one from their defenders.

"Anyone who's had either will follow me to the dispensary immediately," Carlos yelled above all of them. "I have something to help you throw up, and considering what's left inside you may still kill you, I'll be keeping all of you close the rest of the evening."

Sir Drake cursed furiously. "I've had both." He looked up from his plate, noticing Lillian for the first time. "What's happened to Lillian?" he asked worriedly.

She was immediately surrounded by sorcerers, the pack of them behaving like anxious grandmothers.

"Was she poisoned?"

"Is that blood on her sleeve?"

"What happened to her?"

"To the dispensary," Carlos roared. "She's only sleeping."

The disgruntled sorcerers allowed their defenders to herd them after Sir Carlos, and Dan turned back to the dining room. Sir Pescall stood, surveying the tables. "I don't eat meat," he said, frowning. "And I promised Lillian I'd show her the puppies today. They don't like the smell of wine on me."

He stared silently at Lillian a moment before looking to Dan. "I would have watched all my human friends die tonight, and I wouldn't have been able to help them." He stumped closer. "Are you sure she's only sleeping?"

Were his wild hair and beard more tame today, or was it the tenderness in his normally savage eyes that made him look more civilized?

"She sleeps off her big magic." Dan quickly summarized what had happened. "Williams may still be on the grounds with the Kazats, but I don't dare leave her."

Sir Pescall smiled. "Don't worry about them. It will be my pleasure to round them up." He looked into the distance as though listening, then chuckled. "Sounds like some of the idiots took a few of our horses." He paused again before adding, "And a lone soldier a quarter mile out is running directly toward a moose. Have you ever seen someone trampled by a moose?" He caught Dan's look and shrugged. "I'll make sure they're alive enough for questioning." His gruff demeanor returned. "And I'll send a few of the puppies in a basket for Miss Loraine. That way she can't accuse me of breaking my promise." He stomped off, muttering under his breath. Dan could have sworn the defender shadowing Pescall grinned at him.

Lillian

L illian woke when Dan deposited her in her bed.

"Here's your medicine again, Lil," he said coaxingly.

She smiled sleepily at the pet name. "Mmm. You take such good care of me." She closed her eyes. Maybe if she fell asleep quickly, she wouldn't have to take the vile stuff.

"That's what defenders do," he said, shaking her shoulder gently and pressing her vial of medication into her hand. "What defenders do *not* do is let their sorcerer risk their life to save them."

"What an idiotic thing to say, Daniel Forell," Lillian said, squinting open one eye to glare up at him. "You have my friend-ship, even if you don't want it. I help my friends."

His expression softened. "Yes. You do." He shook his head. "I don't think I've ever had such a good friend."

She narrowed her eyes at him. "Are you making fun of me? You don't even *like* me."

He sighed. "Lillian, you terrify me. That doesn't mean I don't care about you."

"That's why you frown at me all the time. You're *scared?*" she scoffed.

He knelt at her bedside and took her hand, looking her in the eye. "No woman has ever scared me more. I'm terrified you could be hurt." His thumb traced lines on hers, and she relaxed deeper into her pillow. "I want to help you, keep you safe. Now take this." He lifted her hand to bring the tiny vial closer to her mouth.

"You think working with the army would make me safer." She took her medicine, making a face.

"I thought it would make you more powerful, so safer, yes."

"Is that what Madsen wants?"

Dan cursed under his breath. "Madsen doesn't have any idea how precious you are. He only thinks about the next big job. He doesn't see your full potential. Your gift is incredible, but coupled with *who* you are, you could *prevent* battles, not just win them. You should negotiate peace treaties, be the king's personal advisor. You could *lead* the army sorcerers."

"How nice, Dan. Do you know, I don't mind at all that you're exceptionally silly." Lillian closed her eyes, sleep beginning to claim her again.

"Thank you for your friendship, Lillian."

She distinctly felt the press of his lips against her hand.

The moment Lillian opened her eyes the next morning, she moaned in horror. How could she have just blurted out to Dan that she loved him? What kind of girl said such a thing to a man without him saying it first?

And he hadn't said it back.

The kind of girl who did that would be the kind of girl who would impersonate a rabid upira to save his life. Well, she was the knight in shining armor this time. She'd risked her life to save him, so it was only right that she professed her love afterward. That's what the hero did in stories. She buried her face in her pillow to muffle her giggles, then snuggled deeper into her covers. He'd think she wouldn't remember anyway, and that would make it easier. Maybe she'd sleep in today.

She was halfway into a dream when something moved beside her. Lillian gave a muffled scream and threw herself to the far side of the bed, looking back to see something white and fluffy regarding her with interest.

One of Sir Pescall's puppies. Lillian grinned and reached out to cuddle it just as Dan burst into the room, his sword drawn. He wore nothing but his trousers.

"What's the matter?" he demanded. He strode quickly around the room, his eyes roving the place for dangers. Lillian didn't say anything at first, just watched him with interest, trying not to ogle. His hair was disheveled, and his feet bare. The hint of a beard shaded his chin, and his eyes were bright with excitement. How could she have thought him only somewhat handsome when she first met him? He was devastatingly perfect.

He finally looked to her, and she shook herself, wondering if she was blushing. "The puppy startled me. I'm sorry to alarm you."

He relaxed visibly and leaned against a wall to chuckle at the ceiling. "Lillian, only *you* would remain absolutely silent when attacked by archers but scream when you're attacked by an affectionate puppy."

"Archers? Yesterday is a little blurred in my mind." She didn't feel the least bit guilty for the deception.

"You'd done some amazing sorcery, and you were tired, a bit out of your mind, I suppose," he said almost wistfully.

"And I woke up in a night dress."

Dan's eyes widened before he shut them tight. He must have finally realized she wasn't dressed for the day. "Lady Teresa got back last night. She woke you up to help you."

He was so adorable.

"She was the only woman available. I hope I did the right thing."

"Of course. Thank you." Lillian remembered Lady Teresa's help perfectly well.

She looked down at her nightdress. It was actually only a slip. She'd thrown off the heavier gown immediately after Lady Teresa had left the night before. The heat had been unbearable. Lillian squashed her own embarrassment in order to enjoy

Dan's discomfort.

He stumbled back into his room and shut the door. Lillian hid her face in her pillow and laughed while the puppy snuffled her hair, and its sister toppled out of the basket nearby.

She rubbed the puppies' ears a few minutes before she bounded out of bed. Her first two romances had been almost accidental on her part. Convenient. They were men who seemed smitten with her. She liked the idea of being adored, but a man she had to chase, to convince... That sounded surprisingly interesting. Dan couldn't be *completely* averse to her. He'd kissed her hair, and later her hand, she was almost certain, and he'd almost kissed her the previous morning in Rosenlen. The memory of their shared kiss at the surprise party warmed her cheeks. Maybe he only needed a little encouragement.

They didn't speak much on the way to breakfast, and once in the dining room, Lillian was surrounded by smiling sorcerers who thanked her repeatedly for finding the spy and saving them from poisoning.

"*Sir Carlos* saved you from poisoning," she said, "though I'm glad I could help."

Lady Teresa Juárez gave her a friendly smile from the other side of the room.

After breakfast, the general beckoned to Lillian and Dan. "The hound has disappeared," he said without preamble. "Our men tracked him past Perch Harbor."

Lillian took a sharp breath at the sound of her home, but the general smiled reassuringly. "He left the harbor quickly, and then we lost track of him. We believe he's gone home."

She could have hugged General Adams.

"You are, of course, free to return home, Lady Lillian, but I hope you will consider staying and working with us here. Your gift is of tremendous value, but it's more than that." He glanced over his shoulder. "The sorcerers are so much happier since you came. Everyone is. You are simply a delight, and we'd be so happy to have you stay. You'd name the terms, of course."

"Thank you, General Adams," Lillian said. "My defender and I will discuss the possibilities."

The general nodded and turned to Dan. "Forell, come with me," he barked. More gently aside to her, the general added, "If that's all right with you, my dear. We've an important matter of security to discuss."

"Of course."

The general moved away to join Uncle Hollis and several other sorcerers clustered at a table.

"You'll be all right for a minute?" Dan asked.

"I'm fine," Lillian said, buttering some bread at the sideboard. "You'd better see what he wants."

He joined the general as Lady Teresa motioned to her from a table near the far wall. Lillian buried her disappointment. She'd wanted to eavesdrop on her defender, but she quickly joined Lady Teresa.

"You'd like to hear their discussion, wouldn't you?" her newest friend asked with a small smile.

"Of course I would."

"The general didn't want to offend your sensitivities, but I think you deserve to hear it."

"You can tell me?"

Lady Teresa smirked while her grand-nephew chuckled behind her. "I can do better than that."

"Sir Hollis brought the truth-teller last night." The general's voice was directly beside her, and Lillian turned, startled, but he wasn't there. Lady Teresa gave her a meaningful look, then glanced at the men at the far table.

"Oh," Lillian breathed. "You can project sound." This went far beyond being able to hear great distances.

"You should eat your breakfast while you listen," murmured Lady Teresa.

Lillian nodded and took a bite as the general said, "The five Kazats and Williams were all questioned. They were working with that fanatic Kazat clan leader, Filip Reznik. He planned his conquest of Kalmar to begin with your deaths. Somehow he learned Oliver was unsatisfied with his current role as defender, and Reznik slowly bought him out."

"I. Should. Have. Seen."

"Not at all, Sir Hollis," Dan said. "If anyone should have noticed, it was I." After a pause, he added, "Has Oliver been questioned yet?"

Lillian tensed, suddenly aware of the pain Dan must be in. She was stupid not to have thought of it before.

CHAPTER 25

Dan

"We haven't questioned him yet," the general said, frowning. "I suspect he knows more than the rest, and is also more capable of withholding information from the truth-teller. It's very likely he'd choose execution over informant and life in prison."

Sir Hollis looked troubled, and Dan frowned more sternly than perhaps was needed. He couldn't think of a better way to cover the turmoil boiling inside. Grief and anger at his cousin's betrayal. The relief of having Lillian safe and the fear of having to leave her. Surprise at General Adams' offer to Lillian and the hope and dread fed by her lack of outright refusal. And of course, the sobering prospect of Oliver's imminent trial and likely execution.

"He tried to kill Lady Lillian," Sir Adivino said. "A quick death is too good for him." He was right, of course.

"He tried to kill all of us," Sir Iloh said. "And I, for one, would like to help him talk. A few of his fingers freezing and falling off might be just the thing to help him remember important details." As much as Dan had learned to dislike Sir Iloh since bringing Lillian to the garrison, the man's reasoning was sound. It still wouldn't be enough to make Oliver talk though.

Sir Pescall seemed to agree. "And if not," he said grimly, "we could tie him down and let a few vultures at him. I guarantee that having your eyes plucked out by the birds would be even more convincing than watching your fingers fall off." Trust Sir Pescall to come up with something like that.

Dan glanced to Lillian, who sat talking with Lady Teresa at a distant table. Lillian's posture held a tension it hadn't before, and he wondered what the two women could be discussing.

"How about having all your clothing turn instantly to hot ash? I've been wanting to try that out on someone," said Sir Drake, his voice laced with hate.

"What say you, Forell?" Sir Carlos' voice cut across a few other suggestions.

"Well, if he still won't talk, I admit I would prefer a quick execution rather than torture. He tried to kill the woman I... defend." It didn't seem the right time to say she was the woman he loved. "And I don't like the idea of him getting another chance at it. However, he is my family, and he intended to kill us all quickly and relatively painlessly. I think we could afford him the same courtesy." He wasn't actually sure he thought that, but he probably would the next day when he'd had time to sort it out.

There were a few grudging murmurs of assent. "Also, Forell," Sir Iloh said, watching Dan closely. "I'm sure you've noticed we feel quite protective of our Miss Loraine. If you should ever consider doing anything to make her sad, I hope you will remember our propensity for... creativity."

There was a pregnant pause while Dan locked eyes with the sorcerer. He wanted a fight if he was suggesting Dan would ever do anything to hurt Lillian. So what if the man could strike him dead where he stood?

Finally he spoke, keeping his words low but measured and solemn. "I will defend Lillian Loraine's happiness and safety to my last dying breath, regardless of whether I remain her defender."

"Well said, man," Sir Drake said, clapping him on the back. The other sorcerers echoed their agreement, and Dan looked to Lillian. She faced away from him, but she brushed at something on her face. Could she be crying? No. Lady Teresa was smiling widely, the sweetest smile he'd ever seen on her face. Lillian did tend to bring out the best in people.

When he joined her a few minutes later, Lillian gave him a radiant smile that threatened to push all rational thought from his mind. Pulling himself together as best he could, Dan asked quietly, "Would you really consider staying with the army sorcerers?"

"I can help here. You were right about that, though I think I could be of value at home too," she said quietly, leaning closer to him as though to keep the conversation private from the few people across the room. She couldn't know what her proximity did to his ability to concentrate.

"I agree," Dan said, not completely sure what he was agreeing to. Sir Iloh looked up at them from across the room. "Why don't we go for a walk around the garrison, and we can talk about it."

"I'm afraid I need a nap," Lillian said with a yawn. "So most of that discussion will have to wait."

Once in the deserted hallway, Dan found the courage to ask the next important question. "And do you already have someone in mind for your next defender?"

"What?" She glanced up at him, her brow furrowed.

"I overheard you talking with Sir Iloh," he said quietly, still walking. "I know you'd like a new defender as soon as possible. I hope you know I'll help you find someone. You won't have to discuss it with Madsen."

She tugged on his arm to stop him. "Dan, we were talking about Uncle Hollis and Oliver, *not about us*."

Oh.

"As a matter of fact," she added primly, not meeting his eye, "I've grown quite fond of my defender and would like to keep working with him."

He stared at her, not quite trusting his hearing.

"Indefinitely," she said. "If he wants."

Oh. After another incredulous pause, he blurted out, "I'd like that too. I mean, I want to."

She gave him a small smile before walking forward again. He'd already searched her room for her before she spoke again. "We will, of course, have to decide what to do about the engagement."

"What do you mean?"

"Well, we can't stay engaged forever, can we?" she said with an angelic smile. And with those horrifying words ringing in his ears, she closed the door between them.

Dan found himself alone in the corridor, all sorts of alarming possibilities flitting through his mind. Would he spend the rest of his life disguised as a female? Lillian could certainly manage that. He wished he dared form the words to tell her how he felt.

The sound of footsteps pulled him from his thoughts. Lady Teresa approached with an assessing look, her defender beside her.

"Ah, Mr. Forell. Just the person I wanted to see," she said.

He bowed.

"I confess I'm curious, Mr. Forell."

"About what, Lady Teresa?"

She glanced toward Lillian's door and lowered her voice. "I'd like to know if you've learned Lillian's secret, why she's so powerful."

"Her illusions?"

"Of course not. They are amazing, to be sure, but they aren't the source of her power."

"The source?" he asked, not following.

Lady Teresa watched him patiently while her defender stood nearby, looking back and forth as any good guard would. His smirk gave him away.

"You mean what motivates her?" Dan asked, a little unnerved.

Lady Teresa folded her hands at her waist, her posture relaxed, as though they had all day for this conversation.

Perhaps she was teasing him. He'd always wondered if she had a sense of humor.

"You haven't noticed any other talents?" she asked.

"Well, she makes people love her, but that isn't part of her sorcery."

"Not in the way you mean, but how do you think she does it?" she prompted. "Make people love her, I mean."

If it had been any other sorcerer asking him, Dan would have made a short remark and excused himself, but Lady Teresa was a woman, and she never heckled anyone. If anything, she had the patient look of someone trying to be helpful.

He thought for a moment before guessing aloud, "She loves them first, right from the time she meets someone. Even the ones she doesn't really like, she still loves them. Well, not me, I suppose," he admitted fairly. "She thought I was horrible. It took her forever to think I was worthwhile."

Lady Teresa smiled as though he'd just recited his lesson perfectly. "Very good, Mr. Forell. I was afraid I might have to explain it to you. Her most remarkable magic is motivated by love." She inclined her head at him and moved away, her defender following in her wake.

Dan stared after her, his mouth open in surprise. Did she actually think he had a chance?

He walked slowly to his room, more troubled than ever.

Lillian

That evening, Lillian dressed carefully for dinner. She rearranged her hair at least three times. Dan needed some sort of incentive to admit he loved her. If he did. Cornering him in his bedroom and kissing him was the most interesting option, but it lacked finesse, and was probably a little inappropriate. Gentle hints hadn't been working. She also had to be sure he wasn't just sorry for her, wasn't just trying to keep the peace between them.

She looked at herself once more in the glass and frowned. She could cheat with her appearance, of course, but she needed her focus elsewhere.

When Dan arrived to escort her to dinner, she immediately resumed their conversation.

"I think we could stay here at the garrison for a while and see how it goes, but there are some things I'll want to do differently."

"Yes?" He studied her quietly, his eyes serious. She thought he'd be more excited at the prospect.

"Well, for one, I'll appear to be a man when we're walking around the garrison. I don't like the way some of the men look at me, even when I'm with you."

"Has anyone done anything offensive?" he asked sharply.

"I would simply be more comfortable." This wasn't the time for him to go hack people up. He was supposed to tell her he loved her.

They walked in silence for a few moments. "And I'd also

want to visit home frequently. Uncle Hollis has already offered to bring us back and forth any time we wish."

"Lillian, I don't think it would be a good idea."

"To visit home? But Dan, just think of the need for—"

He held up her hand to stay her. "No, no. I mean, I don't think you should live here. You're too good to be here. You belong at home."

A rush of relief hit her so unexpectedly, she nearly choked on it. "Are you sure you could stand Perch Harbor?" she asked curiously. "We'd visit the garrison regularly of course, but I mean, to live there?"

He stopped, and she turned to face him. "Lillian Loraine. Wherever you are is where I want to be. It will be my home."

No one could blame her for her response, she reasoned later. It was perfectly instinctual to throw herself into his arms and kiss him fervently.

Dan responded instantly, almost reflexively, his arms clasping her tight and his lips moving against her with a passion that left her breathless. When she pulled him even closer, he lifted her off her feet and deepened their kiss. Being held by him was better than she remembered, and this time she knew the kiss was for her, not because anyone was watching. Things were getting extremely interesting when Dan suddenly froze.

He set her gently on her feet and straightened. "Lillian, I'm sorry," he panted, his gaze panicked.

She refrained from rolling her eyes at him. "For kissing me or for stopping?"

He dropped his face into his hands.

Her racing heart sank in her chest. "You regret it that badly?"

"No," he moaned. "I want to *keep* kissing you. It makes me a bad defender."

Her heart lifted a notch. "Oh, and here I thought you'd come to your senses and were scared."

That made him look up. "Scared?"

"Well, you know what I am." She said it flippantly, but anxiety tore at her insides. It was better to get this part over with.

"What you *are*?" he asked, his brow deeply furrowed.

"You know. The scary part." She conjured several horrific monsters out of thin air and sent them prowling around the two of them. For good measure, she gave one of them hundreds of needle-like teeth and another skin that boiled molten rock.

Dan jumped at their appearance, but then chuckled. "Oh, Lillian, I love you."

Lillian exhaled sharply, and her monsters disappeared.

Dan frowned as though just realizing what he'd said. He took a step back, watching her warily.

She took a cautious step forward. "Did you mean that, Dan?"

"Of course I did," he practically grumbled. "Everyone loves you."

"You mean you love me like my friends love me." Some of the more choice swear words she'd picked up at the garrison came to mind. A treacherous tear began to form in one eye.

Dan sighed. "Not exactly." Their eyes met across the space separating them. "It is very likely you wouldn't want me as your defender if I told you how deeply in love with you I am. I have been for some time." He swallowed, the notch at his throat bobbing deeply. "I didn't want to scare you."

"Scare *me*? Did you learn to make better monsters than I can?"

He closed his eyes and smiled tiredly before looking at her. "It's all right, you know. If you don't return my feelings," he said gently. "We don't have to speak of it again. Or we can find you a different defender as you originally wanted."

What a perfect, wonderful idiot. He really meant it. She took a step forward, intending to tell him she loved him, but a wave of shyness halted her. "Daniel Forell," she said, her voice embarrassingly hoarse. "I don't want anyone but you."

She wasn't sure which of them closed the distance, but there he was, gently tracing her jaw. She lifted her face to him, and he pressed a careful, tender kiss to her lips before looking deeply into her eyes, evidently waiting for her reaction. Lillian didn't hesitate to slide her hands up his shoulders and around his neck, pulling him down for another kiss.

When he instantly drew her back into his embrace, Lillian smiled jubilantly against his lips. Dan's kisses weren't the sort she'd ever been given. She'd been kissed, and they'd been mostly pleasant experiences, but no one else's kisses did this to her. Her head swam, and she had difficulty catching her breath as he drew her tighter to him. One of his hands moved around her waist to the small of her back, pulling her nearer, while his other hand moved to her shoulder and then up to the nape of her neck.

All too soon, distant voices broke the quiet. He released her with obvious reluctance.

"Should we go tell the general our plans?" she whispered.

He threaded her arm through his, making her smile contentedly, and they made their way to the dining hall, where Lady Teresa gave her a knowing look. She didn't seem surprised at all when they announced their plans, though the other sorcerers voiced their disappointment and repeated encouragement for her to come back and join them whenever she wished.

Sir Iloh was the most insistent, and Dan watched him with a frown.

"Let's leave tonight," he said quietly aside to her at the next opportunity.

Lady Teresa laughed aloud from the far side of the room.

"Right. Choice. I. Think," Uncle Hollis told her when she was able to break free of the group and speak with him alone. "He's. Good. For. You. You'll. Be. Happy. At. Home."

"Promise you'll visit me at least a few times a week? Dan said he'll go to his academy with us and help you find a new defender. You'll let us help choose, won't you?"

He'd nodded when she first spoke, but now shrugged his shoulders haltingly. "Don't. Need. One."

"Of course you don't, but I need to know someone is looking out for you." She glanced around before whispering, "If you get sick, or hurt, or have to go somewhere dangerous, I don't want you alone."

He gave her a tolerant smile, "I've. Been. Strange. Places. Alone."

"Stranger than my home?"

He chuckled. "There," he said, nodding to the window.

Lillian turned to look out onto the practice fields, at first not understanding. She looked farther to the horizon, where an almost full moon was rising. His meaning suddenly struck her.

"You've been to the moon, Uncle Hollis?" she choked out. "How could you—" She stared at him in wonder, and he smiled wryly.

"Cold. I. Didn't. Like. It. First. Time. No. Air."

"You've been there more than once?" She kept her voice down with significant effort.

He frowned thoughtfully, then reached haltingly into his pocket. He drew out two small, lumpy, grey stones. "Brought. Back."

She took one of the stones, turning it over in her hands. "Uncle Hollis," she breathed. "Can I go with you next time?"

He quickly shook his head. "Too. Dangerous."

"But then you mustn't go," she said quickly. "I need you too much. You are my only living relative. I love you. I can't do without you."

He reached for her hand and closed it around the rock. "I. Will. Wait. Many. Years. I. Promise."

That was probably the best she could ask for now. "Thank

you." She hugged him fiercely but as gently as she could, and he patted her back.

"Keep. It," he said when she tried to give the moon rock back.

"How can I?" she said, laughing in wonder. "This is impossibly rare and valuable. Like you."

He chuckled again. "But. No. One. Can. Tell."

"I can tell. Your friends can tell. We all want you to have a defender. Please."

He grinned. "You're. Convincing."

She laughed in relief. "Thank you, Uncle Hollis."

It took a long time to bid her new friends a temporary goodbye. When it was Sir Pescall's turn, she was surprised to see a pack of hounds sitting obediently behind him.

"My pack is getting too large for the garrison," he said grumpily. "So I'm sending some of them with you. They're the best guard dogs in the world, and I've explained to them you'll take them with you."

"Really?" Sir Pescall loved his dogs more than any human, she was certain.

"I chose out the ones who'd be happier in a rural setting. Peony here is wild about the ocean." He nodded at a particularly vicious-looking brindle hound with mismatched eyes. She wagged her tail at him. "I'll teach you and Forell their commands. Your defender can't be with you all the time. They'll help keep you safe."

Lillian embraced Sir Pescall tightly, and he awkwardly patted her shoulder.

"You must visit us regularly. They'll be so sad if you don't," she whispered.

"I may visit at that," he said grumpily.

When Sir Iloh took her hand to kiss it, Dan appeared at her side. "Sir Hollis is ready." He gave Sir Iloh a cool look.

"If you ever tire of your defender, Lillian, you always have a place with us," Sir Iloh said. "And I suppose you can bring him with you."

Lillian laughed at his teasing, shaking her head. "I'm sure I'll see all of you soon."

"And the general already explained how to send messages to us?" Sir Adivino asked. "I feel you may need to contact us soon." His brows knit together, and she briefly wondered if he'd seen something coming, but she was going home with the man she loved. Not even dire predictions of the future would sway her mood, though maybe she'd watch carefully for trouble.

CHAPTER 26

Dan

Lillian stood at the balcony, staring out toward the ocean with the first frown Dan had seen on her face since they'd come home to Perch Harbor a week ago. Regardless of her troubled expression, she was still beautiful, loose wisps of hair floating around her head as the breeze from the ocean swept up the hill.

"What's the matter?" Dan asked softly, handing her a pink rose he'd snagged from the garden below. He wondered when he had gotten used to talking softly around her. It didn't bother him, and really, it was better for a defender not to advertise his conversation with his assignment.

She held the rose up to her face and inhaled, smiling contentedly. "Nothing. I don't think so anyway." She glanced toward the water again. "Something just seems a little off, about three miles out. It's silly, but I can't figure it out."

"What do you mean, 'off'?" Dan said, reaching out to smooth one of the wisps of hair back into place. She was lovely with it flying around, but it gave him an excuse to touch her. His uncertainty still pressed on him. He knew of no protocol, no prior example of a defender falling in love with his young and beautiful assignment. He'd heard of a few sorcerers married to their defenders, but the people in question were well into their forties when they'd married, and he didn't know anything else of them. He wanted to ask her to marry him, but was afraid to mis-step. He couldn't be sure she loved him, and she had two prior fiancés, so she might be hesitant to move that direction again.

She looked deeply into his eyes before blinking a few times and answering his question. "I don't know. Something about the light. Would you like to practice again?" They'd spent hours each day with Lillian making imaginary opponents for Dan to battle. With coaching from the army sorcerers, her abilities had grown even further.

He gathered her into his arms. "Maybe in a minute. Will anyone think less of us if I embrace my assignment?"

"I don't think anyone is watching," she whispered.

He immediately pulled her tighter.

"Except Mr. Jensen in the garden below. Oh, and my aunt, through the window to the left."

Dan sighed and loosened his hold, slowly stepping away.

Lillian snickered. "What's the matter, Mr. Forell?" She took a step toward him, and he backed up, trying to frown at her as she advanced.

"Lillian, you'll appear very forward," he warned, unable to keep the smile off his face. She looked so funny, like a kitten stalking a bear.

The whites of her eyes momentarily flashed red, and she smiled to reveal two rows of perfectly sharpened teeth.

Dan burst into laughter, and somewhere behind her mask, Lillian giggled. "What's the matter? I've been waiting for a kiss all day. I'm getting... hungry." She licked her lips invitingly.

"Oh, don't. You know I can hardly breathe when you do

upira." His sword practice the previous evening had involved fifty upira converging on him in the ballroom. He'd hardly been able to move from laughing so hard and had finally asked her to give him faceless attackers so he could get some work in. The complexity of her illusions had grown exponentially since they first left Perch Harbor, and Dan often wondered if Lady Teresa had been right about Lillian's best magic being motivated by love. He'd nearly asked her to marry him half a dozen times, but had always stopped himself, feeling she needed a little more time before he asked.

Her current illusion faded, just as Lillian reached out and fisted the lapels of Dan's jacket.

"Isn't your aunt watching?"

"No. We're just out of her line of sight now. I had double the reason to chase you."

Dan shook his head, looking heavenward and grinning. Lillian reached up and kissed the side of his neck. "Mmm. You taste better than any of my other victims."

At the touch of her lips, a jolt of something powerful raced down Dan's spine, and his chuckle subsided. He looked down into her eyes, and for a long moment, neither of them moved. Then, perhaps of their own volition, Dan's hands came to rest at her waist.

"You're so beautiful, Lillian."

She looked down, and he was ninety percent sure her blush was authentic.

"Thank you," she murmured. "But how would you know, really? Perhaps I'm old enough to be a great-grandmother. I could have been casting a young image on myself the entire time."

Dan's mouth pulled into a smile. "Even you're sleeping?"

"Maybe you only thought I was sleeping."

"Your snoring was certainly convincing."

Her eyes snapped to his. "My what?"

Dan laughed shortly before gathering her close again.

"I'd like to kiss you, Lillian. Without your aunt watching. You are very sure she can't see us?" he murmured.

Lillian inhaled sharply then whispered distractedly, "I moved the light to see from just behind her. We're well out of her line of vision."

Dan didn't hesitate any longer. The first kiss he gave Lillian was gentle. So were the second and third. When her fingers sank into his hair and pulled him closer, he abandoned caution and pulled her tight against him, deepening the kiss until he could taste her. To his relief, she matched his intensity, and they spent an extremely pleasant few minutes in each other's embrace before Lillian pulled back a little.

"Aunt Svea's coming to check on us."

Dan reluctantly loosened his hold and let his forehead rest against hers. "You're sure?"

"Yes," she said with a sigh.

Dan wondered if this was a good time to suggest they find a permanent solution to being able to spend time alone together, but Lillian cocked her head to one side. "Oh, that's what I should have tried."

"What?"

"With the ocean. Looking from behind. Come on," Lillian said resignedly. "We should seem busy anyway. Did your whiskers scratch me much?"

She raised her face, and Dan had to work hard not to kiss her again. "I'm afraid so."

"That's all right." The redness around her mouth disappeared very suddenly.

"That could come in handy."

"Frequently, I hope," Lillian said saucily.

Dan smiled, something he seemed to do a lot recently, and followed Lillian back to the edge of the balcony.

She stared out to sea, her eyes going a little unfocused, and Dan took the opportunity to study her face. Her expression was composed, beautiful, and peaceful.

For all of fifteen seconds.

Then Lillian gave a terrified gasp and latched herself to his side.

His sword was in his hand before he realized it. "What's happened?" he demanded, looking around for threats.

"They're coming!"

Lillian

Lillian took in great gulps of air, fighting back the fear choking her. She tried to explain but couldn't seem to make the right word combinations. "Oh, *here!*" she finally cried out, creating an image before his eyes.

She showed him everything. The five enormous ships, the innumerable Kazat soldiers already on deck in battle garb.

Dan studied the image intently, the muscles of his jaw twitching. "You're sure?"

"I finally looked from behind the disturbance. It isn't a disturbance at all. It's some sort of screen that mimics the ocean behind them. They're only a mile out."

"Show me the leaders?" His voice was calm, but his tense grip on her waist gave him away.

Lillian widened the image, fighting tears.

"There," Dan said, pointing at the first ship. "That's Hessian Fast, the Hound." He shook his head. "He wasn't trying to *capture* sorcerers. He was looking for areas not guarded by any."

Lillian shivered. "And I wasn't here."

"What about these two?" Dan said, indicating a pair at the front of the second ship. "They look like sorcerers."

Lillian wondered how he could guess that, but pulled her image to look at them more closely. "Twins."

"Madsen mentioned them. They'll be the disguise experts. Only instead of disguising people, they're disguising entire ships."

Lillian tried to tamp down her panic, but it was made more difficult by Dan's next words.

"But there must be more sorcerers."

"What?"

"Their ships are moving too quickly. Perhaps wind or water sorcerers. Let's hope they're worn out by the time they get here. And there must be an admiral or a general in command."

They spent a frantic half-minute scanning the ships before Dan pointed. "There. I know him from the paintings at the academy. That's Commander Andrej Strihat. They call him the Carver."

"Why?" Lillian wasn't sure she wanted to know.

Dan looked caught, as though he'd said too much. "He's a talented swordsman. Probably the best in the world." He must have seen Lillian's panic, because he added, "But he's not nearly the best commander, not even close."

"But he has sorcerers, and an army, and we're completely unprepared! No one is here to stop them!"

"Lillian!"

She turned to look at him, and he took her head gently in his hands. He was too calm, a slight smile on his lips. Maybe he'd tell her it wasn't real, that there was a simple answer.

"*You* are here, Lillian. You are more talented than practically any sorcerer in existence. *You* can stop them. *We* can stop them."

That wasn't what she wanted him to say.

His nose was almost touching hers. She wished she could go back to kissing him and pretend there wasn't an army of Kazats only a mile away, ready to kill them all. She wished she could believe her defender.

"Dan, there must be a thousand of them!"

"Closer to two thousand."

"Two thousand," she breathed.

"They're trying to start a war," Dan said, frowning. "There aren't enough of them to take the whole country. There must be other places they'll attack."

"We'll need to—"

"Contact the army sorcerers," they finished together.

They turned and raced back into the house and to the upper balcony, both yelling for the others in the house to come.

Lillian was already in the middle of projecting a call for help over the next three towns when Jensen and Aunt Svea arrived, panting, closely followed by Liv. She kept her back to them, hoping they wouldn't notice what she was doing.

"There's an army coming," Dan quickly explained. "Five ships, about two thousand men strong. And some sorcerers. They'll be here soon. Lillian is... She's hoping to see if the neighboring sorcerer can come."

"We already know she's a sorceress," Liv said impatiently. "What's the plan?"

Lillian looked over her shoulder, her concentration broken.

Aunt Svea and Dan's faces mirrored her amazement.

"We practically live here," Jensen said with a shrug. "How could we not notice?"

"And we've never told anyone," Liv added. "So just trust us."

A desperate laugh escaped Lillian's throat without interrupting her work.

"We've got to warn the village, get the children out," Aunt Svea said, still panting a little.

"I'll do that," Jensen said. "My wife and children will spread word to every house. Will help come in time?"

"No," Dan said decisively. "We might only have half an hour, maybe an hour if we're lucky."

"I can make it look like we have an army waiting for them,"

Lillian said, wondering if she really could. "But I couldn't make the sounds or anything else," she added, hopelessness pulling at her heart.

A manic glint shone in Liv's eyes. "My father was a soldier, and there must be twenty others like him in the village. They have bows, and we have the Mantila fireworks for the queen's birthday next week. We could lob those right down into the invaders."

Lillian's eyes widened at the blood lust in her sweet friend's voice.

"We have at least two drummers in the village," Jensen said. "And I'm still the best trumpeter in the district," he added, matter-of-factly.

"Liv," Dan said, his eyes never leaving Lillian's face. "Lillian will need all the medicine, juice, and cookies you can find."

Liv sprinted away without another word.

"I'll take a horse to the village, spread the word, and gather all able-bodied men," Jensen said. "And I'll send someone to notify the outlying estates."

He left abruptly, passing Sir Malick coming into the room. Aunt Svea quickly filled him in while Lillian finished the last of the distress signals.

Malick barked a short laugh. "Little Lillian a sorceress, eh? Happy to hear it. There's no one I'd trust more with all that power."

Lillian's heart lifted a notch at his instant acceptance.

"What about Hessian Fast?" she asked Dan. "Will he know it's just me?"

"If Madsen is right, he sees magic on people, but he also sees magic being made. He'll know there's magic, but not what it is."

"So if I made some fake sorcerers…"

"Yes, exactly!"

"Well, that's settled," Aunt Svea said firmly. "Sir Malick and I will join the archers. He taught me to shoot long ago."

"I think the beach is the spot for me," Sir Malick said. "But you must stay here, Svea. I love you too well to let you get hurt."

"Don't be an idiot," Aunt Svea said in surprise, her silver eyebrows raising. "I have to help. And you can't love me. I'm too old."

Sir Malick growled a low sound in his throat before pulling Aunt Svea into his arms and kissing her fiercely.

Lillian's surprise was quickly overruled by her worry. Aunt Svea and Sir Malick couldn't run fast enough if the army swarmed across the beach. Dan seemed to understand her silent pleading.

"If you can both fight, you're needed here."

"What?" Malick pulled himself away from a stunned Svea, who looked ready to throw herself back into her old friend's arms.

Good. Dan would convince them.

"You should both guard Lillian," he said. "I have to be on the beach."

Something heavy caught in Lillian's throat, but she swallowed it back. "Absolutely not."

CHAPTER 27

Dan

"I have to, love," he said simply.

"What do you mean, you have to?" Lillian whispered, her face white.

"Someone has to contend with them, neutralize their sorcerers."

She shook her head quickly. "Dan, you have to stay with me. I can't do this without you here."

The hurt in her voice tore at his heart. He snatched her hand and pulled her a little apart from the others.

"You are going to be just fine. Set the hounds to guard. You can do this."

"You can't go to that beach, Daniel Forell. It's too dangerous. You'll be trampled, even if they can't see you. You'd—"

He stopped her hurried speech with a firm kiss.

"Someone has to," he said. "And we can't ask anyone else to do it."

"What if you don't come back? I can't do without you, Dan. If you don't come back…"

He answered with more confidence than he felt. "If it's humanly possible, I'll come back. Of course, I wouldn't mind any help you can give me." He gathered her close, ignoring Svea's scrutiny. "I love you, Lillian. More than my life, more than anything."

Lillian's eyes widened at his words, and Dan allowed himself to kiss her once more before he broke himself away and almost ran from the room. "Don't leave her!" he called over his shoulder at the others. "And make sure she takes her medicine!"

As he hurried away, he heard Svea ask, "What are you going to do, Lillian?"

Panic in her voice, she answered, "I'm going to eat!"

Dan smiled briefly. She was perfect.

Trying not to think of the probable outcome of what he was about to do, he ran to his room and loaded himself with as many of his weapons as he could carry. By the time he mounted his horse and instructed Jake to take the hounds to Lillian and then help guard her, he was cursing the progress of time. He pushed his horse harder than he ever remembered, and by the time he made it to town, he saw Jensen at the center of a small crowd of armed men and women, most of whom he recognized from various parties at Lillian's home. Not far from them, a grandmother ushered several children into a wagon.

"Ah, Mr. Forell," Jensen said seriously when he dismounted. "I've explained everything. We've sent word around. The village is being evacuated. Should be ten or twenty more men on their way here. Some of the young men went to fetch the fireworks."

With the fifteen or so already present, that was more than Dan had hoped for. "We've got less than thirty minutes. Bowmen should divide themselves between the bluffs on either side of the beach. We have a sorcerer in town who will hide your location. Take out any leaders you see, but especially aim for any mature individuals not carrying weapons. They'll be the sorcerers. The Kazats shouldn't be able to see you, but if they figure it out and retaliate, take cover or run to your families. We're only trying to hold them until more sorcerers arrive."

Dan wondered if he was giving them false hope. There was a good chance no one would see Lillian's message or be able to come if they did. From the looks on the villagers' faces, he guessed they understood that already.

Geoffrey and Bennet, Melina's fiancé, arrived on horseback, accompanied by older men who could only be their fathers. Geoffrey averted his eyes from Dan, but Dan was only glad to have more able fighters.

Melina looked anxiously toward Bennet as she and her mother supported an ancient-looking woman toward the wagon of children.

"Once your supply of arrows is gone," Dan said, "make your way quietly off the bluff."

"We've got other ways to irritate the scum," an older man said gruffly, shaking a sling in his fist.

Several others murmured agreement.

"Good," Dan said. "If you ever become surrounded, hide yourselves the best you can, and we'll hope the sorcerer can lead the Kazats away from you."

The next five minutes were spent in hasty planning. When a small cart filled with fireworks arrived, Jensen took it and headed toward the beach, escorted by three weathered men carrying swords and torches.

"Stay behind the boulders," Dan called after them.

Jensen didn't turn around, but only waved over his shoulder in acknowledgement. Geoffrey and his father led a small band of men toward the west bluffs, and Bennet and his father led the other group toward the east.

Words suddenly appeared in the air before Dan, like writing on a page. *The first set are getting in the skiffs.* An image followed of fifty small boats, each carrying about ten men.

Dan gave the last of the instructions before racing toward

the beach. He glanced over his shoulder to see three wagons and a line of women and children working their way quickly toward the forest.

"Lillian," he mouthed the words. "Be safe." He moved forward, passing Jensen, who was setting up the first of the fireworks. "They're in hearing distance now," Dan whispered to him. "Watch for the sorcerer to show the cannons, and then you can start. And don't hit me."

"Hit you?" Jensen hissed back. "Where are you going?"

Dan didn't answer. He strode purposefully toward the beach, stopping just before his feet met sand. The creaking of the boats and the slap of the oars against the water were the only indication Lillian's concerns were real.

More writing appeared in the air before him.

I can hide you from anyone coming in from the beach. The archers are in position and will be able to see you, but no one in front of you will. The children have reached the tree line. My army is just about to come over the rise.

Lillian suddenly stood before him, her image ghost-like. "Come home to me," she mouthed at him.

He nodded, and she disappeared, just as the Kazat sorcerers let go of the disguise they were holding over their men. Almost five hundred soldiers suddenly appeared in formation on the beach a hundred yards away. Well beyond the breakers, five ships materialized, waiting for the skiffs that were already pushing off the beach.

Lillian

Lillian's heart beat painfully in her chest as she looked out from her vantage point on the upper balcony. Over twenty of her friends stood ready on the bluffs with bows and slings. Bennet's jaw twitched as he glared out toward the water, and on the opposite side, Geoffrey stood boldly on the ledge, striking a heroic pose. The idiot. Did he even know he was hidden from the advancing army? To hide the archers, she displaced the image of stands of trees in front of them. It was the easiest approach.

Her heart pounded in her ears, and she gave herself a dose of medicine. She'd already covered Jensen and the men with him by enlarging the rocks they stood near. But could she keep them safe?

She worried over a hundred problems at once. Would the Kazats destroy the town? Did they intend to go inland? Would the army sorcerers come? Did Uncle Hollis even see her message in the sky?

All those thoughts fled her mind when Dan stepped onto the beach opposite five hundred armed men. At that moment, the only thing she could worry about was keeping him alive.

"Here you are, dear," Aunt Svea said grimly, handing Lillian a large glass of juice. "Jake and Sir Malick are locking up the house and collecting weapons. Liv brought all the cookies and medicine we had on hand. I sent her to help evacuate anyone not fighting."

Peony, Sir Pescall's brindle hound with mismatched eyes, leaned her head against Aunt Svea's leg, and she reached down to pet her fiercely.

Lillian nodded and gulped down grape juice as she formed an image in her mind. She set down the cup and released her creation onto the hillside. From the Kazats' view, Kalmarian soldiers began cresting the hill and marching down toward the beach.

The hidden drummers took their cue and began the attack beat. Jensen's trumpet sounded. The body of advancing Kazats stuttered in their march up the beach, and even from so far away, Lillian heard their surprised shouts. She might have

261

laughed at the looks on their faces if she wasn't so overcome with terror. Dan was right in front of them.

"The archers?" Aunt Svea murmured.

Right. The next men that came into the Kazats' view held bows. She paused, making sure her real archers saw the imaginary ones before her false archers took aim.

She couldn't bear to watch the real arrows fly. Instead she focused on bringing the cannon over the hill, hoping that at a distance, no one could see well enough to realize that her soldiers didn't exactly know how to load it. She made a show of having one of them light a fuse, and Jensen took note. A few seconds later, a small explosion sounded directly in the middle of the Kazats. That did it. They broke formation and scattered to the sides.

Dan pointed toward the right of the group where a man was screaming instructions. As Lillian watched, he took an arrow to the chest. She shuddered and looked away. The skiffs moved back through the waves, heading toward the boats where seemingly countless soldiers waited to be ferried to the beach.

It only took a little flashing light to attract the archers' eyes. Seconds later, the oarsmen were showered with arrows. At least half the skiffs were unmanned before the others were cloaked with a screen. Her gaze flitted around the first ship to where Commander Strihat stood shouting, purple-faced, at the twins who gripped the rails, sweating heavily as they gazed out at the returning skiffs. Hessian Fast stood next to them, pointing urgently toward the shore and trying to get the commander's attention.

It took her a moment to realize he was actually pointing up at the manor house, at her.

She quickly drained an entire vial of medicine and released an image of a cloaked figure onto the top of the church tower. Hessian Fast gesticulated toward it, so for good measure, she sent another cloaked figure out from behind the trees next to the school.

Jensen's next round of fireworks was ready, so Lillian's false soldiers prepared the cannon again. By now her army was almost upon the Kazats. She hoped the drums covered the fact that her troops were absolutely silent.

Fast gesticulated forcefully, and Lillian feared what he might be saying, but that fear was nothing compared to her terror when Dan suddenly sprinted toward the center of the body of attackers, leading her false army. She barely heard the squeal of fear erupting from her throat. Making sure the screens guarding her friends were still intact, Lillian put all her energy into making the clash between the real and false armies realistic while at the same time hiding Dan. To the Kazat soldiers' view, the first line of Kalmarian soldiers slipped right through their defenses to attack the second line of Kazats, who then began hacking unknowingly at the backs of their own front line. The other casualties were mostly due to the archers. She never could have managed the images if she hadn't practiced the angles of so many attackers in Dan's daily fighting practice. As it was, she feared her images weren't as clear as they should be, and she counted on the chaos of the battle to keep the Kazats from noticing her soldiers' faces were almost all the same.

Dan danced unseen through their midst, dropping men left and right while the archers rained more arrows down onto the attackers. There were stones in the mix, so the arrow supply was dwindling. Jensen's fireworks exploded regularly within the Kazat ranks, but the men were still pushing their way across the beach. Meanwhile, more Kazats boarded the skiffs.

What they were doing wasn't going to be enough, and Dan was going to be killed. He steadily worked his way to a captain at the back of the group. Another man stood next to the captain, speaking too rapidly in Kazatani for her to lip read. The man took pauses frequently to hold still, as though he listened to something. She focused back on the ship where Commander Strihat spoke urgently, though no one was close to him. When he stopped talking, the Kazat on the beach immediately spoke to the captain again, and then the captain barked orders. The only words Lillian could really discern were, "not an army."

Only some of the Kazats seemed to believe their captain. Most swung their swords at their imaginary opponents, striking their own men in the process.

From some distance away, Dan drew a blade from a sheath at his side and flung it at the listening sorcerer, who went down immediately. Lillian wished she hadn't seen it happen.

The Kazat captain, now without a sorcerer to communicate Strihat's orders, urged his troops on. He then gave instructions to several men who ran to the sides of the beach and began to sneak around the rocks. The bowmen couldn't get a view of them, but Jensen's men were well-armed. Only a handful got past them and into the village, but because everything was displaced to their eyes, they only stumbled about, apparently trying to work their way to the fake sorcerers. Jensen set off more fireworks, and Dan cut his way closer to the Kazat captain. The enemy pressed him on all sides, and some were beginning to notice the disturbance. Lillian filled her soldiers into the path left by Dan, and the Kazats leapt toward them, cutting their comrades down in the process.

The Kazat captain retreated further toward the water, and though arrows and stones rained near him, none took him. Dan was already covered in blood, and Lillian had no idea how much was his. He was going to get himself killed trying to take that man out.

Lillian was doing too much already. A sheen of sweat broke out on her forehead.

She stuffed two cookies into her mouth and chased them with a large glass of grape juice. On her last swallow, something appeared next to her elbow, making her scream, and choke, and spray her juice all over…

"Uncle Hollis?"

Aunt Svea stopped her blade just in time to avoid his head.

Lillian grabbed Sir Hollis' hand. "Dan needs help," she said, pointing to the beach.

Sir Hollis looked pained. "Not. Fighter."

"Can you bring the other sorcerers?"

"Invaders. Everywhere."

The dogs whined, clearly asking for commands.

The dogs.

"Can you take the hounds to Dan?" she asked breathlessly. "He's next to that large rock."

Sir Hollis gave a triumphant smile and disappeared. He reappeared instantaneously next to one of the hounds, and both disappeared together. In a second, he was back, taking another dog.

Svea spoke soothing words to the remaining hounds, and Lillian focused on the beach. Dan had already given the dogs the instruction to attack. They tore down Kazats all around him. Lillian displaced their images by about five feet, enough that the swords swinging toward them missed their mark by far. Then, remembering the Kazats' propensity for superstition, she grew the images of the hounds until they were ten times their natural size. As Sir Hollis transported more hounds, Lillian became more creative. She gave each the back legs of a horse and a single eye. For good measure, the Kazats who were bitten appeared to be ripped apart and eaten by the hounds.

"Psoglav," the Kazat soldiers mouthed in terror. They didn't seem suspicious that these psoglav didn't mind the sunshine.

"It's all fake," their captain seemed to be screaming. Right before Dan took him down.

Lillian would have felt victorious if she couldn't see two hundred more Kazats jumping out of their skiffs.

CHAPTER 28

Dan

Had he been insane, Dan wondered as the Kazat captain fell at his feet. How could he survive long enough to be useful on this beach? The Kazats couldn't see him, but one had already sliced his arm by accident. At least it was his left. When the hounds began appearing, accompanied by flashes of Sir Hollis, Dan wasn't sure if he should be grateful or angry. They were supposed to be guarding Lillian. It was bad enough that *he* had to leave her.

On the other hand, when the horse-dog demons began shredding up the Kazats, Dan felt a surge of pride in Lillian's work. She really was amazing. But Lillian had been doing far greater magic than she'd ever done before. This had to end soon. She couldn't keep it all going forever.

"Sir Hollis," he roared, the next time the sorcerer put in an appearance. Lillian must have been watching and made him visible to her uncle because he flashed to a point on Dan's left while Dan cut down a soldier on his other side. "Is Lillian all right?"

Hollis nodded haltingly and disappeared, reappearing two seconds later with another dog, which instantly turned into a man-eating beast.

The smoke from the fireworks, and the screams of the injured contradicted the words of the Kazats' late captain, and the dogs were demoralizing, to say the least. Unfortunately, at least two hundred more Kazats appeared at the edge of the water, and though they didn't look as confident as the first batch had, the rain of arrows falling on them hit an invisible shield and slid harmlessly to the ground. Dan swore. Another sorcerer.

"Sir Hollis?"

Men around him looked his way but continued to fight against the imaginary foe. Sir Hollis appeared at Dan's shoulder.

"Will you take me to their sorcerer?"

Too late, Dan remembered he'd never travelled with Sir Hollis. A horrible, jarring sensation had his heart thudding to his navel, and then it was over. He stood next to a weathered old man staring up at the sky with a resigned frown.

In the tenth of a second it took for Dan to find his feet, he realized he shouldn't kill the man. Instead he struck him, hard, with the hilt of his sword. Incapacitating the innocent was much better than killing them. The jerking sensation resumed, and Dan found himself back in the center of the dogs. They looked around in confusion, nipping half-heartedly at the men around them.

"Attack," he quickly commanded. The growling resumed, along with a shower of unrestrained arrows and stones.

"Are more sorcerers coming?" Dan asked over the noise of the drums as he cut down the Kazats nearest him.

Sir Hollis shook his head sadly. "All. Busy."

"And more Kazats are coming?"

Lillian had been watching him, reading his lips. An illusion bloomed in front of him of Commander Strihat screaming purple-faced at his soldiers, who moved unwillingly into lines, awaiting the skiffs rowing back to the ships.

None of them wanted to be there, not the soldiers, not the sorcerers, but Strihat was terrifying. They were more afraid of him than Lillian's man-eating monster dogs. He had to be dealt with.

"Can you bring me their commander without getting hurt?"

Sir Hollis nodded once, a worried expression on his face, before disappearing. It took only as long as it had to retrieve a dog.

Andrej Strihat was still shouting orders when he landed on the sand in front of Dan, but faster than seemed possible, the man's sword was out and whipping in circles.

Sir Hollis was gone, thank goodness. Hopefully back to Lillian.

Dan wished he had time to rest. He was facing a fresh fighter, the most renowned swordsman in the world, and Dan had already been on the beach at least half an hour.

He paused to plan his attack, and in that time, one of the snarling hounds moved in on Strihat. He shouldn't have been able to see the dog coming, not with Lillian displacing its image by several feet, but Strihat's blade whipped out, and in a moment, the dog fell to the ground, dead.

Dan swore again.

Strihat raced toward another hound, and Dan quickly relieved a dead Kazat soldier of his bow and quiver.

His arrow flew straight. He knew it had. But Strihat's blade moved in a motion too fast to see, and the arrow hit steel.

"I know you're there," Strihat spat out with a thick accent. "And I know you're alone out here. Your little charade will end with your death. The other sorcerers are being hunted now. My men will not be stopped. All your fake arrows and monster hounds cannot save your little town. We will sweep through like a—"

Strihat flicked his blade again, and the knife Dan had hurled at his chest was deflected.

"Why don't you come closer? Or did you already know that my blade never misses my target? A convenient little magic trick. You Kalmarians think you're the only sorcerers, just because we don't advertise it like you do."

Dan didn't answer. He moved stealthily around the circle opened by the remaining hounds, not wanting to give away his position. All the while, the battle went on around them.

Some of the Kazats looked to their commander, but none of them seemed tempted to try passing Lillian's monsters.

Dan was certain that if the commander was defeated, his men would retreat. *Almost* certain. It probably wouldn't be enough for Lillian to only make it *look* like he was defeated.

He thought of Lillian, of her laugh, her beautiful eyes, her thoughtfulness. He considered what she might feel watching the outcome of this fight, and his heart felt leaden. He'd never hold her again, but if the army made it through to the valley, countless people would die.

Dan took a mental inventory of his remaining weapons: his sword, a few throwing knives, a blade in his boot. None of those could match a magic sword, but perhaps all of them, along with the one thing Andrej Strihat wouldn't be expecting.

Lillian

Five minutes prior

Controlling the screens hiding her friends while she gave the dogs their appearance from every angle, as well as displacing an entire village and creating sorcerers out of thin air, was nearly driving Lillian mad. The magic had never felt so slippery. She crammed another cookie in her mouth and washed it down with another cup of her medicine. Her stomach churned in protest, and Lillian prayed she wouldn't throw up.

Her fake archers released another volley of arrows, and sweat trickled down her face.

Lillian timed another cannon blast to coincide with Jensen's fireworks. His wagon of explosives was more than half-depleted.

The hounds who'd stood near Lillian suddenly erupted in growls and barks. Peony snarled aggressively.

"Lillian, look out," Aunt Svea suddenly shrieked.

Lillian ducked instinctively, and in the split-second she spared to glance over her shoulder, her concentration almost faltered. Several paces away, Sir Malick jumped between her and a Kazat soldier, while Aunt Svea loosed an arrow at another running at Lillian from the other direction.

Lillian pulled herself back to her work, hoping her images hadn't flickered and endangered her loved ones. She listened intently to the clash of swords behind her and bent some light to see over her shoulder. Sir Malick's work was gruesome, but effective, and the man he faced crumpled to the ground. Malick strode a few paces to the Kazat who'd taken Aunt Svea's arrow. Lillian didn't watch the death blow. Aunt Svea's cheeks were pale, but she nodded fiercely at Sir Malick. The two shared a measured look then went back to scouring the balcony for other assassins.

"More juice, Lillian," Svea called to her.

Lillian instantly obeyed, taking the next cup from the tray. Apple juice. She didn't even care how horrible it tasted. She gulped it down.

Sir Hollis reappeared, his eyes wide as he surveyed the dead men. Svea explained about the attack.

"I'll. Look. For. More."

Sir Hollis disappeared and came back several seconds later. "One. More. In. Garden."

Sir Malick and Aunt Svea notched arrows and stepped to the edge of the balcony.

"There," Sir Malick said, nodding his head toward the right.

Two thuds below told Lillian the arrows hit their target. She didn't need to look.

"How did they see you?" Sir Malick said, panting.

"Didn't you hide yourself, dear?" Aunt Svea asked.

Lillian shook her head, wanting to cry. Those three men were probably following orders, and if she'd been smarter, they wouldn't have had to die.

Aunt Svea seemed to read her mind. "They would have killed us all, dear, and Dan would've died in seconds."

Lillian nodded with a sniff.

"You are protecting everyone, darling."

"And doing a wonderful job of it," Sir Malick added.

Lillian sniffed again but nodded her head. She had to keep going.

"Army. Sorcerers. Fight. Assassins. At. Palace. I. Moved. King. Must. Check. On. Him."

They wouldn't come. The sorcerers had to protect the king.

"I'll. Leave. One. Dog. Here," Sir Hollis said, nodding to Peony.

He disappeared with another dog.

Lillian watched as Jensen and the men with him set up the last of the fireworks. One of them lit fuses while the others buckled swords about their waists, clearly intending to join the fight. She'd have to displace their images too.

She watched Dan and her uncle work together to neutralize the old Kazat sorcerer, and she loved Dan for not killing him.

The next thing Dan did wasn't quite so tender or confidence-inspiring. He asked Uncle Hollis to bring him Commander Strihat.

No! she wrote in the air in front of him. He never noticed. She was too slow. The commander appeared only yards from

Dan. She saw a flicker of her uncle's form before he disappeared again, back to check on the king. And if she read their conversation correctly, Dan now faced an unparalleled swordsman who was actually a *sorcerer*. She couldn't protect him.

Her army was deep in the ranks of the Kazats, but she had to let go of some of their angles. If the soldiers turned to look behind them, they'd see their comrades swinging swords at empty air, but it was too much. Her strength was fading.

That's what she thought—until Dan sheathed his sword and picked up two shields from fallen Kazats. He mouthed the words, "I love you, Lillian," and rushed Commander Strihat.

Lillian cried out in anger and surprise. He was going to be killed.

Willing all her other images to stay in place, Lillian made five Dans, all rushing the commander with raised swords. His real form remained invisible.

It made no difference.

Strihat's sword was too fast for her to follow. It flicked out three times, at last burying itself deep in Dan's leg.

Lillian gasped but couldn't look away, not if she could help Dan.

With a grimace of pain, he slammed one of his shields into Strihat's face. Stunned, the sorcerer took a step backward, but his sword stayed lodged in Dan's thigh. Dan lunged, somehow pulling out a hidden blade and burying it in the commander's navel.

Strihat screamed in pain and rage.

Then Dan punched him in the face, and then in the throat.

The commander pulled at his sword with all his might, and the blade came free, just as Dan buried another knife in the commander's heart.

Strihat dropped to his knees, his unbeatable sword falling from his limp hand. Several of his men shouted to each other, forgetting about the psoglav in their shock.

Afraid they would try to avenge their leader, Lillian turned an image of Strihat's face toward his men while the real commander collapsed to the ground.

"Retreat," the fake Strihat mouthed at his men in Kazatani. Dan understood immediately. "Retreat," the commander seemed to yell toward his men just as Dan's mouth formed the word.

Three more times the commander gave the order.

Then, as the Kazats began to obey, Dan fell limply to the ground, his face draining of color.

Lillian moaned in despair. His body was going to be trampled by the fleeing Kazats.

CHAPTER 29

Dan

It had been a risk, but Dan had been right. Strihat's sword whipped into him with unbelievable speed, but with two large shields protecting his upper body, it couldn't find its mark. The sword then buried itself in the most lethal place still available.

Even on the battlefield, Dan had never seen bleeding quite like the fountain jetting from his upper leg. Thankfully, he still had the energy to kill Strihat and yell the retreat. With an order from a supreme commander, the Kazat soldiers could run without fear of execution waiting for them at home. He was grateful Mendine had taught them the word in Kazatani, and that he'd had the energy to shout it before he collapsed.

Dan fell to his back, the pain in his leg fading as he grew sleepy. He looked up into the blue sky, relieved that Lillian would be safe now. The Kazats fled back toward the water, dragging their wounded. Some thundered nearer, obviously intending to retrieve the commander's body. They'd probably trample him, but he didn't want to live any longer, knowing he'd never hold Lillian again, never marry her. He closed his eyes and waited to die.

Hundreds of terrified screams roused him enough to open his eyes. He would have flinched if he'd had the energy.

A horrific vision stood directly above him. Dan had never seen such a creature. It was as though a demon had mated with a dragon. Thick, dark scales protected a muscular body, and whipping around behind it was a tail covered in deadly sharp spikes. It was taller than a building, and when it opened its mouth, hundreds of razor-sharp teeth glinted in the sunshine. Long arms, almost human-like, met thick paws, each at least as large as a man and ending in heavy, blood-stained claws. It reached down toward Dan.

The creature would kill him, and it would be over.

But the monster never touched him. Instead it picked up the body of Andrej Strihat. The commander struggled weakly, encircled by two enormous paws.

That was odd. Dan had been so certain he'd killed him.

The demon sniffed the struggling commander before ripping off one of his legs and swallowing it whole. Blood sprayed down on Dan, but he didn't feel a drop.

Oh. He would have smiled if he could have. Lillian truly was the most amazing woman. Half-dazed, he watched as the creature ripped off pieces of the commander, eating him piece by piece.

The screaming seemed louder, but none of the Kazat soldiers approached, not with Lillian's monster frightening the spit out of them. How he loved her.

The light of mid-day faded to a grey haze, growing darker until Dan couldn't tell if his eyes were open anymore.

There was a sudden, odd, jerking motion, as though he'd fallen sideways across a field. How strange. It didn't feel at all like he'd imagined dying would. It felt a lot more like traveling with Sir Hollis.

His mind sank into darkness.

~

Two days later
Dan dreamed the most incredible dreams. Most were centered on Lillian. Horrific monsters followed her like loyal hounds, and she murmured urgently to them, repeating the words, "I love you," and "come back to me," over and over. He dreamed of others too. Jensen kept promising to take someone fishing once they woke up. He also dreamed of Sir Carlos, but those dreams were accompanied by terrible pain. Sir Carlos kept stabbing him in the leg, or moving his limbs in excruciating positions.

After the last dream about the healer, understanding began to trickle into Dan's mind. He wasn't dead. Sir Hollis must have brought Sir Carlos.

Voices came closer, but Dan found he still couldn't move. Carlos must have given him a sedative.

"I'd like to see him for myself, you understand." Coordinator Madsen didn't sound happy. "You said he fought Strihat, and I find it unlikely he's going to live."

Dan had to agree. No one fought Strihat and lived.

Lillian said something...angry? Lillian was never angry.

A door opened nearby, and still Dan couldn't fully rouse himself.

Two sets of footsteps approached. One was Lillian's. Dan wondered when he'd memorized the sound of her tread.

"Well, he's breathing, but even if he lives, he won't be fit to be your defender," Madsen said clinically.

"I think I'll be the judge of that," Lillian said, steel in her quiet voice.

"Be reasonable, my dear," Madsen said placatingly. "There's no doubt he was very brave and that the two of you did amazing work together, but you are among the most valuable sorcerers we have, possibly *the* most valuable. You need the most capable defender, and after these injuries…"

"Sir Carlos said he might only have an occasional limp," Lillian hissed. "How *dare* you imply he's not capable?"

An occasional limp?

"In battle, that could mean the difference between success and defeat."

Madsen was right.

"You know you can't produce a defender half as good as he is, even if he does have a limp."

Madsen's voice became annoyed, and Dan wished he could throw him from the room.

"As the coordinator, it is my choice, which defender serves which sorcerer, and I say…Wait. What are you doing?"

"Do you really think you'll remain in your current position if you lose your sight?" Lillian's voice was quiet, measured, and dangerous.

"I thought you said you couldn't block out the sun," Madsen said angrily.

"I can't, but I've been practicing, and I can certainly angle the light away from *one* person's eyes. If you ever threaten to take my defender away again, I'll make this permanent."

There was a long, tense, silence before Madsen spoke again. "Of course you can keep him if you wish," he said stiffly.

"As though he was a puppy you could give away," Lillian said, her voice rising. "You'd better leave before I do something you'll regret."

"Lillian?" Svea's voice came from a distance. "You have visitors."

"In here," Lillian called back in a low voice.

"Melina is here with half the town, dear. They've come to check on Dan. You'd better give them an update."

"Will you please stay with him?" Lillian asked, furious

undercurrents still lacing her voice. "I don't trust his safety with this man in the room."

Lillian stomped away, and Svea said wryly, "Wore out your welcome already?"

"She's fabulous," Madsen said fervently, as though he was a child seeing his very first warship. "Do you know what she just did to me? We were right. He's perfect for her."

Dan could almost hear Svea frowning. "Did you really just threaten to take him away? We spent forever choosing the perfect man for my niece, and I refuse to go through that process again."

"Just testing the waters," Madsen said before adding seriously, "but if I ever feel he can't keep her safe, I'll come kill him myself."

"You and what army?" Svea said snidely. "Oh, wait, you'd need *more* than that. An army wasn't enough for the Kazats."

"It wasn't, was it?" Madsen said smugly.

Dan stopped listening. They thought he was going to live. He didn't have to leave Lillian. At least, not yet. He drifted back to sleep.

Lillian

Lillian sent off her friends as quickly as possible, assuring them that their hero was well and resting. She hurried back toward Dan's room, but paused at the library when she heard Madsen's voice.

"She made what?"

"A monster, of course," said Aunt Svea. "The Kazats would have trampled Mr. Forell otherwise."

Lillian could still taste the medicine in her mouth. She drank an entire vial in two swallows to make that monster.

"It was frightening beyond words, Mr. Madsen." Lillian leaned closer to the doorway to make out Jensen's low rumble. "The men running on to the beach with me to recover Mr. Forell's body retreated back to the fireworks wagon. I'm going to be known as the bravest man in the village because I kept walking forward, blowing the Kazat retreat on my trumpet." He chuckled. "I was the only one who knew the monster wasn't real."

It hadn't been funny at all to Lillian. She'd sobbed her way through the creation of her monster, and when Uncle Hollis had shown up with Sir Carlos, she'd nearly lost control of the image while trying to speak coherently about where Dan was. In the end, she'd just pointed, and Uncle Hollis, with one wild-eyed look at the demon, disappeared, reappearing a moment later with Dan's lifeless form. She felt a surge of guilt for not being able to articulate to Uncle Hollis that the creature was perfectly safe, but she loved him even more for fetching Dan anyway.

"What happened to it?" Sir Carlos' voice drew Lillian into the library.

Uncle Hollis smiled at her from the sofa, and she quickly joined him.

"Lillian retired the monster into the sand once most of the Kazats retreated," Aunt Svea explained. Carlos had missed that part as he'd been busy saving Dan's life.

"But she kept her army guarding the beach for another hour," Jensen supplied. "Until the ships were out of sight. Then they marched back over the hill and disappeared."

"And what of Fast?" Madsen asked, looking to Lillian.

"He stood watching us with a spyglass," she said, "until his ship sank into the horizon." She'd kept the other "sorcerers" visible until he was gone. Lillian almost thought his fingers flicked out at her in a mocking salute. He'd be back someday.

If it hadn't been for Fast, she could have checked on Dan immediately. As it was, she made it to his room just in time to hear Sir Carlos announce he was going to live. Too exhausted to consider all she'd done, Lillian crumpled onto the large bed next to Dan. She hadn't regained full consciousness until the following evening when Aunt Svea tearfully explained she'd had another seizure, the worst ever. Thankfully, Sir Carlos had been there to lessen its effects.

The healer now showed obvious signs of overwork. His face was haggard and lined, though still smiling.

"How is Dan now?" Lillian asked him while Madsen listened intently.

"It will take time for him to regain his strength. I can't conjure blood to fill his veins. He's got to do that part himself, so make sure he eats well, drinks well, and gets enough sleep."

"We. Must. Go," Uncle Hollis told her.

"With over a dozen coordinated attacks, there are many people still to heal," said Sir Carlos. "Thanks to Sir Hollis taking the army sorcerers where they were needed, there are far fewer than there should be. Once the Kazats realized our sorcerers were very much alive and capable of fighting them, most of them retreated. And none of the other locations had half the number you dealt with. Fast and Strihat saw this as the easiest way in and concentrated their force here." He patted Lillian's arm and gave her a proud smile. "We'll be back as soon as we can."

"We can't leave yet," Madsen said with an indignant frown. "I've hardly had any details about this battle. I need to make a full report to His Majesty."

Aunt Svea, Uncle Hollis, Jensen, and Sir Carlos turned hard stares on the coordinator.

"My work is important too," he blustered. "I haven't nearly enough understanding of what went on, and—"

He cut himself off, jumping in his seat when Lillian's image of Perch Harbor expanded in the air before him. She recreated a tiny version of the battle for him to watch, but at twenty times the speed.

"No wonder Adivino thought he was having nightmares," he said a few minutes later, gaping openly at the images before him. "Are you certain that's what happened?"

"Actually, I think the demon was about twice that large," Jensen said, eyeing the coordinator with dislike.

"And the archers were completely hidden from the Kazats," Aunt Svea said. "Andrej Strihat's army would have broken through a harbor you didn't consider important enough for a sorcerer to guard. Whether or not Reznik's invasion was successful, Strihat would have killed thousands of people."

"I know you want me to join the army sorcerers," Lillian told him quietly. "Dan and I have decided that's not where I'm needed most. This is. Of course, I'll consider doing some work with the army sorcerers on a case by case basis. When I want to," she qualified, "and if my defender feels it would be safe for me."

"Oh, that's what Forell and you have decided, is it?" Madsen said, narrowing his gaze.

"Yes," Lillian said firmly. "It is."

"It. Is," Uncle Hollis echoed with a steely gaze for Madsen.

Madsen's eyes widened at Uncle Hollis, who disappeared and reappeared beside the coordinator. Madsen protested, "But —" before they both winked out of view.

Jensen and Sir Carlos chuckled, and Uncle Hollis soon reappeared next to the healer.

"One minute please, Hollis," Sir Carlos said. "I need to give instructions for Dan's care." He moved aside with Jensen, and Lillian hurried to hug her uncle.

"Thank you for everything," she said as he patted her shoulder haltingly.

"You'll join us for dinner tonight, won't you, Sir Hollis?" Aunt Svea said.

"Yes, please," Lillian said. "I still have so many questions about Mother and Father."

"Of. Course," Uncle Hollis said with a grin.

Lillian embraced him once more, and he disappeared with Sir Carlos.

"I need to check on Mr. Forell," Jensen said with a respectful nod to Lillian and her aunt.

Lillian waited a few minutes before following him and pressing an ear to Dan's door.

"Oh, you should have seen it, Mr. Forell," Jensen said. "That dragon-demon scared the Kazats witless. The injured filled the boats, others swam. Only a few were left behind. They're being interrogated by a truth-teller." He paused and then said shrewdly, "You know, Mr. Forell, I've been wonderin'. Aside from those that took arrows, there weren't many dead Kazats on that beach. I saw you dropping them right and left. You're obviously an experienced fighter. It would have been just as easy for you to kill them. Why didn't you?"

"Ah, Jensen," Dan said tiredly. Lillian's heart rose into her throat at the sound of his voice. "Those men didn't want to be there, and Lillian didn't want to see them die. It was bad enough she had to see what she did. You're sure she's all right?"

"She's shocked for sure at all the going's on, but I think she's been too worried about you to really consider everything she did. 'Course, she might just be shocked about all those assassins that came after her."

"What?" Dan demanded hoarsely, and Lillian bit her lip. Why did Jensen have to tell him about that? He needed rest, not more worry.

"Well, it was nothing to worry about. Young Jake Harper took out four of them on his own, and then Sir Malick and Lady Ellstrom took care of the three that got past him."

Dan cursed fluently. Maybe that meant he was feeling more energetic. Lillian stifled a nervous giggle.

Jensen misunderstood. "Well, you couldn't have all the fun, and poor Jake. He was in a special unit in the army before his parents convinced him to come home and study for the cloth. The poor man deserved some of the action. Come on, your pants now."

She waited another minute, then knocked lightly on the door. Jensen opened it and smiled broadly. "Well, Miss Lillian. Look who's up and walking around." He hefted a basket of linens and left, winking at her as he passed.

Silence followed, and she found herself nervous under Dan's searching gaze.

"I'm so sorry about your injury," she murmured.

He walked slowly forward, testing his mended leg. "It was my fault. I couldn't think of another way to get rid of Strihat."

She wanted to scold him for taking so many risks, but he reached out to caress a lock of her hair, and she lost her train of thought.

"Thanks for not letting me get trampled," he said, now close enough that she could make out the tiny pattern etched on the buttons of his shirt.

She wanted to kiss him so badly, but after everything that had happened, she found herself shy and uncertain. What if her monster had scared him into sensibility, and he *didn't* want her anymore? "Thank you for getting rid of the Kazats," she said quietly.

"Me?" He threw back his head and laughed. Lillian couldn't help smiling at the sound. "Oh, Lil. I was very glad I could help you, but that's all I did. *You* saved everyone."

She shrugged, uncertain what to make of his assessment. She looked up at him anxiously. "Dan? I talked to Madsen. I told him we'd stay together, but is that what you still want?"

"You think we can make it work?" His lips twitched.

She took a breath and started over. "If you don't want to—"
She broke off and paused before saying as quickly as she could,

"You don't have to stay, but I—" She swallowed. "I really hope you will."

"You're sure you don't want someone else?"

She was only about half sure he was teasing. She took a deep breath and looked into his grey-blue eyes. "I promise I'll be stronger and braver, that I'll—"

He interrupted with another tired but good-humored laugh. "Lillian, I've never met anyone stronger. You fought off an entire army and kept everyone safe at the same time. And as for bravery, not too long ago, I saw you walk into a room full of Kazats and traitors bent on murder, and you fought them singlehandedly."

"I couldn't have done any of that without you."

"I'm very glad you wanted me with you for all that, but Lillian, you are a force of nature. You don't *need* me."

"Well, I happen to *love* you, Dan Forell," she said, frowning up at him. "So yes. I *do* think I need you."

At her words, his lips parted, and he inhaled sharply, his eyebrows furrowed. Had she just made an enormous mistake?

CHAPTER 30

Dan

Lillian's words somehow buried themselves between his ribs and just under his heart. She'd said she loved him before, but never when she'd been in her right mind. He didn't realize how anxiously he'd been waiting for those words until she actually said them, just as he hadn't realized that an over-abundance of happiness could bring moisture to his eyes.

His first impulse was to snatch her into his arms and kiss her breathless, but her eyes were worried, and he didn't want to scare her. Moving slowly, he gently tugged her toward him, burying one hand in her hair and pressing his lips to her forehead. "You are my life, Lillian. I love you, and I never want to be without you."

She sighed and moved her arms around him, leaning her head against his shoulder.

"Lillian," he murmured into her hair. "Since I didn't die, could I convince you to marry me?"

She made a choking noise, and he pulled away to make sure she was all right. But she was laughing. "Dan! I thought I was going to have to ask *you*, and then bully you into it. I love you. Of course I'll marry you!"

Dan choked out a laugh of his own, just before Lillian stepped more snugly into his embrace and turned her face up to him. He didn't hesitate. Their smiling lips met quickly, triumphantly. She pulled away almost at once. "Are you sure you want—"

He didn't let her finish her question. He snatched her into his arms and pressed another kiss to her perfect lips. She sighed and melted against him, snaking her arms around his neck and returning his kiss with such sweetness that it pulled another tear from his eye. He swiped it away, hoping to catch it before she noticed. Whether she did or not, she pulled him tighter, deepening their kiss without a hint of restraint.

"I love you, Lillian," he whispered when they paused a few minutes later. She leaned back to study him, and he added, "I will want you forever."

She exhaled sharply and reached up on tiptoe to kiss him fiercely. He clasped her tight, practically lifting her off her feet as he deepened their kiss. She was perfection. And he wasn't dead. He pulled her even closer.

O ne month later

The baron quieted the crowd with a wave of his hand. Somehow Dan had been expecting a more imposing figure. Lillian's adopted father was a thin man, hardly any taller than his sister, and Dan thought the Loraine nose and chin looked much better on Svea than they did on the baron.

"I present the happy couple," he said loudly.

The people of Perch Harbor cheered as Svea and Sir Malick stepped forward, Svea looking ten years younger. Dan was almost sure Lillian had nothing to do with it, and that it was simply that a broad smile had replaced Svea's usual shrewd expression. Sir Malick's smile was so filled with pride and elation that Dan half expected him to burst with it.

The evening rounded out with a spectacular display of fireworks.

Dan gave Lillian a glass of chilled juice as she stood staring up at the spectacle.

"Have you decided yet?" he asked. In gratitude for Lillian's service, and to entice her to continue to guard Perch Harbor, the crown had offered to build her a home there or to purchase the baron's for her.

Lillian shook her head, and Dan didn't press her. There was time.

"These are the most amazing fireworks I've ever seen," he said, nodding toward the distant lights. She smiled until he added, "It's strange that no one notices how silent they are."

"Oh, don't spoil my fun."

"I wouldn't dream of it." And he wouldn't have. After seeing the way the baron had inched away from her during the ceremony, Dan would have done anything to please her.

He'd quietly offered to kill the man, but she'd only laughed. "There's no rule in heaven or earth that says the people you love have to love you back." The words were light, flippant even, but the tightness in her eyes contradicted her tone.

"*I* love you back," Dan said savagely.

"That's everything I need," she said.

He'd worked very hard to make sure Lillian's day was otherwise perfect. He hadn't even struck down Geoffrey when the idiot tried to take sole credit for the victory at the beach. Luckily Jensen had been within hearing and had laughed heartily until Geoffrey's face was an unbecoming shade of scarlet.

Another multicolored explosion blossomed over their heads and streaked downward before melting away.

"Will you take a break from the fireworks to kiss your

husband?" He loved saying the word aloud. He was far prouder of that title than of defender. He'd tried to convince her to marry him three days after the battle at the beach, but she'd insisted on waiting another week so the army sorcerers could come. He suspected she was also concerned he'd regret the decision and that she wanted to give him time to back out. He'd never been more certain of anything in his life, had never felt so completely at peace.

A few days before their wedding, Lillian brought him a book and pointed to a page she'd marked. "Defenders are supposed to swear loyalty to their sorcerer in a ceremony. Did you know that?"

"I did."

"Well?"

Her smile when he'd repeated his vow may have had a self-congratulatory glint, but he couldn't really tell because she'd sniffed into a handkerchief through the entire thing. Considering that her aunt and Jensen stood in as witnesses, the kiss she gave him afterward to seal the vow (instead of the usual handshake) was more energetic than he would have thought appropriate. Not that he wished to complain. Only later did she admit to him that she never had trouble with her memory after working illusions and that it had been so beautiful the first time that she wanted to enjoy it again. That explained a lot more than Dan cared to examine at the time.

On their wedding day, the sorcerers brought the news that Oliver had disappeared from his prison cell. "It was as though someone spirited him away," Sir Adivino had said. Everyone turned to Sir Hollis, who glanced guiltily to the floor.

"Where did you take him?" Lillian asked worriedly, looking up at the faint outline of the moon in the afternoon sky.

"Not. There," Sir Hollis said, with his uneven smile.

How strange that Lillian would consider such an impossible thing.

With another guilty look at Dan and the assembled sorcerers, Sir Hollis admitted, "Deep. Jungle. Island. Other. Side. Of. The. World. No. People."

Dan clasped Sir Hollis' shoulder. "Thank you. Truly."

Dan and Lillian's wedding ceremony had been simple and beautiful, Jake looking extremely dignified as he pronounced them sealed for life. Thousands of pink roses scented the small chapel and later the reception, courtesy of Sir Mendine. Their heavenly appearance was nothing compared to Lillian. Her honey brown hair hung in waves past her shoulders, and her simple white gown fit her form perfectly, but his favorite thing had been the way she'd looked at him as Jake performed the ceremony. Her smile was radiantly happy and her eyes mischievous. He would never grow tired of looking at her, of talking with her, of being with her.

Now, outside Sir Malick's and Svea's reception, she grinned wickedly at him. "I suppose the fireworks are almost done anyway." A hundred fireworks exploded in an awesome finale before the sky went black.

The next second she was in his arms, kissing him breathless. "You need a shave, my love," she whispered. He tried to ease back, but she pulled him closer. "I don't mind it." She smiled against his lips.

"I can't believe when I first met you, I thought you were—" He caught himself.

She only laughed. "Spoiled? Weak? With an unhealthy taste for romance novels?"

He chuckled and kissed her brow. "Turns out you were none of those things. Not even close."

"Oh, I don't know," she said.

He leaned back to frown at her.

"I don't mind the occasional romance novel."

He grinned. "Well, it's like the monster books. Why read it when you can live it?"

"Is that an invitation?"

"I think it was."

They were instantly surrounded by a pack of prowling wolves, blood dripping from razor-sharp teeth. Impossibly large vipers appeared at their feet, their mouths wide and ready to strike. A few reanimated corpses shuffled toward them from the garden.

A startled chuckle ripped out of his chest, and then he laughed uncontrollably a half-minute more before he could speak. "I meant the romance novel," he finally clarified.

"Right. Let's see," Lillian said thoughtfully. "How's this?" She took a half-step back and clasped her hands in front of her chest, her lips trembling in apparent fright. "Oh, my hero, won't you save me?"

"That's it," Dan said, lunging for her and snatching her up. "The real thing is definitely better," he said in a low voice before his lips met hers. The monsters might have disappeared. He didn't know or care. All he could think of in that moment was the way her lips moved against his, hungrily, enthusiastically. After several extremely enjoyable minutes, their kisses slowed, and Lillian sighed contentedly. "I love you, Daniel Forell. I'm so glad you aren't frightened by my illusions."

"I'm terrified by them," he said seriously.

She stiffened in his arms.

"Turns out I like to be scared." He laughed at her as she pulled away, her brows contracted.

"Dan, you are the most—"

He never found out what he was, because instead of finishing her sentence, she pulled him back down for another kiss. She didn't seem to have any intention of letting go, and that was just fine with him.

~

I hope you enjoyed *Disillusioned*. Please consider leaving a review. For occasional announcements, free content, and information on future releases, including the next Love and Sorcery book, sign up for my newsletter at https://roxannemcneil.com/newsletter/.

ALSO BY ROXANNE MCNEIL

LOVE AND SORCERY: BAITED

An arranged marriage to a dangerous man calls for an escape plan. Too bad his kisses are completely addictive.

Biated is a sweet romance with fantasy elements for fans of Jane Austen and The Princess Bride.

LOVE AND SORCERY: DISGUISED

His heart belongs to someone else. She's a danger to those around her. They have no business falling in love.

Disguised is a sweet romance with fantasy elements for fans of Jane Eyre and happily ever afters.

SISTER TO BEAUTY

What if Beauty tricked her ordinary sister into taking her place with the beast?

Sister to Beauty is a sweet historical romance set in the lavender fields of Provence.

ACKNOWLEDGMENTS

A big thank you to my family members and critique partners who've helped me so many times. Many thanks to my editors, Cara Seger and Laura Walker. The biggest thank you, of course, goes to Benjamin, the love of my life and my biggest support.

ABOUT THE AUTHOR

Roxanne writes sweet, chemistry-driven romance. Her bookshelves are full of happy endings, and she would never consider writing anything else. Roxanne loves the Pacific Northwest and has a long-standing relationship with See's chocolate. She lives with a sweet, 45-pound ball of fur named Queenie, who is much more of a princess than Roxanne is.

Made in United States
North Haven, CT
01 May 2022

18776923R00181